# THE SACRED FOUNT

OTHER WORKS BY HENRY JAMES

PUBLISHED BY GROVE PRESS

*Italian Hours*

*A London Life*

*The Reverberator*

HENRY JAMES

# THE SACRED FOUNT

*With an Introductory Essay*
*By Leon Edel*

GROVE PRESS, INC.
NEW YORK

First Black Cat Edition 1979
First Printing 1979
ISBN: 0-394-17081-4
Grove Press ISBN: 0-8021-4239-7
Library of Congress Catalog Card Number: 53-6867

*The Library of Congress Cataloged the First Printing of This Title as Follows:*

James, Henry, 1843–1916.

The sacred fount. With an introductory essay by Leon Edel. New York, Grove Press [1953]

319 p. 20 cm.
I. Title.

PZ3.J234S4 53-6867
Library of Congress

Manufactured in the United States of America

Distributed by Random House, Inc., New York

GROVE PRESS, INC., 196 West Houston Street,
New York, N.Y. 10014

# AN INTRODUCTORY ESSAY

## I. THE LABYRINTH

Half a century has elapsed since Henry James wrote *The Sacred Fount,* and criticism, on the whole, still tends to regard it in a mood of weary bafflement. Over none of his novels have the critical waves melted so helplessly into their own shimmering foam. When the book appeared in 1901, the few reviewers who attempted to read it either masked their bewilderment in derision or candidly admitted they could not understand. Henry James had "out-Jamesed" himself; he was "intent on making nothing out of nothing"; he had written a "brilliantly stupid piece of work." And so it has been, with one or two rare exceptions, in the ensuing decades. In a work as recent as the brief sketch of the novelist by Michael Swan, *The Sacred Fount* is still "that strange and baffling book." And Mr. Swan's curious account of it reveals just how baffled he is.

Criticism of the book has run to strange extremes: from coyness to elaborate speculation. When he read it, William Dean Howells, a staunch defender of Henry James and a devoted friend, announced he had "mastered the secret" of the novel but "wouldn't for the present divulge it." That was in 1903 and the "secret" remained undivulged when Howells died seventeen years later. In 1936 Wilson Follett, in an article couched in the sensational terms of journalism rather than the more sober evaluative terms of criticism, described the book as "Henry James's Portrait of Henry James." The novelist, he wrote in the *New York Times Book Review,* had been "leering" at his critics for many years, in "one of the most stupendous parodies ever concocted . . . it is Henry James deliberately turning a searchlight on Henry James." The novel, he said, was a parody, a parable, an allegory, a lampoon on his own fictional methods. It is difficult to reconcile our knowledge of Henry James with this gratuitous flight of fancy. James could turn the light (but never the searchlight!) of irony on himself on occasions, as in "Pandora," where he makes fun of "Daisy Miller." But he took the art of fiction too seriously ever to burlesque or parody his own practice of it. He believed in the novelist as an historian, and accordingly a realist, and all his fiction was addressed to the demonstration of this fundamental truth. He once chided Anthony Trollope for an aside in a novel that fiction was, after all, "making believe." Henry James's point in *The Sacred Fount* is not, as Follett argued, that "life" destroys the artist's "make-believe," but that the "make-believe" has a reality of its own. This James often said. His short story "The Real Thing" is his best fictional statement of it.

Rebecca West wittily showed her impatience with *The Sacred Fount* when she described it as "a small, mean story" that "worries one like a rat nibbling at the wainscot." And her description of the book has often been quoted, how "a week-end visitor spends more intellectual force than Kant can have used on *The Critique of Pure Reason,* in an unsuccessful attempt to discover whether there exists between certain of his fellow-guests a relationship not more interesting among these vacuous people than it is among sparrows."

But, as Miss West would be perhaps the first to recognize, *The Sacred Fount* was the work of a serious artist, and however much vacuity she might find in it, there was also a great deal of applied art. And Edmund Wilson, some fifteen years after Miss West, set himself in his essay on Henry James's "ambiguity" to unraveling the meaning of the art. He saw promptly the significance of the narrator and the relationship between this work and *The Turn of the Screw.* Unfortunately he did not pursue his inquiry further. In fact he quite suddenly dropped it with a baffled: "*The Sacred Fount* is mystifying, even maddening." No greater tribute could have been paid to James, who had boasted he worked for "mystification." Wilson observed that "if anyone got to the bottom of it, he would throw a good deal of light on James."

A significant attempt at a critical examination of the book was made by R. P. Blackmur in the *Kenyon Review* in 1942. His essay showed a closer and more sensitive reading of the text than any critic had hitherto vouchsafed it. He recognized it as a viable work of fiction, closer to Joyce and Proust, Virginia Woolf and Franz Kafka, than to nineteenth-century fiction. And he established the important relationship between the method in the ghostly tales—the process of "mystification," of evoking a fairy-tale fascination in the reader—and the method of this novel. In his essay, criticism is no longer baffled, even if it does not attempt a full explication. It is at least performing its function of attempting to see into a work and to catch its dominant mood. Similarly in 1947, in England, Edward Sackville West gave the book the close reading it deserves. He was enchanted. He found it a "supreme exercise in the spirit of poetic analysis," a "profound inquiry" into human relationships. As an artistic *tour de force,* he wrote, "the book is extraordinarily perfect."

When criticism throws up its hands in bewilderment over a work of art or waivers between such extremes, it is reasonable to inquire whether the work in question is really art. Has there been a failure in communication or a failure in perception—or both? The precise question—particularly at this moment when the work is being reprinted—is the extent to which criticism now, after fifty years, can illuminate and assess an admittedly intricate novel written by a master of the craft of fiction, who, therefore, whatever his lapses, presumably knew what he was about.

Our method will be quite simply to begin with the text, as all criticism worthy of the name must begin, to determine what a close reading may yield. This done, we shall seek further light by relating this work to other works of James and to other Jamesian modes of representation. Finally, since no work is created in a void but is the projection of a given mind at a given time (and we might add in a given place), we will seek the illumination of biography. It will be shown that any one of these approaches to *The Sacred Fount* can clarify the work and that by using all three we may arrive at the richest understanding.

### 2. PALACE OF THOUGHT, HOUSE OF CARDS

*The Sacred Fount* is a first person narrative. The narrator, instead of telling us something about himself in the traditional manner of such self-revelatory fiction, plunges us at once into the story itself. Indeed, we must determine for ourselves, whether he is (as we suspect) a man. It is clear from the outset, therefore, that we have a very difficult problem in this book: the reader may not remain passive and receive from the narrator the whole story. He must actively deduce from the things said to him by the narrator, and from the things said to the narrator by other characters, what sort of a person the narrator himself is. This is where criticism can stumble. To read the book inattentively is to take everything on the narrator's terms.

The narrator, never named or identified, and never described physically to us, takes a train from Paddington Station to Newmarch where he is to join a house party for the week-end. He shares a compartment with two acquaintances who are also bound for Newmarch: Gilbert Long, a man the narrator has always found to be depressingly dull, and Mrs. Brissenden, who seems much younger and prettier than she had appeared before.

Thus in a few paragraphs the stage is set. We discover the narrator to be a man addicted to close and subtle observation, inordinately curious, and constantly piecing together the evidence presented to him by his eyes and ears. He is deeply puzzled by the strange transformation in Mrs. Brissenden. "How could a woman who had been plain so long become pretty so late?" How could she have acquired this second youth?

We learn from a conversation between Long and the narrator that she had married Guy Brissenden, a man many years younger than herself. "What was it they called it?—a case of child-stealing. Everyone made jokes. Briss isn't yet thirty." But Mrs. Brissenden, who is now over forty, looks twenty-five. It is Gilbert Long who makes the remark about "child-stealing"; he concludes that Mrs. Brissenden has simply ceased to grow older. The narrator is hardly satisfied. Moreover he is puzzled by something else: Long, too, is changed. He discusses this with Mrs. Brissenden at the first opportunity.

Long had always been a "heavy Adonis," banal and quite unfriendly. Now he is not only amiable but shows signs of alertness and intelligence. Mrs. Brissenden confirms to the narrator his view that Long somehow is different. She suggests that "a very clever woman has for some time past . . ." but the eager narrator, with that exasperating habit certain of James's characters have of butting in, finishes the sentence for her ". . . taken a particular interest in him?" Mrs. Briss toys with the idea that this woman has given him "steadily, more and more intellect." She thinks a certain Lady John is the source of Long's new wit, and Lady John is also due at Newmarch.

At their destination, on this August day, the narrator sees Guy Brissenden and is struck by the way he has aged. Gradually therefore the central theme of the book has been unfolded for us: Mrs. Brissenden seems to be draining Guy Briss of his youth in her process of growing younger and more beautiful. The narrator promptly translates this equation into a question: whose sacred fount is Long therefore draining to acquire his greater mental capacities? He sees this as a challenging puzzle: the solution is to look for a lady once clever, now dull. If we examine the equations, we arrive at this generalization: women exercise a two-fold influence on men; they can sometimes deprive men of their manhood, wither their very being, and grow young in the process. Or they can endow men with superior intelligence and insight. Otherwise stated, physical relations with women can be perilous to men; but the Platonic relationship of the mind can be a life-giving force to men, and depleting to women.

It is this vampire theme which preoccupies the narrator during the remaining day and a half at Newmarch. He discovers soon enough that Lady John is hardly a great fountain of wit and intelligence. She is thoroughly down-to-earth, a hat "askew on the bust of Virgil." Later the narrator speaks of her as having a "vision as closed as Obert's was open." Ford Obert, R. A., is an artist encountered at the week-end party. He sees *into* life and people since he has the "painter-sense deeply applied."

Something he says focuses the narrator's attention on another woman, May Server, as a possible source for Long's mental rejuvenation. He had painted her portrait when she was a creature of great beauty and calm. Now her beauty is fading and she is a restless flirt, flitting from man to man at the party in a pathetic effort to recover something that she has lost. We learn, too, that she is a woman depleted apparently not only of her calm and her fugitive beauty: she has lost her three children.

As the narrator becomes increasingly absorbed in his speculation, he is disturbed by the thought that he is invading other people's privacy. Ford Obert offers reassurance. When the narrator wonders whether he should "nose about for a relation that a lady has her reasons for keeping secret," Obert replies this is harmless and "positively honorable" so long as the investigator sticks to "psychologic evidence." He observes that "resting on psychologic signs alone, it's a high application of the intelligence. What's ignoble," he adds, "is the detective and the keyhole."

The narrator indeed pursues his researches as a "high application of the intelligence." He studies the persons present at Newmarch; he wanders through the rooms and in the grounds; his observation is merciless; he watches for signs, listens for stray remarks; he is a detective of the intelligence, terribly proud of his ratiocinative capacity and his insights. Yet doubts begin to arise. Isn't he the victim of a "ridiculous obsession?" He admits to agitation and anxiety. Early in the book he refers to "the common fault of minds for which the vision of life is an obsession" to seek "a law that would fit certain given facts." He warns himself against the grouping of such facts "into a larger mystery . . . than the facts as observed, yet warranted."

Later "the curiosity to which I had so freely surrendered myself began to strike me as wanting in taste." Nevertheless there remained Obert's reminder about the detective and the keyhole; and so while the narrator has occasional qualms—"the amusing question was stamped for me as none of my business"—he continues his fascinating cerebration. He reads what he can in the relationships—and into them, perhaps—until he is brought up short: "I remember feeling seriously warned," he says to himself during dinner on the second evening, "not to yield further to my idle habit of reading into mere human things an interest so much deeper than mere human things were in general prepared to supply." And as he watches May Server's pathetic struggle—or what seems to him to be such—he says: "It would have been almost as embarrassing to have had to tell them how little experience I had had in fact as to have had to tell them how much I had had in fancy. . . ."

He is extraordinarily vain over his powers of observation and insight. *"I* alone was magnificently and absurdly aware—everyone else was benightedly out of it. . . ." Lady John bluntly warns him against this belief in his omniscience. "Give up . . . the attempt to be providence. . . . A real providence *knows;* whereas you . . . have to find out." Her warning falls on deaf ears. *"I,* in my supernatural acuteness," he again remarks at another point of his self-laudation, and goes on to speak of "my plunges of insight" and the "joy of the intellectual mastery of things unamenable, that joy of determining, almost of creating results!"

*Almost creating results!* Then he does think himself a providence! For he goes on to boast of "my relish of the way I was keeping things together" and "my accumulations of lucidity" which are "such as to defy all leakage." He describes himself—as the end of his Newmarch week-end approaches—as having created a veritable "palace of thought." And there is a sense of exaltation at twilight of the second day that the novelist works up into one of his soaring moods that evoke the "spirit of the place." What follows is the anti-climax: the palace of thought seems to become, by a few swift strokes, a collapsing house of cards.

Mrs. Brissenden, apparently stirred up by the narrator's continuing "researches," asks to see him late in the evening. They have a long talk—a big final scene. The narrator unrolls his speculations, with great subtlety, stating some of them as hard fact, only to find that Mrs. Brissenden is no longer helpful. Was Gilbert Long really more intelligent and witty than he had been? "There's really nothing in him at all," says Mrs. Brissenden. Was there anything going on between Mrs. Server and Long? Between Long and Lady John? "Of course you could always imagine—which is precisely what is the matter with you," Mrs. Brissenden observes at one point as she deflates the narrator's theories. Long was, apparently, having an affair with Lady John, not with May Server, and May in turn had been making up to Guy. As for the vampire situation between Mr. and Mrs. Briss, the narrator is too much of a gentleman to allude to that.

"You see too much," she says at one point. At others she tells him: "You talk too much." Again: "You're abused by a fine fancy." And still again: "You build up houses of cards." And: "You overestimate the penetration of others."

And finally, point-blank: "I think you're crazy."

The narrator must protect himself. He decides Mrs. Brissenden is "suffering and stammering and lying"—trying to cover up her own strange conduct, perhaps not only her "eating poor Briss" but possible infidelities, perhaps her own interest in Long. "I was there to save my priceless pearl of an inquiry and to harden, to that end, my heart." Mrs. Brissenden has shaken and continues to shake him. She tells him "people have such a notion of what you embroider on things that they're rather afraid to commit themselves or to lead you on." In other words, the very testimony he has accumulated becomes questionable.

"You're costing me a perfect palace of thought," he mourns. There's nothing he can do. She opposes to his speculations what seems like blunt reality at every turn, and yet reality seems impossible to him beside the beauty of the imagined and the imaginative, which, to him, are just as real.

"I *should* certainly never again, on the spot, quite hang together, even though it wasn't really that I hadn't three times her method. What I too fatally lacked was her tone." With these words James ends his novel. Nothing has been solved; nothing is settled. We have had an hypothesis, a series of assumptions and speculations. There have been precious few facts to go on. The reader can only take the narrator at his word; and *his* word has been based largely upon appearance. As for the reality——!

### 3. MASK OF DEATH, MASK OF LIFE

That indeed is what this book is about: appearance and reality. It is written over the face of it, visible to every reader providing he can remind himself at each stage that the story belongs exclusively to the ingenious narrator. When the unnamed and undescribed narrator tells us that he alone "was magnificently and absurdly aware," we must remember that this is what *he* thinks. He may indeed be; and again he may be as "crazy" as Mrs. Brissenden suggests he is. When he speaks of "my accumulations of lucidity" we must by the same token remember that someone else may not find these accumulations lucid at all. In this light, Mrs. Brissenden's charge "you build up houses of cards" has as much value as the narrator's remark about "my plunges of insight." We are asked by Henry James to determine the credibility of the witness, but we are not given enough evidence to arrive at an answer. It was this, we suspect, that Edmund Wilson found "maddening." What we do have is more than ample evidence of the narrator's hungry, subtle imagination, his curiosity, his feeling for people, his sense of place and mood, his fine artistic being, his artistic vanity. We are ready to believe that such a mind enjoys "the intellectual mastery" of which it boasts. We also can believe that it experiences that "joy of determining, almost of creating results."

The results are created for us. Yet what we end up with is a fantasy, a series of hypotheses, an atmosphere, a tone, a surfeit of analysis. Mrs. Server's three lost children are among the few concrete facts vouchsafed us along with the description of the beauties of Newmarch. One important scene, however, does permit us to search a little further.

It occurs in the fourth chapter, on the morning of the second day. The narrator asks Mrs. Server to come with him to examine certain pictures in one of the rooms at Newmarch. When they arrive in the great saloon they find that Ford Obert and Gilbert Long are already there. The narrator looks at Mrs. Server closely. She strikes him as "all pale pinks and blues and pearly whites and candid eyes—an old dead pastel under glass." Since they are looking at pastels, this seems to be an attempt to identify her with the inanimate works of art on the walls. Gilbert Long, hitherto dumb, but now in possession of the wit he has—in the narrator's view—derived from another's fount, is expatiating on the pictures and seems, in Obert's view, to be an "unexpected demon of a critic." This noted, we find on glancing again at the text that Obert never says so. The narrator has planted that idea with us. It was what Obert's eyes "most seemed to throw over to me." It is the narrator who is reading the evidence. Once again we must take it on his say-so. Obert's eyes alone have spoken, and we have no guarantee that they might not have been saying something else. And Obert never confirms the interpretation. Indeed he is unaware of it.

Contemplating the picture under discussion, Mrs. Server wonders "what in the world does it mean?" We wonder as well. It is that of a young man in black, the dress of another era, with a "pale, lean, livid face" and a stare "from eyes without eyebrows, like that of some whitened old-world * clown." In his hand he holds an object that "strikes the spectator at first simply as some obscure, some ambiguous work of art." On a second glance this is seen by the narrator to be a "representation of a human face, modelled and colored, in wax, in enamelled metal, in some substance not human. The object thus appears a complete mask, such as might have been fantastically fitted and worn."

Mrs. Server suggests the picture might be called "The Mask of Death." "Why so?" the narrator queries. "Isn't it much rather the Mask of Life? It's the man's own face that's Death. The other one, blooming and beautiful——"

"Ah, but with an awful grimace!" Mrs. Server rejoins.

The narrator ignores the interruption and continues blandly: "The other one, blooming and beautiful, is Life, and he's going to put it on; unless indeed he has just taken it off."

* This is one of Henry James's rare lapses and a revelation of his sense of his new-world identity. He is writing a novel set in the old world, and is probably thinking of the clowns seen as a boy in the Cirque d'Hiver and the Cirque d'Été; but he speaks as if from a distance, as if he were in the New World and were recalling something from the Old World.

"He's dreadful, he's awful—that's what I mean," says Mrs. Server.

The narrator pursues the matter, insisting the artificial face is "extremely studied and, when you carefully look at it, charmingly pretty. I don't see the grimace."

"I don't see anything else!" Mrs. Server replies.

When Obert is asked about the picture he says nothing; he escapes by paying Mrs. Server a compliment instead. There is no return anywhere else in the book to the pastel and we are left to make what we can of this episode. It cannot be regarded as a scene accidentally thrown in by Henry James. It is clearly not a momentary conceit that welled up in his fancy. By the time he wrote this book Henry James had been a master of his craft for a quarter of a century; he had reached that state of mastery in which every incident, every name, every scene was calculated not to "pad" the story but to advance its movement or light up character or situation.

Yet the introduction of the pastel of a man with a mask does seem a piece of such obvious and hackneyed symbolism as to be almost unworthy of the subtle mind of the novelist. We say this and promptly catch ourselves up: for is this not still another instance in which the description is furnished by the narrator? It is *he* who tells us what's in the picture and who promptly draws our attention to the fact that the face is Death and that it is the mask that is really alive. This is not challenged by Mrs. Server, and we must take it as given: indeed we have no alternative. There ensues, however, a sharp difference between

Mrs. Server and the narrator about the aspect of the mask. *Blooming, beautiful, charmingly pretty*—this is his description to which we must oppose Mrs. Server's, *dreadful, awful* and *awful grimace.* And the entire episode is all the more striking for the fact that but two pages earlier Mrs. Server herself has been seen by the narrator not as a person alive but as one "all Greuze tints . . . an old dead pastel under glass."

What has been underlined here for us if not the very theme of the book? We are again confronted with appearance and reality: and the difference of opinion over which aspect is Life and which Death, which Beauty and which a mere grimace, is a measure of how a palace of thought can also be a house of cards.

### 4. RAGE OF WONDERMENT

What world are we in when we have wandered into that strange week-end at Newmarch and found ourselves at the mercy of the narrator, limited to his vision of everything, limited to his view of his own creative sense and of his own "magnificence"? He resembles very much the governess of *The Turn of the Screw* who face to face with her ghosts insists in telling us: "I was wonderful." There is a passage in *The Sacred Fount* which is filled with extraordinary echoes of the ghostly tale. The governess in *The Turn of the Screw* describes how, walking at Bly at the end of a June day, in the long English twilight, she is haunted by the thought that she will meet, at some turn of the path, the handsome man whom she saw but twice in Harley Street, and who is her employer. "What arrested me on the spot—and with a shock much greater than any vision had allowed for —was the sense that my imagination had, in a flash, turned real. He did stand there!—but high up, beyond the lawn and at the very top of the tower. . . ." Then she becomes aware of her mistake. So in *The Sacred Fount,* in the twilight of the August day at Newmarch, the narrator goes for a walk. He has no such adventure as the governess. He meets no ghosts, he sees only the twilight, the trees, the rooks, but he encounters May Server . . .

I scarce know what odd consciousness I had of roaming at close of day in the grounds of some castle of enchantment. I had positively encountered nothing to compare with this since the days of fairy-tales and of the childish imagination of the impossible. *Then* I used to circle round enchanted castles, for then I moved in a world in which the strange "came true." It was the coming true that was the proof of the enchantment, which, moreover, was naturally never so great as when such coming was, to such a degree and by the most romantic stroke of all, the fruit of one's own wizardry. I was positively—so had the wheel revolved—proud of my work. . . . Yet I recall how I even then knew on the spot that there was something supreme I should have failed to bring unless I had happened suddenly to become aware of the very presence of the haunting principle, as it were, of my thought. This was the light in which Mrs. Server, walking alone now, apparently, in the grey wood and pausing at sight of me, showed herself in her clear dress at the end of a vista. It was exactly as if she had been there by the operation of my intelligence, or even by that—in a still happier way—of my feeling.

Decidedly at dusk, in the works of Henry James, one could dream, and the dreams seemed to come true. "We were in a beautiful old picture, we were in a beautiful old tale. . . ." The question was: where did the dream end and the reality begin? *The Sacred Fount* and *The Turn of the Screw* were not isolated works which posed this problem. They were two works in a chain of fiction that began in 1897 and extended past the turn of the century, each concerned with fathoming a surrounding world or reducing a series of "facts," a certain amount of data, to a reasonable order. The works follow in an extraordinarily logical progression, and seem to move through the stages from childhood to maturity. *What Maisie Knew* of 1897 is concerned with a "light vessel of consciousness," and the question of what exactly Maisie did know carries over to what did the governess know in *The Turn of the Screw* (1898). The governess also is trying to piece together a mystifying situation. What did the little telegraph girl *In the Cage* (1898) piece together from her angle of vision and out of the evidence presented to her by the laconic texts of other people's telegrams? And what did Nanda, emerging from late adolescence, know and discover in *The Awkward Age* (1899)? And finally, what did the narrator really fathom in *The Sacred Fount*? James himself pointed to the similarities between *What Maisie Knew* and *In the Cage:* "The rage of wonderment attributed in our tale to the young woman employed at Cocker's differs little in essence from the speculative thread on which the pearls of Maisie's experience . . . pearls of so strange an iridescence—are mostly strung." *In the Cage,* James agrees, does endow his little heroine with a great deal of "divination." And he warns in his preface, in words akin to the narrator's in *The Sacred Fount,* of "the danger . . . of imparting to too many others, right and left, the critical impulse and the acuter vision. . . ."

It is *The Turn of the Screw* which, of this entire group, invites closest comparison with *The Sacred Fount.* Newmarch and Bly are country residences; and in both places, as Edmund Wilson discerned, there are "the same passages of a strange and sad beauty, the same furtive happenings in an atmosphere of clarity and brightness, the same dubious central figure, the same almost inscrutable ambiguity." Mr. Wilson goes on to see, with great clarity, James's theory of the omniscient narrator. Both the story of the governess and that of the preoccupied observer in *The Sacred Fount* contain, he writes, "two separate stories to be kept distinct: a romance which the narrator is spinning and a reality which we are supposed to divine from what he tells us about what actually happens." This is the heart of James's method. Fully grasped, it would have obviated the long-spun controversy over the ghostly tale. But Mr. Wilson does not seem to take advantage of his insight. He goes on to say: "The truth is, I believe, that Henry James was not clear about the book in his own mind." This seems highly doubtful. An author who planned his works as carefully as Henry James and endowed his narrators with special and consistent "points of view," not only knew what he was about, but was actually constructing a puzzle, a maze, a labyrinth, with diabolical ingenuity. He is constantly on guard against making any slips likely to disturb his plan of composition. There seem to be no slips in *The Sacred Fount*. Whatever ambiguity there is, has been willed by James. (We speak of course of the conscious part of his work and not the subterranean unconscious part, which is another question entirely.) The novelist's goal is above all his "mystification." He will not unravel the mystery for us; he is stubbornly determined to leave that to his reader.

In *The Turn of the Screw* James achieved his mystification in a way which readers usually overlook. There are, so to speak, three narrators in this story. The first is the individual, perhaps James himself, who begins by telling us "The story had held us, round the fire. . . ." This unidentified First Narrator goes on to mention a second personage, Douglas. Douglas now briefly takes over the narrative: he tells of a ghost story with a special "turn of the screw." It is in an old manuscript; and Douglas then describes the writer of the manuscript, the governess. He is, in a sense, a Second Narrator—but not in reality; his account, in turn, is being quoted, or summarized, by the First Narrator. Then it is Douglas who begins to read the story, and the Third and most important Narrator—the governess, takes over. The story we finally are given is hers. Douglas and the First Narrator disappear.

Readers usually forget this extremely elaborate setting provided for us by the author—a setting by which he withdraws and places between himself and his audience a series of narrators. Each narrator provides a certain set of "facts" which are not evaluated for us. The question at issue is the credibility of the principal witness. And James's attitude is one of complete *neutrality*. So neutral is he that he leaves a wide imaginative margin for the reader who, if he is not careful, will be adding material from his own mind to the story. This is what most readers of *The Turn of the Screw* have done. The same trap is set for readers of *The Sacred Fount*.

### 5. BLISS AND BALE

In Henry James's essay "The Art of Fiction" he observes that "the deepest quality" of a work of art will always be the "quality of mind of the person who produced it." This means, what must be obvious to us all (as it was to the novelist), that in the last resort, try as he may, the author cannot cut the umbilical cord that attaches him to the work he has created. He may be able to provide a multitude of narrators but his is the hand that performs the magic, his the mind that nourishes the minds of the narrators. He provides the tone, the voice, the elements of the story, the lucidity and the imagination. In other words, the critic can attempt to probe the "quality of mind" that informed the work, even a work as artfully vague as *The Sacred Fount*.

The idea of depletion is a common one among many men who think of sex as a depleting force. Henry James seems to have held some such view. Yet in his case there was a much deeper view of the relations between men and women, going back to the primary scene of his own childhood. In his own family, his mother appeared as a woman of strength compared with his father who expressed his feelings with much greater openness than the mother. Henry James seems to have believed all his life that it was his mother's strength which sustained the father. The father, who had lost a leg when he was a boy, struck him as a vacillating and rather ineffectual figure, as indeed he often was, in spite of his great nobility of character and his vigorous life as an intellectual. The weight of these contradictions, both paternal and maternal, weighed upon the young Henry James and played an important part in his insistence, later, on his own autonomy and sovereignty: in his fear of involvements of any kind with men and women. It was safest to stand firmly on his own feet

There is ample evidence of this in his work. A striking statement of it is to be found in the opening pages of *The Portrait of a Lady* where he describes the Touchett parents as seen by their son Ralph: "His father, as he had often said to himself, was the more motherly; his mother, on the other hand, was paternal, and even, according to the slang of the day, gubernatorial." Henry James might have been writing of his own parents. In his recollections of his boyhood he has very little to say about his mother so that everything that he does say takes on great significance. And the sketch he gives of her is that of a woman depleted, like May Server, through devotion to her husband and children. "The only thing I might well have questioned . . ." he muses, "was the possibility on the part of a selflessness so consistently and unabatedly active, of its having anything ever left *acutely* to offer."

This was his first view of the operation of the "sacred fount" by which a process of nourishment and depletion was carried out; and he saw it all around him, in "strong" female relatives and in a grandmother who survived her husband by many years; and later, in middle life, in the spectacle of his own father who lost all will to live after the death of the mother. In Henry James's mind—and in his fiction—love was a force capable of depleting and destroying. Women could influence men, change them for good or bad, and what resulted usually was a stultifying dependency. The significant relationship was what a woman of feeling and perception could impart to a man, what a maternal, all-serving figure could do for a man's mind. It is no accident that in discussing the woman who parted with her wit in *The Sacred Fount* the narrator invokes Egeria—"We shall find the right woman—our friend's mystic Egeria." Egeria was one of the nymphs in Rome from whom King Numa, the successor to Romulus, received instruction; he met her in a grove which had a kind of sacred fount, a spring gushing from a dark recess and from which the Vestal Virgins drew water for their rites. Ovid has told how Egeria, disconsolate when Numa died, melted into tears and became a fountain herself, attaining definitive form as a source.

In James's works men sometimes draw their mental strength from women but can also be physically destroyed by them. James's first short story, published anonymously, was that of a Balzacian heroine who plots with a boatman to destroy her lame husband. The young Henry James was sufficiently attracted to Mérimée's *La Vénus d'Ille* to have translated it. It tells how a statue of Venus comes alive, not beneficently, like Pygmalion's statue, but to crush and kill a man who had placed his engagement ring on the statue's finger. The hero of one of James's early stories, "Osborne's Revenge," sees the heroine as a woman who "drained honest men's hearts to the last drop, and bloomed white upon the monstrous diet." This story is one of his earliest experiments in appearance and reality; for while the heroine gives this impression of being a vampire, she turns out to be wholly innocent of the charge. The heroine of another early blood-and-thunder tale, "De Grey: A Romance," fights the family curse which dooms De Grey heirs to early death and only succeeds in reversing it ". . . she blindly, senselessly, remorselessly drained the life from his being. As she bloomed and prospered, he drooped and languished. While she was living for him, he was dying for her." It was a case of bliss and bale. James was twenty-five when he wrote this story and twenty-six when his cousin Minny Temple died. Minny, to whom he was deeply attached, promptly was converted into a May Server figure in a letter written by Henry to his brother William: "Among the sad reflections that her death provokes for me, there is none sadder than this view of the gradual change and reversal of our relations: I slowly crawling from weakness and inaction and suffering into strength and health and hope: she sinking out of brightness and youth into decline and death. It's almost as if she had passed away—as far as I am concerned—from having served her purpose, that of standing well within the world, inviting and inviting me onward by all the bright intensity of her example. . . ." This is strangely like the narrator's musing in *The Sacred Fount* as to what would happen to Mrs. Brissenden if her fount, Guy, her husband, were to die. "She would have loved his youth, and have made it her own, in death as in life, and he would have quitted the world, in truth, only the more effectually to leave it to her."

When James was thirty-four the fantasy still haunted him. In "Longstaff's Marriage," as in "De Grey," one or the other of the lovers must die; their attraction for each other means depletion or extinction. And in this story it is the woman who dies—like Minny—and the man who survives. Finally, at fifty-seven, James gave the fantasy its most elaborate statement in *The Sacred Fount*.

Henry James himself regarded *The Sacred Fount* as a trifle, a *jeu d'esprit* intended as a short story but which he found had grown to 20,000 words. When this happened to the novelist, his usual procedure was to go through with his work no matter where it would lead him, on the professional theory that having expended so much labor he must get some return for it. He always made it a rule to finish any work once it was started. Not to finish would be a waste of effort, a sign of failure in ingenuity. James accordingly tossed off another 60,000 words of this "fine flight . . . into the high fantastic" with his characteristic vigor. His professional sense was sound. He collected $3,500 in advances on royalties from the American and English publishers and, having thus cleared his desk and earned his money, he set to work on *The Ambassadors.* That novel, as a matter of fact, has in it an interesting carry-over from *The Sacred Fount*—for what is Lambert Strether doing but once more being the sensitive observer seeking to fathom a relationship, that between Madame de Vionnet and Chad? Madame de Vionnet is again a May Server, at whose sacred fount Chad has acquired poise and a measure of polish. It is she who is left depleted at the end.

In an unpublished letter to the Duchess of Sutherland the novelist spoke of his book as a "profitless labyrinth" and as "fantastic and insubstantial: I mean to serve, in future, to make up for it, nothing but boiled mutton and potatoes." In another unpublished letter, to Mrs. Humphry Ward,* he offered more details. Mrs. Ward, as a fellow novelist, was entitled, he felt, to a fuller answer to her puzzled inquiry after reading the book. Closely read, the answer provides us with an important clue to Henry James's intention. After asserting that the book wasn't "worth discussing" and dismissing it as "the merest of *jeux d'esprit*" and "a small fantasticality" and also as "a consistent joke," he nevertheless adds: "Let me say for it, however, that it has, I assure you, and applied quite rigorously and constructively, I believe, its own little law of composition." And he

* I am indebted to Miss Dorothy Ward for this letter and to Mr. Donald Brien for the letter to the Duchess of Sutherland.

adds "As I give but the phantasmagoric I have, for clearness, to make it *evidential. . . .*"

The key words for us are *own little law of composition, phantasmagoric,* and *evidential.* For *phantasmagoric* is that which is appearance, and *evidential* is that which deals with reality. And we have seen how Henry James adhered consistently to his "law of composition," that of keeping the story entirely within the eye-view and the mind of the narrator. We might translate James's sentence as follows: "As I give but the appearance of things, I have, for clearness, to make them offer such evidence as they can. . . ."

We return now to our point of departure. Is this elaborately written book an independent work of art or must it be set down as a failure, even if it stemmed from a great master of fiction? Its theme is tenuous, it is a flight into fantasy, it is slight indeed when set into the long shelf of Henry James's substantial fictions. Yet it is, taken as a technical performance, a masterpiece of the story-teller's art. Having predicated a situation, Henry James does create a vivid little drama of shadow and substance; on artistic ground there is much to commend the work. The narrative is tight, the action confined to a brief compass of time, and after the prelude, the unity of place is carefully observed. We are conscious of the lapse of the hours, of movement from bright sunlight to sunset and twilight; we stroll on lawn and terrace; and only the characters involved in the action are presented to us. We are told nothing more than is necessary to keep the story going, and the drama is built wholly out of the tensions of human relationships. Above all there is the striking compositional method that reminds one of those experimental films in which the camera eye is ours, but is also the eye of the person in the film. This process of self-revelation, exercised by an omniscient narrator, leaves us with two levels of reading: the narrative itself, and the evidence in it which we must appraise in order to evaluate the credibility of the narrator. As a "high application of the intelligence" *The Sacred Fount* is to be cherished and studied. It deserves its honored little place on the Jamesian shelf. And it deserves better of its critics.

LEON EDEL

# THE SACRED FOUNT

## I

IT was an occasion, I felt—the prospect of a large party—to look out at the station for others, possible friends and even possible enemies, who might be going. Such premonitions, it was true, bred fears when they failed to breed hopes, though it was to be added that there were sometimes, in the case, rather happy ambiguities. One was glowered at, in the compartment, by people who on the morrow, after breakfast, were to prove charming; one was spoken to first by people whose sociability was subsequently to show as bleak; and one built with confidence on others who were never to reappear at all—who were only going to Birmingham. As soon as I saw Gilbert Long, some way up the platform, however, I knew him as an element. It was not so much that the wish was father to the thought as that I remembered having already more than once met him at Newmarch. He was a friend of the house—he wouldn't be going to Birmingham. I so little expected him, at the same time, to recognise me that I stopped short of the carriage near which he stood—I looked for a seat that wouldn't make us neighbours.

I had met him at Newmarch only—a place of a charm so special as to create rather a bond among its guests; but he had always, in the interval, so failed to know me that I could only hold him as stupid unless I held him as impertinent. He was stupid in fact, and in that character had no business at Newmarch; but he had also, no doubt, his system, which he applied without discernment. I wondered, while I saw my things put into my corner, what Newmarch could see in him—for it always had to see something before it made a sign. His good looks, which were striking, perhaps paid his way—his six feet and more of stature, his low-growing, tight-curling hair, his big, bare, blooming face. He was a fine piece of human furniture—he made a small party seem more numerous. This, at least, was the impression of him that had revived before I stepped out again to the platform, and it armed me only at first with surprise when I saw him come down to me as if for a greeting. If he had decided at last to treat me as an acquaintance made, it was none the less a case for letting him come all the way. That, accordingly, was what he did, and with so clear a conscience, I hasten to add, that at the end of a minute we were talking together quite as with the tradition of prompt intimacy. He was good-looking enough, I now again saw, but not such a model of it as I had seemed to remember; on the other hand his manners had distinctly gained in ease. He referred to our previous encounters and common contacts—he was glad I was going; he peeped into my compartment and thought it better than his own. He called a porter, the next minute, to shift his things, and while his attention was so taken I made out some of the rest of the contingent, who were finding or had already found places.

This lasted till Long came back with his porter, as well as with a lady unknown to me and to whom he had apparently mentioned that our carriage would pleasantly accommodate her. The porter carried in fact her dressing-bag, which he put upon a seat and the bestowal of which left the lady presently free to turn to me with a reproach: "I don't think it very nice of you not to speak to me." I stared, then caught at her identity through her voice; after which I reflected that she might easily have thought me the same sort of ass as I had thought Long. For she was simply, it appeared, Grace Brissenden. We had, the three of us, the carriage to ourselves, and we journeyed together for more than an hour, during which, in my corner, I had my companions opposite. We began at first by talking a little, and then as the train—a fast one—ran straight and proportionately bellowed, we gave up the effort to compete with its music. Meantime, however, we had exchanged with each other a fact or two to turn over in silence. Brissenden was coming later—not, indeed, that that was such a fact. But his wife was informed—she knew about the numerous others; she had mentioned, while we waited, people and things: that Obert, R.A., was somewhere in the train, that her husband was to bring on Lady John, and that Mrs. Froome and Lord Lutley were in the wondrous new fashion—and their servants too, like a single household—starting, travelling, arriving together. It came back to me as I sat there that when she mentioned Lady John as in charge of Brissenden the other member of our trio had expressed interest and surprise—expressed it so as to have made her reply with a smile: "Didn't you really know?" This passage had taken place on the platform while, availing ourselves of our last minute, we hung about our door.

"Why in the world *should* I know?"

To which, with good nature, she had simply returned: "Oh, it's only that I thought you always did!" And they both had looked at me a little oddly, as if appealing from each other. "What in the world does she mean?" Long might have seemed to ask; while Mrs. Brissenden conveyed with light profundity: "*You* know why he should as well as I, don't you?" In point of fact I didn't in the least; and what afterwards struck me much more as the beginning of my anecdote was a word dropped by Long after someone had come up to speak to her. I had then given him his cue by alluding to my original failure to place her. What in the world, in the year or two, had happened to her? She had changed so extraordinarily for the better. How could a woman who had been plain so long become pretty so late?

It was just what he had been wondering. "I didn't place her at first myself. She had to speak to me. But I hadn't seen her since her marriage, which was—wasn't it?—four or five years ago. She's amazing for her age."

"What then *is* her age?"

"Oh—two or three-and-forty."

"She's prodigious for that. But can it be so great?"

"Isn't it easy to count?" he asked. "Don't you remember, when poor Briss married her, how immensely she was older? What was it they called it?—a case of child-stealing. Everyone made jokes. Briss isn't yet thirty." No, I bethought myself, he wouldn't be; but I hadn't remembered the difference as so great. What I had mainly remembered was that she had been rather ugly. At present she was rather handsome. Long, however, as to this, didn't agree. "I'm bound to say I don't quite call it beauty."

"Oh, I only speak of it as relative. She looks so well—and somehow so 'fine.' Why else shouldn't we have recognised her?"

"Why indeed? But it isn't a thing with which beauty has to do." He had made the matter out with an acuteness for which I shouldn't have given him credit. "What has happened to her is simply that—well, that nothing has."

"Nothing has happened? But, my dear man, she has been married. That's supposed to be something."

"Yes, but she has been married so little and so stupidly. It must be desperately dull to be married to poor Briss. His comparative youth doesn't, after all, make more of him. He's nothing but what he is. Her clock has simply stopped. She looks no older—that's all."

"Ah, and a jolly good thing too, when you start where she did. But I take your discrimination," I added, "as just. The only thing is that if a woman doesn't grow older she may be said to grow younger; and if she grows younger she may be supposed to grow prettier. That's all—except, of course, that it strikes me as charming also for Brissenden himself. *He* had the face, I seem to recall, of a baby; so that if his wife did flaunt her fifty years——!"

"Oh," Long broke in, "it wouldn't have mattered to him if she had. That's the awfulness, don't you see? of the married state. People have to get used to each other's charms as well as to their faults. He wouldn't have noticed. It's only you and I who do, and the charm of it is for *us*."

"What a lucky thing then," I laughed, "that, with Brissenden so out of it and relegated to the time-table's obscure hereafter, it should be you and I who enjoy her!" I had been struck in what he said with more things than I could take up, and I think I must have looked at him, while he talked, with a slight return of my first mystification. He talked as I had never heard him—less and less like the heavy Adonis who had so often "cut" me; and while he did so I was proportionately more conscious of the change in him. He noticed in fact after a little the vague confusion of my gaze and asked me—with complete good nature—why I stared at him so hard. I sufficiently disembroiled myself to reply that I could only be fascinated by the way he made his points; to which he—with the same sociability—made answer that he, on the contrary, more than suspected me, clever and critical as I was, of amusement at his artless prattle. He stuck none the less to his idea that what we had been discussing was lost on Brissenden. "Ah, then I hope," I said, "that at least Lady John isn't!"

"Oh, Lady John——!" And he turned away as if there were either too much or too little to say about her.

I found myself engaged again with Mrs. Briss while he was occupied with a newspaper-boy—and engaged, oddly, in very much the free view of him that he and I had just taken of herself. She put it to me frankly that she had never seen a man so improved: a confidence that I met with alacrity, as it showed me that, under the same impression, I had not been astray. She had only, it seemed, on seeing him, made him out with a great effort. I took in this confession, but I repaid it. "He hinted to me that he had not known you more easily."

"More easily than you did? Oh, nobody does that; and, to be quite honest, I've got used to it and don't mind. People talk of our changing every seven years, but they make me feel as if I changed every seven minutes. What will you have, at any rate, and how can I help it? It's the grind of life, the wear and tear of time and misfortune. And, you know, I'm ninety-three."

"How young you must feel," I answered, "to care to talk of your age! I envy you, for nothing would induce me to let you know mine. You look, you see, just twenty-five."

It evidently too, what I said, gave her pleasure—a pleasure that she caught and held. "Well, you can't say I dress it."

"No, you dress, I make out, ninety-three. If you *would* only dress twenty-five you'd look fifteen."

"Fifteen in a schoolroom charade!" She laughed at this happily enough. "Your compliment to my taste is odd. I know, at all events," she went on, "what's the difference in Mr. Long."

"Be so good then, for my relief, as to name it."

"Well, a very clever woman has for some time past——"

"Taken"—this beginning was of course enough—"a particular interest in him? Do you mean Lady John?" I inquired; and, as she evidently did, I rather demurred. "Do you call Lady John a very clever woman?"

"Surely. That's why I kindly arranged that, as she was to take, I happened to learn, the next train, Guy should come with her."

"You arranged it?" I wondered. "She's not so clever as you then."

"Because you feel that *she* wouldn't, or couldn't? No doubt she wouldn't have made the same point of it—for more than one reason. Poor Guy hasn't pretensions—has nothing but his youth and his beauty. But that's precisely why I'm sorry for him and try whenever I can to give him a lift. Lady John's company *is*, you see, a lift."

"You mean it has so unmistakably been one to Long?"

"Yes—it has positively given him a mind and a tongue. *That's* what has come over him."

"Then," I said, "it's a most extraordinary case—such as one really has never met."

"Oh, but," she objected, "it happens."

"Ah, so very seldom! Yes—I've positively never met it. Are you very sure," I insisted, "that Lady John *is* the influence?"

"I don't mean to say, of course," she replied, "that he looks fluttered if you mention her, that he doesn't in fact look as blank as a pickpocket. But that proves nothing—or rather, as they're known to be always together, and she from morning till night as pointed as a hat-pin, it proves just what one sees. One simply takes it in."

I turned the picture round. "They're scarcely together when she's together with Brissenden."

"Ah, that's only once in a way. It's a thing that from time to time such people—don't you know?—make a particular point of: they cultivate, to cover their game, the appearance of other little friendships. It puts outsiders off the scent, and the real thing meanwhile goes on. Besides, you yourself acknowledge the effect. If she hasn't made him clever, what has she made him? She has given him, steadily, more and more intellect."

"Well, you may be right," I laughed, "though you speak as if it were cod-liver oil. Does she administer it, as a daily dose, by the spoonful? or only as a drop at a time? Does he take it in his food? Is he supposed to know? The difficulty for me is simply that if I've seen the handsome grow ugly and the ugly handsome, the fat grow thin and the thin fat, the short grow long and the long short; if I've even, likewise, seen the clever, as I've too fondly, at least, supposed them, grow stupid: so have I *not* seen—no, not once in all my days—the stupid grow clever."

It was a question, none the less, on which she could perfectly stand up. "All I can say is then that you'll have, the next day or two, an interesting new experience."

"It *will* be interesting," I declared while I thought—"and all the more if I make out for myself that Lady John *is* the agent."

"You'll make it out if you talk to her—that is, I mean, if you make *her* talk. You'll see how she *can*."

"She keeps her wit then," I asked, "in spite of all she pumps into others?"

"Oh, she has enough for two!"

"I'm immensely struck with yours," I replied, "as well as with your generosity. I've seldom seen a woman take so handsome a view of another."

"It's because I like to be kind!" she said with the best faith in the world; to which I could only return, as we entered the train, that it was a kindness Lady John would doubtless appreciate. Long rejoined us, and we ran, as I have said, our course; which, as I have also noted, seemed short to me in the light of such a blaze of suggestion. To each of my companions—and the fact stuck out of them—something unprecedented had happened.

## II

THE day was as fine and the scene as fair at Newmarch as the party was numerous and various; and my memory associates with the rest of the long afternoon many renewals of acquaintance and much sitting and strolling, for snatches of talk, in the long shade of great trees and through the straight walks of old gardens. A couple of hours thus passed, and fresh accessions enriched the picture. There were persons I was curious of—of Lady John, for instance, of whom I promised myself an early view; but we were apt to be carried away in currents that reflected new images and sufficiently beguiled impatience. I recover, all the same, a full sequence of impressions, each of which, I afterwards saw, had been appointed to help all the others. If my anecdote, as I have mentioned, had begun, at Paddington, at a particular moment, it gathered substance step by step and without missing a link. The links, in fact, should I count them all, would make too long a chain. They formed, nevertheless, the happiest little chapter of accidents, though a series of which I can scarce give more than the general effect.

One of the first accidents was that, before dinner, I met Ford Obert wandering a little apart with Mrs. Server, and that, as they were known to me as agreeable acquaintances, I should have faced them with confidence had I not immediately drawn from their sequestered air the fear of interrupting them. Mrs. Server was always lovely and Obert always expert; the latter straightway pulled up, however, making me as welcome as if their converse had dropped. She was extraordinarily pretty, markedly responsive, conspicuously charming, but he gave me a look that really seemed to say: "Don't—there's a good fellow—leave me any longer alone with her!" I had met her at Newmarch before—it was indeed only so that I had met her—and I knew how she was valued there. I also knew that an aversion to pretty women—numbers of whom he had preserved for a grateful posterity—was his sign neither as man nor as artist; the effect of all of which was to make me ask myself what she could have been doing to him. Making love, possibly—yet from that he would scarce have appealed. She wouldn't, on the other hand, have given him her company only to be inhuman. I joined them, at all events, learning from Mrs. Server that she had come by a train previous to my own; and we made a slow trio till, at a turn of the prospect, we came upon another group. It consisted of Mrs. Froome and Lord Lutley and of Gilbert Long and

Lady John—mingled and confounded, as might be said, not assorted according to tradition. Long and Mrs. Froome came first, I recollect, together, and his lordship turned away from Lady John on seeing me rather directly approach her. She had become for me, on the spot, as interesting as, while we travelled, I had found my two friends in the train. As the source of the flow of "intellect" that had transmuted our young man, she had every claim to an earnest attention; and I should soon have been ready to pronounce that she rewarded it as richly as usual. She was indeed, as Mrs. Briss had said, as pointed as a hat-pin, and I bore in mind that lady's injunction to look in her for the answer to our riddle.

The riddle, I may mention, sounded afresh to my ear in Gilbert Long's gay voice; it hovered there—before me, beside, behind me, as we all paused—in his light, restless step, a nervous animation that seemed to multiply his presence. He became really, for the moment, under this impression, the thing I was most conscious of; I heard him, I felt him even while I exchanged greetings with the sorceress by whose wand he had been touched. To be touched myself was doubtless not quite what I wanted; yet I wanted, distinctly, a glimpse; so that, with the smart welcome Lady John gave me, I might certainly have felt that I was on the way to get it. The note of Long's predominance deepened during these minutes in a manner I can't describe, and I continued to feel that though we pretended to talk it was to him only we listened. He had us all in hand; he controlled for the moment all our attention and our relations. He was in short, as a consequence of our attitude, in possession of the scene to a tune he couldn't have dreamed of a year or two before—inasmuch as at that period he could have figured at no such eminence without making a fool of himself. And the great thing was that if his eminence was now so perfectly graced he yet knew less than any of us what was the matter with him. He was unconscious of how he had "come out"—which was exactly what sharpened my wonder. Lady John, on her side, was thoroughly conscious, and I had a fancy that she looked at me to measure how far *I* was. I cared, naturally, not in the least what she guessed; her interest for me was all in the operation of her influence. I am afraid I watched to catch it in the act—watched her with a curiosity of which she might well have become aware.

What an intimacy, what an intensity of relation, I said to myself, so successful a process implied! It was of course familiar enough that when people were so deeply in love they rubbed off on each other—that a great pressure of soul to soul usually left on either side a sufficient show of tell-tale traces. But for Long to have been so stamped as

I found him, how the pliant wax must have been prepared and the seal of passion applied! What an affection the woman working such a change in him must have managed to create as a preface to her influence! With what a sense of her charm she must have paved the way for it! Strangely enough, however—it was even rather irritating—there was nothing more than usual in Lady John to assist my view of the height at which the pair so evoked must move. These things—the way other people could feel about each other, the power not one's self, in the given instance, that made for passion—were of course at best the mystery of mysteries; still, there were cases in which fancy, sounding the depths or the shallows, could at least drop the lead. Lady John, perceptibly, was no such case; imagination, in her presence, was but the weak wing of the insect that bumps against the glass. She was pretty, prompt, hard, and, in a way that was special to her, a mistress at once of "culture" and of slang. She was like a hat—with one of Mrs. Briss's hat-pins—askew on the bust of Virgil. Her ornamental information—as strong as a coat of furniture-polish—almost knocked you down. What I felt in her now more than ever was that, having a reputation for "point" to keep up, she was always under arms, with absences and anxieties like those of a celebrity at a public dinner. She thought too much of her "speech"—of how soon it would have to come.

It was none the less wonderful, however, that, as Grace Brissenden had said, she should still find herself with intellect to spare—have lavished herself by precept and example on Long and yet have remained for each other interlocutor as fresh as the clown bounding into the ring. She cracked, for my benefit, as many jokes and turned as many somersaults as might have been expected; after which I thought it fair to let her off. We all faced again to the house, for dressing and dinner were in sight.

I found myself once more, as we moved, with Mrs. Server, and I remember rejoicing that, sympathetic as she showed herself, she didn't think it necessary to be, like Lady John, always "ready." She was delightfully handsome—handsomer than ever; slim, fair, fine, with charming pale eyes and splendid auburn hair. I said to myself that I hadn't done her justice; she hadn't organised her forces, was a little helpless and vague, but there was ease for the weary in her happy nature and her peculiar grace. These last were articles on which, five minutes later, before the house, where we still had a margin, I was moved to challenge Ford Obert.

"What was the matter just now—when, though you were so fortunately occupied, you yet seemed to call me to the rescue?"

"Oh," he laughed, "I was only occupied in being frightened!"

"But at what?"

"Well, at a sort of sense that she wanted to make love to me."

I reflected. "Mrs. Server? Does Mrs. Server make love?"

"It seemed to me," my friend replied, "that she began on it to *you* as soon as she got hold of you. Weren't you aware?"

I debated afresh; I didn't know that I had been. "Not to the point of terror. She's so gentle and so appealing. Even if she took one in hand with violence, moreover," I added, "I don't see why terror—given so charming a person—should be the result. It's flattering."

"Ah, you're brave," said Obert.

"I didn't know you were ever timid. How can you be, in your profession? Doesn't it come back to me, for that matter, that—only the other year—you painted her?"

"Yes, I faced her to that extent. But she's different now."

I scarcely made it out. "In what way different? She's as charming as ever."

As if even for his own satisfaction my friend seemed to think a little. "Well, her affections were not then, I imagine, at her disposal. I judge that that's what it must have been. They were fixed—with intensity; and it made the difference with *me*. Her imagination had, for the time, rested its wing. At present it's ready for flight—it seeks a fresh perch. It's trying. Take care."

"Oh, I don't flatter myself," I laughed, "that I've only to hold out my hand! At any rate," I went on, "*I* sha'n't call for help."

He seemed to think again. "I don't know. You'll see."

"If I do I shall see a great deal more than I now suspect." He wanted to get off to dress, but I still held him. "Isn't she wonderfully lovely?"

"Oh!" he simply exclaimed.

"Isn't she as lovely as she seems?"

But he had already broken away. "What has that to do with it?"

"What has anything, then?"

"She's too beastly unhappy."

"But isn't that just one's advantage?"

"No. It's uncanny." And he escaped.

The question had at all events brought us indoors and so far up our staircase as to where it branched towards Obert's room. I followed it to my corridor, with which other occasions had made me acquainted, and I reached the door on which I expected to find my card of designation. This door, however, was open, so as to show me, in momentary possession of the room, a gentleman, unknown to me, who, in unguided quest of his quarters, appeared to have arrived from the other end of the passage. He had just seen, as the property of another, my unpacked things, with which he immediately connected me. He moreover, to my surprise, on my entering, sounded my name, in response to which I could only at first remain blank. It was in fact not till I had begun to help him place himself that, correcting my blankness, I knew him for Guy Brissenden. He had been put by himself, for some reason, in the bachelor wing and, exploring at hazard, had mistaken the signs. By the time we found his servant and his lodging I had reflected on the oddity of my having been as stupid about the husband as I had been about the wife. He had escaped my notice since our arrival, but I had, as a much older man, met him—the hero of his odd union—at some earlier time. Like his wife, none the less, he had now struck me as a stranger, and it was not till, in his room, I stood a little face to face with him that I made out the wonderful reason.

The wonderful reason was that I was *not* a much older man; Guy Brissenden, at any rate, was not a much younger. It was he who was old—it was he who was older—it was he who was oldest. That was so disconcertingly what he had become. It was in short what he would have been had he been as old as he looked. He looked almost anything—he looked quite sixty. I made it out again at dinner, where, from a distance, but opposite, I had him in sight. Nothing could have been stranger than the way that, fatigued, fixed, settled, he seemed to have piled up the years. They were there without having had time to arrive. It was as if he had discovered some miraculous short cut to the common doom. He had grown old, in fine, as people you see after an interval sometimes strike you as having grown rich—too quickly for the honest, or at least for the straight, way. He had cheated or inherited or speculated. It took me but a minute then to add him to my little gallery—the small collection, I mean, represented by his wife and by Gilbert Long, as well as in some degree doubtless also by Lady John: the museum of those who put to me with such intensity the question of what had happened to them. His wife, on the same side, was not out of my range, and now, largely exposed, lighted, jewelled, and enjoying moreover visibly the sense of these things—his wife, upon my honour, as I soon remarked to the lady next me, his wife (it was too prodigious!) looked about twenty.

"Yes—isn't it funny?" said the lady next me.

It was so funny that it set me thinking afresh and that, with the interest of it, which became a positive excitement, I had to keep myself in hand in order not too publicly to explain, not to break out right and left with my reflections. I don't know why—it was a sense instinctive and unreasoned, but I felt from the first that if I was on the scent of something ultimate I had better waste neither my wonder nor my wisdom. I *was* on the scent—that I was sure of; and yet even after I was sure I should still have been at a loss to put my enigma itself into words. I was just conscious, vaguely, of being on the track of a law, a law that would fit, that would strike me as governing the delicate phenomena — delicate though so marked—that my imagination found itself playing with. A part of the amusement they yielded came, I daresay, from my exaggerating them—grouping them into a larger mystery (and thereby a larger "law") than the facts, as observed, yet warranted; but that is the common fault of minds for which the vision of life is an obsession. The obsession pays, if one will; but to pay it has to borrow. After dinner, but while the men were still in the room, I had some talk again with Long, of whom I inquired if he had been so placed as to see "poor Briss."

He appeared to wonder, and poor Briss, with our shifting of seats, was now at a distance. "I think so—but I didn't particularly notice. What's the matter with poor Briss?"

"That's exactly what I thought you might be able to tell me. But if nothing, in him, strikes you——!"

He met my eyes a moment—then glanced about. "Where is he?"

"Behind you; only don't turn round to look, for he knows——" But I dropped, having caught something directed toward me in Brissenden's face. My interlocutor remained blank, simply asking me, after an instant, what it was he knew. On this I said what I meant. "He knows we've noticed."

Long wondered again. "Ah, but I *haven't!*" He spoke with some sharpness.

"He knows," I continued, noting the sharpness too, "what's the matter with him."

"Then what the devil is it?"

I waited a little, having for the moment an idea on my hands. "Do you see him often?"

Long disengaged the ash from his cigarette. "No. Why should I?"

Distinctly, he was uneasy—though as yet perhaps but vaguely—at what I might be coming to. That was precisely my idea, and if I pitied him a little for my pressure my idea was yet what most possessed me. "Do you mean there's nothing in him that strikes you?"

On this, unmistakably, he looked at me hard. "'Strikes' me—in that boy? Nothing in him, that I know of, ever struck me in my life. He's not an object of the smallest interest to me!"

I felt that if I insisted I should really stir up the old Long, the stolid coxcomb, capable of rudeness, with whose redemption, reabsorption, supersession—one scarcely knew what to call it—I had been so happily impressed. "Oh, of course, if you haven't noticed, you haven't, and the matter I was going to speak of will have no point. You won't know what I mean." With which I paused long enough to let his curiosity operate if his denial had been sincere. But it hadn't. His curiosity never operated. He only exclaimed, more indulgently, that he didn't know what I was talking about; and I recognised after a little that if I had made him, without intention, uncomfortable, this was exactly a proof of his being what Mrs. Briss, at the station, had called cleverer, and what I had so much remarked while, in the garden before dinner, he held our small company. Nobody, nothing could, in the time of his inanity, have made him turn a hair. It was the mark of his aggrandisement. But I spared him—so far as was consistent with my wish for absolute certainty; changed the subject, spoke of other things, took pains to sound disconnectedly, and only after reference to several of the other ladies, the name over which we had just felt friction. "Mrs. Brissenden's quite fabulous."

He appeared to have strayed, in our interval, far. "'Fabulous'?"

"Why, for the figure that, by candle-light and in cloth-of-silver and diamonds, she is still able to make."

"Oh dear, yes!" He showed as relieved to be able to see what I meant. "She has grown so very much less plain."

But that wasn't at all what I meant. "Ah," I

said, "you put it the other way at Paddington—which was much more the right one."

He had quite forgotten. "How then did I put it?"

As he had done before, I got rid of my ash. "She hasn't grown very much less plain. She has only grown very much less old."

"Ah, well," he laughed, but as if his interest had quickly dropped, "youth is—comparatively speaking—beauty."

"Oh, not always. Look at poor Briss himself."

"Well, if you like better, beauty is youth."

"Not always, either," I returned. "Certainly only when it *is* beauty. To see how little it may be either, look," I repeated, "at poor Briss."

"I thought you told me just now not to!" He rose at last in his impatience.

"Well, at present you can."

I also got up, the other men at the same moment moved, and the subject of our reference stood in view. This indeed was but briefly, for, as if to examine a picture behind him, the personage in question suddenly turned his back. Long, however, had had time to take him in and then to decide. "I've looked. What then?"

"You don't see anything?"

"Nothing."

"Not what everyone else must?"

"No, confound you!"

I already felt that, to be so tortuous, he must have had a reason, and the search for his reason was what, from this moment, drew me on. I had in fact half guessed it as we stood there. But this only made me the more explanatory. "It isn't really, however, that Brissenden has grown less lovely — it's only that he has grown less young."

To which my friend, as we quitted the room, replied simply: "Oh!"

The effect I have mentioned was, none the less, too absurd. The poor youth's back, before us, still as if consciously presented, confessed to the burden of time. "How old," I continued, "did we make out this afternoon that he would be?"

"That who would?"

"Why, poor Briss."

He fairly pulled up in our march. "Have you got him on the brain?"

"Don't I seem to remember, my dear man, that it was you yourself who knew? He's thirty at the most. He can't possibly be more. And there he is: as fine, as swaddled, as royal a mummy, to the eye, as one would wish to see. Don't pretend! But it's all right." I laughed as I took myself up. "I must talk to Lady John."

I did talk to her, but I must come to it. What is most to the point just here is an observation or two that, in the smoking-room, before going to bed, I exchanged with Ford Obert. I forbore, as I have hinted, to show all I saw, but it was lawfully open to me to judge of what other people did; and I had had before dinner my little proof that, on occasion, Obert could see as much as most. Yet I said nothing more to him for the present about Mrs. Server. The Brissendens were new to him, and his experience of every sort of facial accident, of human sign, made him just the touchstone I wanted. Nothing, naturally, was easier than to turn him on the question of the fair and the foul, type and character, weal and woe, among our fellow-visitors; so that my mention of the air of disparity in the couple I have just named came in its order and produced its effect. This effect was that of my seeing—which was all I required—that if the disparity was marked for him this expert observer could yet read it quite the wrong way. Why had so fine a young creature married a man three times her age? He was of course astounded when I told him the young creature was much nearer three times Brissenden's, and this led to some interesting talk between us as to the consequences, in general, of such association on such terms. The particular case before us, I easily granted, sinned by over-emphasis, but it was a fair, though a gross, illustration of what almost always occurred when twenty and forty, when thirty and sixty, mated or mingled, lived together in intimacy. Intimacy of course had to be postulated. Then either the high number or the low always got the upper hand, and it was usually the high that succeeded. It seemed, in other words, more possible to go back than to keep still, to grow young than to remain so. If Brissenden had been of his wife's age and his wife of Brissenden's, it would thus be he who must have redescended the hill, it would be she who would have been pushed over the brow. There was really a touching truth in it, the stuff of—what did people call such things?—an apologue or a parable. "One of the pair," I said, "has to pay for the other. What ensues is a miracle, and miracles are expensive. What's a greater one than to have your youth twice over? It's a second wind, another 'go'—which isn't the sort of thing life mostly treats us to. Mrs. Briss had to get her new blood, her extra allowance of time and bloom, somewhere; and from whom could she so conveniently extract them as from Guy himself? She *has*, by an extraordinary feat of legerdemain, extracted them; and he, on his side, to supply her, has had to tap the sacred fount. But the sacred fount is like the greedy man's description of the turkey as an 'awkward' dinner dish. It may be sometimes too much for a single share, but it's not enough to go round."

Obert was at all events sufficiently struck with my view to throw out a question on it. "So that, paying to his last drop, Mr. Briss, as you call him, can only die of the business?"

"Oh, not yet, I hope. But before *her*—yes: long."

He was much amused. "How you polish them off!"

"I only talk," I returned, "as you paint; not a bit worse! But one must indeed wonder," I conceded, "how the poor wretches feel."

"You mean whether Brissenden likes it?"

I made up my mind on the spot. "If he loves her he must. That is if he loves her passionately, sublimely." I saw it all. "It's in fact just because he does so love her that the miracle, for her, is wrought."

"Well," my friend reflected, "for taking a miracle coolly——!"

"She hasn't her equal? Yes, she does take it. She just quietly, but just selfishly, profits by it."

"And doesn't see then how her victim loses?"

"No. She can't. The perception, if she had it, would be painful and terrible—might even be fatal to the process. So she hasn't it. She passes round it. It takes all her flood of life to meet her own chance. She has only a wonderful sense of success and well-being. The *other* consciousness——"

"Is all for the other party?"

"The author of the sacrifice."

"Then how beautifully 'poor Briss,'" my companion said, "must have it!"

I had already assured myself. He had gone to bed, and my fancy followed him. "Oh, he has it so that, though he goes, in his passion, about with her, he dares scarcely show his face." And I made a final induction. "The agents of the sacrifice are uncomfortable, I gather, when they suspect or fear that you see."

My friend was charmed with my ingenuity. "How you've worked it out!"

"Well, I feel as if I were on the way to something."

He looked surprised. "Something still more?"

"Something still more." I had an impulse to tell him I scarce knew what. But I kept it under. "I seem to snuff up——"

"*Quoi donc?*"

"The sense of a discovery to be made."

"And of what?"

"I'll tell you to-morrow. Good-night."

## III

I DID on the morrow several things, but the first was not to redeem that vow. It was to address myself straight to Grace Brissenden. "I must let you know that, in spite of your guarantee, it doesn't go at all—oh, but not at all! I've tried Lady John, as you enjoined, and I can't but feel that she leaves us very much where we were." Then, as my listener seemed not quite to remember where we had been, I came to her help. "You said yesterday at Paddington, to explain the change in Gilbert Long — don't you recall? — that that woman, plying him with her genius and giving him of her best, is clever enough for two. She's not clever enough then, it strikes me, for three—or at any rate for four. I confess I don't see it. Does she really dazzle *you?*"

My friend had caught up. "Oh, you've a standard of wit!"

"No, I've only a sense of reality—a sense not at all satisfied by the theory of such an influence as Lady John's."

She wondered. "Such a one as whose else then?"

"Ah, that's for us still to find out! Of course

this can't be easy; for as the appearance is inevitably a kind of betrayal, it's in somebody's interest to conceal it."

This Mrs. Brissenden grasped. "Oh, you mean in the lady's?"

"In the lady's most. But also in Long's own, if he's really tender of the lady—which is precisely what our theory posits."

My companion, once roused, was all there. "I see. You call the appearance a kind of betrayal because it points to the relation behind it."

"Precisely."

"And the relation—to do that sort of thing—must be necessarily so awfully intimate."

"*Intimissima.*"

"And kept therefore in the background exactly in that proportion."

"Exactly in that proportion."

"Very well then," said Mrs. Brissenden, "doesn't Mr. Long's tenderness of Lady John quite fall in with what I mentioned to you?"

I remembered what she had mentioned to me. "His making her come down with poor Briss?"

"Nothing less."

"And is that all you go upon?"

"That and lots more."

I thought a minute—but I had been abundantly thinking. "I know what you mean by 'lots.' Is Brissenden in it?"

"Dear no—poor Briss! He wouldn't like that. *I* saw the manœuvre, but Guy didn't. And you must have noticed how he stuck to her all last evening."

"How Gilbert Long stuck to Lady John? Oh yes, I noticed. They were like Lord Lutley and Mrs. Froome. But is that what one can call being tender of her?"

My companion weighed it. "He must speak to her *sometimes*. I'm glad you admit, at any rate," she continued, "that it does take what you so prettily call some woman's secretly giving him of her best to account for him."

"Oh, that I admit with all my heart—or at least with all my head. Only, Lady John has none of the signs——"

"Of being the beneficent woman? What then *are* they—the signs—to be so plain?" I was not yet quite ready to say, however; on which she added: "It proves nothing, you know, that *you* don't like her."

"No. It would prove more if she didn't like *me*, which—fatuous fool as you may find me—I verily believe she does. If she hated me it would be, you see, for my ruthless analysis of her secret. She *has* no secret. She would like awfully to have—and she would like almost as much to be believed to have. Last evening, after dinner, she could feel perhaps for a while that she *was* believed. But it won't do. There's nothing in it. You asked me just now," I pursued, "what the signs of such a secret would naturally be. Well, bethink yourself a moment of what the secret itself must naturally be."

Oh, she looked as if she knew all about *that!* "Awfully charming—mustn't it?—to act upon a person, through an affection, so deeply."

"Yes—it can certainly be no vulgar flirtation." I felt a little like a teacher encouraging an apt pupil; but I could only go on with the lesson. "Whoever she is, she gives all she has. She keeps nothing back—nothing for herself."

"I see—because *he* takes everything. He just cleans her out." She looked at me—pleased at last really to understand—with the best conscience in the world. "Who *is* the lady then?"

But I could answer as yet only by a question. "How can she possibly be a woman who gives absolutely nothing whatever; who scrapes and saves and hoards; who keeps every crumb for herself? The whole show's there — to minister to Lady John's vanity and advertise the business—behind her smart shop-window. You can see it, as much as you like, and even amuse yourself with pricing it. But she never parts with an article. If poor Long depended on *her*——"

"Well, what?" She was really interested.

"Why, he'd be the same poor Long as ever. He

would go as he used to go—naked and unashamed. No," I wound up, "he deals—turned out as we now see him—at another establishment."

"I'll grant it," said Mrs. Brissenden, "if you'll only name me the place."

Ah, I could still but laugh and resume! "He doesn't screen Lady John—she doesn't screen herself—with your husband or with anybody. It's she who's herself the screen! And pleased as she is at being so clever, and at being thought so, she doesn't even know it. She doesn't so much as suspect it. She's an unmitigated fool about it. 'Of course Mr. Long's clever, because he's in love with me and sits at my feet, and don't you see how clever *I* am? Don't you hear what good things I say—wait a little, I'm going to say another in about three minutes; and how, if you'll only give him time too, he comes out with them after me? They don't perhaps sound so good, but you see where he has got them. I'm so brilliant, in fine, that the men who admire me have only to imitate me, which, you observe, they strikingly do.' Something like that is all her philosophy."

My friend turned it over. "You do sound like her, you know. Yet how, if a woman's stupid——"

"Can she have made a man clever? She can't. She can't at least have begun it. What we shall know the real person by, in the case that you and

I are studying, is that the man himself will have made her what she has become. She will have done just what Lady John has not done—she will have put up the shutters and closed the shop. She will have parted, for her friend, with her wit."

"So that she may be regarded as reduced to idiocy?"

"Well—so I can only see it."

"And that if we look, therefore, for the right idiot——"

"We shall find the right woman—our friend's mystic Egeria? Yes, we shall be at least approaching the truth. We shall 'burn,' as they say in hide-and-seek." I of course kept to the point that the idiot would have to *be* the right one. *Any* idiot wouldn't be to the purpose. If it was enough that a woman was a fool the search might become hopeless even in a house that would have passed but ill for a fool's paradise. We were on one of the shaded terraces, to which, here and there, a tall window stood open. The picture without was all morning and August, and within all clear dimness and rich gleams. We stopped once or twice, raking the gloom for lights, and it was at some such moment that Mrs. Brissenden asked me if I then regarded Gilbert Long as now exalted to the position of the most brilliant of our companions. "The cleverest man of the party?"—it pulled me up a little. "Hardly that, perhaps—for don't you see the proofs I'm myself giving you? But say he *is*"—I considered—"the cleverest but one." The next moment I had seen what she meant. "In that case the thing we're looking for ought logically to be the person, of the opposite sex, giving us the maximum sense of depletion for his benefit? The biggest fool, you suggest, *must*, consistently, be the right one? Yes again; it would so seem. But that's not really, you see, the short cut it sounds. The biggest fool is what we want, but the question is to discover who *is* the biggest."

"I'm glad then *I* feel so safe!" Mrs. Brissenden laughed.

"Oh, you're not the biggest!" I handsomely conceded. "Besides, as I say, there must be the other evidence—the evidence of relations."

We had gone on, with this, a few steps, but my companion again checked me, while her nod toward a window gave my attention a lead. "Won't *that*, as it happens, then do?" We could just see, from where we stood, a corner of one of the rooms. It was occupied by a seated couple, a lady whose face was in sight and a gentleman whose identity was attested by his back, a back somehow replete for us, at the moment, with a guilty significance. There *was* the evidence of relations. That we had suddenly caught Long in the act of presenting his receptacle at the sacred fount seemed announced by the tone in which Mrs. Brissenden named the other party—"Mme. de Dreuil!" We looked at each other, I was aware, with some elation; but our triumph was brief. The Comtesse de Dreuil, we quickly felt—an American married to a Frenchman—wasn't at all the thing. She was almost as much "all there" as Lady John. She was only another screen, and we perceived, for that matter, the next minute, that Lady John was also present. Another step had placed us within range of her; the picture revealed in the rich dusk of the room was a group of three. From that moment, unanimously, we gave up Lady John, and as we continued our stroll my friend brought out her despair. "Then he has nothing *but* screens? The need for so many does suggest a fire!" And in spite of discouragement she sounded, interrogatively, one after the other, the names of those ladies the perfection of whose presence of mind might, when considered, pass as questionable. We soon, however, felt our process to be, practically, a trifle invidious. Not one of the persons named could, at any rate—to do them all justice—affect us as an intellectual ruin. It was natural therefore for Mrs. Brissenden to conclude with scepticism. "She may exist—and exist as you require her; but what, after all, proves that she's here? She mayn't have come down with him. Does it necessarily follow that they always go about together?"

I was ready to declare that it necessarily followed.

I had my idea, and I didn't see why I shouldn't bring it out. "It's my belief that he no more goes away without her than you go away without poor Briss."

She surveyed me in splendid serenity. "But what have we in common?"

"With the parties to an abandoned flirtation? Well, you've in common your mutual attachment and the fact that you're thoroughly happy together."

"Ah," she good-humouredly answered, "we don't flirt!"

"Well, at all events, you don't separate. He doesn't really suffer you out of his sight, and, to circulate in the society you adorn, you don't leave him at home."

"Why shouldn't I?" she asked, looking at me, I thought, just a trifle harder.

"It isn't a question of why you shouldn't—it's a question of whether you do. You don't—do you? That's all."

She thought it over as if for the first time. "It seems to me I often leave him when I don't want him."

"Oh, when you don't want him—yes. But when don't you want him? You want him when you want to be right, and you want to be right when you mix in a scene like this. I mean," I continued for my private amusement, "when you want to be happy. Happiness, you know, is, to a lady in the full tide of social success, even more becoming than a new French frock. You have the advantage, for your beauty, of being admirably married. You bloom in your husband's presence. I don't say he need always be at your elbow; I simply say that you're most completely yourself when he's not far off. If there were nothing else there would be the help given you by your quiet confidence in his lawful passion."

"I'm bound to say," Mrs. Brissenden replied, "that such help is consistent with his not having spoken to me since we parted, yesterday, to come down here by different trains. We haven't so much as met since our arrival. My finding him so indispensable is consistent with my not having so much as looked at him. Indispensable, please, for what?"

"For your not being without him."

"What then do I do *with* him?"

I hesitated—there were so many ways of putting it; but I gave them all up. "Ah, I think it will be only *he* who can tell you! My point is that you've the instinct—playing in you, on either side, with all the ease of experience—of what you are to each other. All I mean is that it's the instinct that Long and *his* good friend must have. They too perhaps haven't spoken to each other. But where he comes she does, and where she comes he does. That's why I know she's among us."

"It's wonderful what you know!" Mrs. Brissenden again laughed. "How can you think of them as enjoying the facilities of people in *our* situation?"

"Of people married and therefore logically in presence? I don't," I was able to reply, "speak of their facilities as the same, and I recognise every limit to their freedom. But I maintain, none the less, that so far as they *can* go, they do go. It's a relation, and they work the relation: the relation, exquisite surely, of knowing they help each other to shine. Why are they not, therefore, like you and Brissenden? What I make out is that when they do shine one will find—though only after a hunt, I admit, as you see—they must both have been involved. Feeling their need, and consummately expert, they will have managed, have arranged."

She took it in with her present odd mixture of the receptive and the derisive. "Arranged what?"

"Oh, ask *her!*"

"I would if I could find her!" After which, for a moment, my interlocutress again considered. "But I thought it was just your contention that *she* doesn't shine. If it's Lady John's perfect repair that puts that sort of thing out of the question, your image, it seems to me, breaks down."

It did a little, I saw, but I gave it a tilt up. "Not at all. It's a case of shining as Brissenden shines."

I wondered if I might go further—then risked it. " By sacrifice."

I perceived at once that I needn't fear: her conscience was too good — she was only amused. " Sacrifice, for mercy's sake, of what? "

" Well—for mercy's sake—of his time."

" His time? " She stared. " Hasn't he all the time he wants? "

" My dear lady," I smiled, " he hasn't all the time *you* want! "

But she evidently had not a glimmering of what I meant. " Don't I make things of an ease, don't I make life of a charm, for him? "

I'm afraid I laughed out. " That's perhaps exactly it! It's what Gilbert Long does for *his* victim—makes things, makes life, of an ease and a charm."

She stopped yet again, really wondering at me now. " Then it's the woman, simply, who's happiest? "

" Because Brissenden's the man who is? Precisely! "

On which for a minute, without her going on, we looked at each other. " Do you really mean that if you only knew *me* as I am, it would come to you in the same way to hunt for my confederate? I mean if he weren't made obvious, you know, by his being my husband."

I turned this over. " If you were only in flirtation—as you reminded me just now that you're not? Surely!" I declared. "I should arrive at him, perfectly, after all eliminations, on the principle of looking for the greatest happiness——"

"Of the smallest number? Well, he may be a small number," she indulgently sighed, "but he's wholly content! Look at him now there," she added the next moment, "and judge." We had resumed our walk and turned the corner of the house, a movement that brought us into view of a couple just round the angle of the terrace, a couple who, like ourselves, must have paused in a sociable stroll. The lady, with her back to us, leaned a little on the balustrade and looked at the gardens; the gentleman close to her, with the same support, offered us the face of Guy Brissenden, as recognisable at a distance as the numbered card of a "turn" —the black figure upon white—at a music-hall. On seeing us he said a word to his companion, who quickly jerked round. Then his wife exclaimed to me—only with more sharpness—as she had exclaimed at Mme. de Dreuil: "By all that's lovely—May Server!" I took it, on the spot, for a kind of "Eureka!" but without catching my friend's idea. I was only aware at first that this idea left me as unconvinced as when the other possibilities had passed before us. Wasn't it simply the result of this lady's being the only one we had happened not to eliminate? She had not even occurred to us. She was pretty enough perhaps for any magic, but she hadn't the other signs. I didn't believe, somehow—certainly not on such short notice—either in her happiness or in her flatness. There was a vague suggestion, of a sort, in our having found her there with Brissenden: there would have been a pertinence, to our curiosity, or at least to mine, in this juxtaposition of the two persons who paid, as I had amused myself with calling it, so heroically; yet I had only to have it marked for me (to see them, that is, side by side,) in order to feel how little—at any rate superficially—the graceful, natural, charming woman ranged herself with the superannuated youth.

She had said a word to him at sight of us, in answer to his own, and in a minute or two they had met us. This had given me time for more than one reflection. It had also given Mrs. Brissenden time to insist to me on her identification, which I could see she would be much less quick to drop than in the former cases. "We have her," she murmured; "we have her; it's *she!*" It was by her insistance in fact that my thought was quickened. It even felt a kind of chill—an odd revulsion—at the touch of her eagerness. Singular perhaps that only then—yet quite certainly then—the curiosity to which I had so freely surrendered myself began to strike me as wanting in taste. It was reflected in Mrs. Brissenden quite by my fault, and I can't say just what cause for shame, after so much talk of our search and our scent, I found in our awakened and confirmed keenness. Why in the world hadn't I found it before? My scruple, in short, was a thing of the instant; it was in a positive flash that the amusing question was stamped for me as none of my business. One of the reflections I have just mentioned was that I had not had a happy hand in making it so completely Mrs. Brissenden's. Another was, however, that nothing, fortunately, that had happened between us really signified. For what had so suddenly overtaken me was the consciousness of this anomaly: that I was at the same time as disgusted as if I had exposed Mrs. Server and absolutely convinced that I had yet *not* exposed her.

While, after the others had greeted us and we stood in vague talk, I caught afresh the effect of their juxtaposition, I grasped, with a private joy that was quite extravagant—as so beyond the needed mark—at the reassurance it offered. This reassurance sprang straight from a special source. Brissenden's secret was so aware of itself as to be always on the defensive. Shy and suspicious, it was as much on the defensive at present as I had felt it to be—so far as I was concerned—the night before. What was there accordingly in Mrs. Server—frank and fragrant in the morning air—to correspond to any such consciousness? Nothing whatever—not a symptom. Whatever secrets she might have had, she had not *that* one; she was not in the same box; the sacred fount, in her, was not threatened with exhaustion. We all soon re-entered the house together, but Mrs. Brissenden, during the few minutes that followed, managed to possess herself of the subject of her denunciation. She put me off with Guy, and I couldn't help feeling it as a sign of her concentration. She warmed to the question just as I had thrown it over; and I asked myself rather ruefully what on earth I had been thinking of. I hadn't in the least had it in mind to "compromise" an individual; but an individual would be compromised if I didn't now take care.

## IV

I HAVE said that I did many things on this wonderful day, but perhaps the simplest way to describe the rest of them is as a sustained attempt to avert that disaster. I succeeded, by vigilance, in preventing my late companion from carrying Mrs. Server off: I had no wish to see her studied—by anyone but myself at least—in the light of my theory. I felt by this time that I understood my theory, but I was not obliged to believe that Mrs. Brissenden did. I am afraid I must frankly confess that I called deception to my aid; to separate the two ladies I gave the more initiated a look in which I invited her to read volumes. This look, or rather the look she returned, comes back to me as the first note of a tolerably tight, tense little drama, a little drama of which our remaining hours at Newmarch were the all too ample stage. She understood me, as I meant, that she had better leave me to get at the truth—owing me some obligation, as she did, for so much of it as I had already communicated. This step was of course a tacit pledge that she should have the rest from me later on. I knew of some pictures in one of the rooms that had not been lighted the previous evening, and I made these my pretext for the effect I desired. I asked Mrs. Server if she wouldn't come and see them with me, admitting at the same time that I could scarce expect her to forgive me for my share in the invasion of the quiet corner in which poor Briss had evidently managed so to interest her.

"Oh, yes," she replied as we went our way, "he *had* managed to interest me. Isn't he curiously interesting? But I hadn't," she continued on my being too struck with her question for an immediate answer—"I hadn't managed to interest *him*. Of course you know why!" she laughed. "No one interests him but Lady John, and he could think of nothing, while I kept him there, but of how soon he could return to her."

These remarks—of which I give rather the sense than the form, for they were a little scattered and troubled, and I helped them out and pieced them together—these remarks had for me, I was to find, unexpected suggestions, not all of which was I prepared on the spot to take up. "And is Lady John interested in our friend?"

"Not, I suppose, given her situation, so much as he would perhaps desire. You don't know what her situation *is?*" she went on while I doubtless appeared to be sunk in innocence. "Isn't it rather marked that there's only one person she's interested in?"

"One person?" I was thoroughly at sea.

But we had reached with it the great pictured saloon with which I had proposed to assist her to renew acquaintance and in which two visitors had anticipated us. "Why, here he is!" she exclaimed as we paused, for admiration, in the doorway. The high frescoed ceiling arched over a floor so highly polished that it seemed to reflect the faded pastels set, in rococo borders, in the walls and constituting the distinction of the place. Our companions, examining together one of the portraits and turning their backs, were at the opposite end, and one of them was Gilbert Long.

I immediately named the other. "Do you mean Ford Obert?"

She gave me, with a laugh, one of her beautiful looks. "Yes!"

It was answer enough for the moment, and the manner of it showed me to what legend she was committed. I asked myself, while the two men faced about to meet us, why she was committed to it, and I further considered that if Grace Brissenden, against every appearance, was right, there would now be something for me to see. Which of the two—the agent or the object of the sacrifice—would take most precautions? I kept my companion purposely, for a little while, on our side of the room, leaving the others, interested in their observations, to take their time to join us. It gave me occasion to wonder if the question mightn't be cleared up on the spot. There *was* no question, I had compunctiously made up my mind, for Mrs. Server; but now I should see the proof of that conclusion. The proof of it would be, between her and her imputed lover, the absence of anything that was not perfectly natural. Mrs. Server, with her eyes raised to the painted dome, with response charmed almost to solemnity in her exquisite face, struck me at this moment, I had to concede, as more than ever a person to have a lover imputed. The place, save for its pictures of later date, a triumph of the florid decoration of two centuries ago, evidently met her special taste, and a kind of profane piety had dropped on her, drizzling down, in the cold light, in silver, in crystal, in faint, mixed delicacies of colour, almost as on a pilgrim at a shrine. I don't know what it was in her—save, that is, the positive pitch of delicacy in her beauty—that made her, so impressed and presented, indescribably touching. She was like an awestruck child; she might have been herself—all Greuze tints, all pale pinks and blues and pearly whites and candid eyes—an old dead pastel under glass.

She was not too reduced to this state, however, not to take, soon enough, her own precaution—if a precaution it was to be deemed. I was acutely conscious that the naturalness to which I have just alluded would be, for either party, the only precaution worth speaking of. We moved slowly round the room, pausing here and there for curiosity; during which time the two men remained where we had found them. She had begun at last to watch them and had proposed that we should see in what they were so absorbed; but I checked her in the movement, raising my hand in a friendly admonition to wait. We waited then, face to face, looking at each other as if to catch a strain of music. This was what I had intended, for it had just come to me that one of the voices was in the air and that it had imposed close attention. The distinguished painter listened while—to all appearance—Gilbert Long did, in the presence of the picture, the explaining. Ford Obert moved, after a little, but not so as to interrupt—only so as to show me his face in a recall of what had passed between us the night before in the smoking-room. I turned my eyes from Mrs. Server's; I allowed myself to commune a little, across the shining space, with those of our fellow-auditor. The occasion had thus for a minute the oddest little air of an æsthetic lecture prompted by accidental, but immense, suggestions and delivered by Gilbert Long.

I couldn't, at the distance, with my companion, quite follow it, but Obert was clearly patient enough to betray that he was struck. His impression was at any rate doubtless his share of surprise at Long's gift of talk. This was what his eyes indeed most seemed to throw over to me—"What an unexpected demon of a critic!" It was extraordinarily interesting—I don't mean the special drift of Long's eloquence, which I couldn't, as I say, catch; but the phenomenon of his, of all people, dealing in that article. It put before me the question of whether, in these strange relations that I believed I had thus got my glimpse of, the action of the person "sacrificed" mightn't be quite out of proportion to the resources of that person. It was as if these elements might really multiply in the transfer made of them; as if the borrower practically found himself—or herself—in possession of a greater sum than the known property of the creditor. The surrender, in this way, added, by pure beauty, to the thing surrendered. We all know the French adage about that *plus belle fille du monde* who can give but what she has; yet if Mrs. Server, for instance, *had* been the heroine of this particular connection, the communication of her intelligence to her friend would quite have falsified it. She would have given much more than she had.

When Long had finished his demonstration and his charged voice had dropped, we crossed to claim acquaintance with the work that had inspired him. The place had not been completely new to Mrs. Server any more than to myself, and the impression now made on her was but the intenser vibration of a chord already stirred; nevertheless I was struck with her saying, as a result of more remembrance than I had attributed to her "Oh yes,—the man with the mask in his hand!" On our joining the others I expressed regret at our having turned up too late for the ideas that, on a theme so promising, they would have been sure to produce, and Obert, quite agreeing that we had lost a treat, said frankly, in reference to Long, but addressing himself more especially to Mrs. Server: "He's perfectly amazing, you know—he's perfectly amazing!"

I observed that as a consequence of this Long looked neither at Mrs. Server nor at Obert; he looked only at me, and with quite a penetrable shade of shyness. Then again a strange thing happened, a stranger thing even than my quick sense, the previous afternoon at the station, that he was a changed man. It was as if he were still more changed—had altered as much since the evening before as during the so much longer interval of which I had originally to take account. He had altered almost like Grace Brissenden—he looked fairly distinguished. I said to myself that, without his stature and certain signs in his dress, I should probably not have placed him. Engrossed an instant with this view and with not losing touch of the uneasiness that I conceived I had fastened on him, I became aware only after she had spoken that Mrs. Server had gaily and gracefully asked of Obert why in the world so clever a man should *not* have been clever. "Obert," I accordingly took upon myself to remark, "had evidently laboured under some extraordinary delusion. He must literally have doubted if Long *was* clever."

"Fancy!" Mrs. Server explained with a charming smile at Long, who, still looking pleasantly competent and not too fatuous, amiably returned it.

"They're natural, they're natural," I privately reflected; "that is, he's natural to *her*, but he's not so to me." And as if seeing depths in this, and to try it, I appealed to him. "Do, my dear man, let us have it again. It's the picture, of all pictures, that most needs an interpreter. *Don't* we want," I asked of Mrs. Server, "to know what it means?" The figure represented is a young man in black—a quaint, tight black dress, fashioned in years long past; with a pale, lean, livid face and a stare, from eyes without eyebrows, like that of some whitened old-world clown. In his hand he holds an object that strikes the spectator at first simply as some obscure, some ambiguous work of art, but that on a second view becomes a representation of a human face, modelled and coloured, in wax, in enamelled metal, in some substance not human. The object thus appears a complete mask, such as might have been fantastically fitted and worn.

"Yes, what in the world does it mean?" Mrs. Server replied. "One could call it—though that doesn't get one much further — the Mask of Death."

"Why so?" I demanded while we all again looked at the picture. "Isn't it much rather the Mask of Life? It's the man's own face that's Death. The other one, blooming and beautiful——"

"Ah, but with an awful grimace!" Mrs. Server broke in.

"The other one, blooming and beautiful," I repeated, "is Life, and he's going to put it on; unless indeed he has just taken it off."

"He's dreadful, he's awful—that's what I mean," said Mrs. Server. "But what does Mr. Long think?"

"The artificial face, on the other hand," I went on, as Long now said nothing, "is extremely studied and, when you carefully look at it, charmingly pretty. I don't see the grimace."

"I don't see anything else!" Mrs. Server good-humouredly insisted. "And what does Mr. Obert think?"

He kept his eyes on her a moment before replying. "He thinks it looks like a lovely lady."

"That grinning mask? What lovely lady?"

"It does," I declared to him, really seeing what he meant — "it does look remarkably like Mrs. Server."

She laughed, but forgivingly. "I'm immensely

obliged. You deserve," she continued to me, " that I should say the gentleman's own face is the image of a certain other gentleman's."

" It isn't the image of yours," Obert said to me, fitting the cap, " but it's a funny thing that it should really recall to one some face among us here, on this occasion—I mean some face in our party—that I can't think of." We had our eyes again on the ominous figure. " We've seen him yesterday—we've seen him already this morning." Obert, oddly enough, still couldn't catch it. " Who the deuce is it? "

" I know," I returned after a moment — our friend's reference having again, in a flash, become illuminating. " But nothing would induce me to tell."

" If *I* were the flattered individual," Long observed, speaking for the first time, " I've an idea that you'd give me the benefit of the compliment. Therefore it's probably not me."

" Oh, it's not you in the least," Mrs. Server blandly took upon herself to observe. " This face is so bad——"

" And mine is so good?" our companion laughed. " Thank you for saving me! "

I watched them look at each other, for there had been as yet between them no complete exchange. Yes, they were natural. I couldn't have made it out that they were not. But there was something, all the same, that I wanted to know, and I put it immediately to Long. "Why do you bring against me such an accusation?"

He met the question—singularly enough—as if his readiness had suddenly deserted him. "I don't know!"—and he turned off to another picture.

It left the three of us all the more confronted with the conundrum launched by Obert, and Mrs. Server's curiosity remained. "*Do* name," she said to me, "the flattered individual."

"No, it's a responsibility I leave to Obert."

But he was clearly still at fault; he was like a man desiring, but unable, to sneeze. "I see the fellow—yet I don't. Never mind." He turned away too. "He'll come to me."

"The resemblance," said Long, on this, at a distance from us and not turning, "the resemblance, which I shouldn't think would puzzle anyone, is simply to 'poor Briss'!"

"Oh, of course!"—and Obert gave a jump round.

"Ah—I do see it," Mrs. Server conceded with her head on one side, but as if speaking rather for harmony.

I didn't believe she saw it, but that only made her the more natural; which was also the air she had on going to join Long, in his new contemplation, after I had admitted that it was of Brissenden I myself had thought. Obert and I remained together in the presence of the Man with the Mask, and, the others being out of earshot, he reminded me that I had promised him the night before in the smoking-room to give him to-day the knowledge I had then withheld. If I had announced that I was on the track of a discovery, pray had I made it yet, and what was it, at any rate, that I proposed to discover? I felt now, in truth, more uncomfortable than I had expected in being kept to my obligation, and I beat about the bush a little till, instead of meeting it, I was able to put the natural question: "What wonderful things was Long just saying to you?"

"Oh, characteristic ones enough—whimsical, fanciful, funny. The things he says, you know."

It was indeed a fresh view. "They strike you as characteristic?"

"Of the man himself and his type of mind? Surely. Don't *you?* He talks to talk, but he's really amusing."

I was watching our companions. "Indeed he is—extraordinarily amusing." It was highly interesting to me to hear at last of Long's "type of mind." "See how amusing he is at the present moment to Mrs. Server."

Obert took this in; she was convulsed, in the extravagance always so pretty as to be pardonable, with laughter, and she even looked over at us as if to intimate with her shining, lingering eyes that we wouldn't be surprised at her transports if we suspected what her entertainer, whom she had never known for such a humourist, was saying. Instead of going to find out, all the same, we remained another minute together. It was for me, now, I could see, that Obert had his best attention. "What's the matter with them?"

It startled me almost as much as if he had asked me what was the matter with myself—for that something *was*, under this head, I was by this time unable to ignore. Not twenty minutes had elapsed since our meeting with Mrs. Server on the terrace had determined Grace Brissenden's elation, but it was a fact that my nervousness had taken an extraordinary stride. I had perhaps not till this instant been fully aware of it—it was really brought out by the way Obert looked at me as if he fancied he had heard me shake. Mrs. Server might be natural, and Gilbert Long might be, but I should not preserve that calm unless I pulled myself well together. I made the effort, facing my sharp interlocutor; and I think it was at this point that I fully measured my dismay. I had grown—that was what was the matter with me—precipitately, preposterously anxious. Instead of dropping, the discomfort produced in me by Mrs. Brissenden had deepened to agitation, and this in spite of the fact that in the brief interval nothing worse, nothing but what was right, had happened. Had I myself suddenly fallen so much in love with Mrs. Server that the care for her reputation had become with me an obsession? It was of no use saying I simply pitied her: what did I pity her for if she wasn't in danger? She *was* in danger: that rushed over me at present —rushed over me while I tried to look easy and delayed to answer my friend. She *was* in danger—if only because she had caught and held the searchlight of Obert's attention. I took up his inquiry. "The matter with them? I don't know anything but that they're young and handsome and happy—children, as who should say, of the world; children of leisure and pleasure and privilege."

Obert's eyes went back to them. "Do you remember what I said to you about her yesterday afternoon? She darts from flower to flower, but she clings, for the time, to each. You've been feeling, I judge, the force of my remark."

"Oh, she didn't at all 'dart,'" I replied, "just now at me. I darted, much rather, at *her*."

"Long didn't, then," Obert said, still with his eyes on them.

I had to wait a moment. "Do you mean he struck you as avoiding her?"

He in turn considered. "He struck me as having noticed with what intensity, ever since we came down, she has kept alighting. She inaugurated it, the instant she arrived, with *me*, and every man of us has had his turn. I dare say it's only fair, certainly, that Long should have."

"He's lucky to get it, the brute! She's as charming as she can possibly be."

"That's it, precisely; and it's what no woman ought to be—as charming as she possibly can!—more than once or twice in her life. This lady is so every blessed minute, and to every blessed male. It's as if she were too awfully afraid one wouldn't take it in. If she but knew how one does! However," my friend continued, "you'll recollect that we differed about her yesterday—and what does it signify? One should of course bear lightly on anything so light. But I stick to it that she's different."

I pondered. "Different from whom?"

"Different from herself—as she was when I painted her. There's something the matter with her."

"Ah, then, it's for me to ask *you* what. I don't myself, you see, perceive it."

He made for a little no answer, and we were both indeed by this time taken up with the withdrawal of the two other members of our group. They moved away together across the shining floor, pausing, looking up at the painted vault, saying the inevitable things—bringing off their retreat, in short, in the best order. It struck me somehow as a retreat, and yet I insisted to myself, once more, on its being perfectly natural. At the high door, which stood open, they stopped a moment and looked back at us—looked frankly, sociably, as if in consciousness of our sympathetic attention. Mrs. Server waved, as in temporary farewell, a free explanatory hand at me; she seemed to explain that she was now trying somebody else. Obert moreover added *his* explanation. "That's the way she collars us."

"Oh, Long doesn't mind," I said. "But what's the way she strikes you as different?"

"From what she was when she sat to me? Well, a part of it is that she can't keep still. She was as still then as if she had been paid for it. Now she's all over the place." But he came back to something else. "I like your talking, my dear man, of what you 'don't perceive.' I've yet to find out what that remarkable quantity is. What you do perceive has at all events given me so much to think about that it doubtless ought to serve me for the present. I feel I ought to let you know that you've made me also perceive the Brissendens." I of course remembered what I had said to him, but it was just this that now touched my uneasiness, and I only echoed the name, a little blankly, with the instinct of gaining time. "You put me on them wonderfully," Obert continued, "though of course I've kept your idea to myself. All the same it sheds a great light."

I could again but feebly repeat it. "A great light?"

"As to what may go on even between others still. It's a jolly idea—a torch in the darkness; and do you know what I've done with it? I've held it up, I don't mind telling you, to just the question of the change, since this interests you, in Mrs. Server. If you've got your mystery I'll be hanged if I won't have mine. If you've got your Brissendens I shall see what I can do with *her*. You've given me an analogy, and I declare I find it dazzling. I don't see the end of what may be done with it. If Brissenden's paying for his wife, for her amazing second bloom, who's paying for Mrs. Server? Isn't *that*—what do the newspapers call it?—the missing word? Isn't it perhaps in fact just what you told me last night you were on the track of? But don't add now," he went on, more and more amused with his divination, "don't add now that the man's obviously Gilbert Long—for I won't be put off with anything of the sort. She collared him much too markedly. The real man must be one she doesn't markedly collar."

"But I thought that what you a moment ago made out was that she so markedly collars all of us." This was my immediate reply to Obert's blaze of ingenuity, but I none the less saw more things in it than I could reply to. I saw, at any rate, and saw with relief, that if he should look on the principle suggested to him by the case of the Brissendens, there would be no danger at all of his finding it. If, accordingly, I was nervous for Mrs. Server, all I had to do was to keep him on this false scent. Since it was not she who was paid for, but she who possibly paid, his fancy might harmlessly divert him till the party should disperse. At the same time, in the midst of these reflections, the question of the "change" in her, which he was in so much better a position than I to measure, couldn't help having for me its portent, and the sense of that was, no doubt, in my next words. "What makes you think that what you speak of was what I had in my head?"

"Well, the way, simply, that the shoe fits. She's absolutely not the same person I painted. It's exactly like Mrs. Brissenden's having been for you yesterday not the same person you had last seen bearing her name."

"Very good," I returned, "though I didn't in the least mean to set you digging so hard. However, dig on your side, by all means, while I dig on mine. All I ask of you is complete discretion."

"Ah, naturally!"

"We ought to remember," I pursued, even at the risk of showing as too sententious, "that success in such an inquiry may perhaps be more embarrassing than failure. To nose about for a relation that a lady has her reasons for keeping secret——"

"Is made not only quite inoffensive, I hold"—

he immediately took me up—" but positively honourable, by being confined to psychologic evidence."

I wondered a little. " Honourable to whom? "

" Why, to the investigator. Resting on the *kind* of signs that the game takes account of when fairly played—resting on psychologic signs alone, it's a high application of intelligence. What's ignoble is the detective and the keyhole."

" I see," I after a moment admitted. " I did have, last night, my scruples, but you warm me up. Yet I confess also," I still added, " that if I do muster the courage of my curiosity, it's a little because I feel even yet, as I think you also must, altogether destitute of a material clue. If I had a material clue I should feel ashamed: the fact would be deterrent. I start, for my part, at any rate, quite in the dark—or in a darkness lighted, at best, by what you have called the torch of my analogy. The analogy too," I wound up, " may very well be only half a help. It was easy to find poor Briss, because poor Briss is here, and it's always easy, moreover, to find a husband. But say Mrs. Server's poor Briss —or his equivalent, whoever it may be — *isn't* here."

We had begun to walk away with this, but my companion pulled up at the door of the room. " I'm sure he is. She tells me he's near."

" ' Tells ' you? " I challenged it, but I uncomfortably reflected that it was just what I had myself told Mrs. Brissenden.

"She wouldn't be as she is if he weren't. Her being as she is is the sign of it. He wasn't present—that is he wasn't present in her life at all—when I painted her; and the difference we're impressed with is exactly the proof that he is now."

My difficulty in profiting by the relief he had so unconsciously afforded me resided of course in my not feeling free to show for quite as impressed as he was. I hadn't really made out at all what he was impressed *with*, and I should only have spoiled everything by inviting him to be definite. This was a little of a worry, for I should have liked to know; but on the other hand I felt my track at present effectually covered. "Well, then, grant he's one of us. There are more than a dozen of us—a dozen even with you and me and Brissenden counted out. The hitch is that we're nowhere without a primary lead. As to Brissenden there *was* the lead."

"You mean as afforded by his wife's bloated state, which was a signal——?"

"Precisely: for the search for something or other that would help to explain it. Given his wife's bloated state, his own shrunken one was what was to have been predicated. I knew definitely, in other words, what to look for."

"Whereas we don't know here?"

"Mrs. Server's state, unfortunately," I replied, "is not bloated."

He laughed at my "unfortunately," though recognising that I spoke merely from the point of view of lucidity, and presently remarked that he had his own idea. He didn't say what it was, and I didn't ask, intimating thereby that I held it to be in this manner we were playing the game; but I indulgently questioned it in the light of its not yet having assisted him. He answered that the minutes we had just passed were what had made the difference; it had sprung from the strong effect produced on him after she came in with me. "It's but now I really see her. She did and said nothing special, nothing striking or extraordinary; but that didn't matter—it never does: one saw how she *is*. She's nothing but *that*."

"Nothing but what?"

"She's all *in* it," he insisted. "Or it's all in *her*. It comes to the same thing."

"Of course it's all in her," I said as impatiently as I could, though his attestation—for I wholly trusted his perception—left me so much in his debt. "That's what we start with, isn't it? It leaves us as far as ever from what we must arrive at."

But he was too interested in his idea to heed my question. He was wrapped in the "psychologic" glow. "I *have* her!"

"Ah, but it's a question of having *him!*"

He looked at me on this as if I had brought him back to a mere detail, and after an instant the light went out of his face. " So it is. I leave it to you. I don't care." His drop had the usual suddenness of the drops of the artistic temperament. " Look for the last man," he nevertheless, but with more detachment, added. " I daresay it would be he."

" The last? In what sense the last? "

" Well, the last sort of creature who could be believed of her."

" Oh," I rejoined as we went on, " the great bar to that is that such a sort of creature as the last won't *be* here! "

He hesitated. " So much the better. I give him, at any rate, wherever he is, up to you."

" Thank you," I returned, " for the beauty of the present! You do see, then, that our psychologic glow doesn't, after all, prevent the thing——"

" From being none of one's business? Yes. Poor little woman! " He seemed somehow satisfied; he threw it all up. " It isn't any of one's business, is it? "

" Why, that's what I was telling you," I impatiently exclaimed, " that *I* feel! "

## V

THE first thing that happened to me after parting with him was to find myself again engaged with Mrs. Brissenden, still full of the quick conviction with which I had left her. "It *is* she—quite unmistakably, you know. I don't see how I can have been so stupid as not to make it out. I haven't your cleverness, of course, till my nose is rubbed into a thing. But when it *is*—!" She celebrated her humility in a laugh that was proud. "The two are off together."

"Off where?"

"I don't know where, but I saw them a few minutes ago most distinctly 'slope.' They've gone for a quiet, unwatched hour, poor dears, out into the park or the gardens. When one knows it, it's all there. But what's that vulgar song?—'You've got to know it first!' It strikes me, if you don't mind my telling you so, that the way *you* get hold of things is positively uncanny. I mean as regards what first marked her for you."

"But, my dear lady," I protested, "nothing at all first marked her for me. She *isn't* marked for me, first or last. It was only you who so jumped at her."

My interlocutress stared, and I had at this moment, I remember, an almost intolerable sense of her fatuity and cruelty. They were all unconscious, but they were, at that stage, none the less irritating. Her fine bosom heaved, her blue eyes expanded with her successful, her simplified egotism. I couldn't, in short, I found, bear her being so keen about Mrs. Server while she was so stupid about poor Briss. She seemed to recall to me nobly the fact that *she* hadn't a lover. No, she was only eating poor Briss up inch by inch, but she hadn't a lover. "I don't," I insisted, "see in Mrs. Server any of the right signs."

She looked almost indignant. "Even after your telling me that you see in Lady John only the wrong ones?"

"Ah, but there are other women here than Mrs. Server and Lady John."

"Certainly. But didn't we, a moment ago, think of them all and dismiss them? If Lady John's out of the question, how can Mrs. Server possibly *not* be in it? We want a fool——"

"Ah, *do* we?" I interruptingly wailed.

"Why, exactly by your own theory, in which you've so much interested me! It was you who struck off the idea."

"That we want a fool?" I felt myself turning

gloomy enough. "Do we really want anyone at all?"

She gave me, in momentary silence, a strange smile. "Ah, you want to take it back now? You're sorry you spoke. My dear man, you may be——" but that didn't hinder the fact, in short, that I had kindled near me a fine, if modest and timid, intelligence. There did remain the truth of our friend's striking development, to which I had called her attention. Regretting my rashness didn't make the prodigy less. "You'll lead me to believe, if you back out, that there's suddenly someone you want to protect. Weak man," she exclaimed with an assurance from which, I confess, I was to take alarm, "something has happened to you since we separated! Weak man," she repeated with dreadful gaiety, "you've been squared!"

I literally blushed for her. "Squared?"

"Does it inconveniently happen that you find you're in love with her yourself?"

"Well," I replied on quick reflection, "do, if you like, call it that; for you see what a motive it gives me for being, in such a matter as this wonderful one that you and I happened to find ourselves for a moment making so free with, absolutely sure about her. I *am* absolutely sure. There! She won't do. And for your postulate that she's at the present moment in some sequestered spot in Long's company, suffer me without delay to correct it.

It won't hold water. If you'll go into the library, through which I have just passed, you'll find her there in the company of the Comte de Dreuil."

Mrs. Briss stared again. "Already? She *was*, at any rate, with Mr. Long, and she told me on my meeting them that they had just come from the pastels."

"Exactly. They met there—she and I having gone together; and they retired together under my eyes. They must have parted, clearly, the moment after."

She took it all in, turned it all over. "Then what does that prove but that they're afraid to be seen?"

"Ah, they're *not* afraid, since both you and I saw them!"

"Oh, only just long enough for them to publish themselves as not avoiding each other. All the same, you know," she said, "they do."

"Do avoid each other? How is your belief in that," I asked, "consistent with your belief that they parade together in the park?"

"They ignore each other in public; they foregather in private."

"Ah, but they *don't*—since, as I tell you, she's even while we talk the centre of the mystic circle of the twaddle of M. de Dreuil; chained to a stake if you *can* be. Besides," I wound up, "it's not only that she's not the 'right fool'—it's simply that she's not a fool at all. We want the woman who has been rendered most inane. But this lady hasn't been rendered so in any degree. She's the reverse of inane. She's in full possession."

"In full possession of what?"

"Why, of herself."

"Like Lady John?"

I had unfortunately to discriminate here. "No, not like Lady John."

"Like whom then?"

"Like anyone. Like me; like you; like Brissenden. Don't I satisfy you?" I asked in a moment.

She only looked at me a little, handsome and hard. "If you wished to satisfy me so easily you shouldn't have made such a point of working me up. I daresay I, after all, however," she added, "notice more things than you."

"As for instance?"

"Well, May Server last evening. I was not quite conscious at the time that I did, but when one has had the 'tip' one looks back and sees things in a new light."

It was doubtless because my friend irritated me more and more that I met this with a sharpness possibly excessive. "She's perfectly natural. What I saw was a test. And so is he."

But she gave me no heed. "If there hadn't been so many people I should have noticed of myself after dinner that there was something the matter with her. I should have seen what it was. She was all over the place."

She expressed it as the poor lady's other critic had done, but this didn't shut my mouth. "Ah, then, in spite of the people, you did notice. What do you mean by 'all over the place'?"

"She couldn't keep still. She was different from the woman one had last seen. She used to be so calm—as if she were always sitting for her portrait. Wasn't she in fact always being painted in a pink frock and one row of pearls, always staring out at you in exhibitions, as if she were saying 'Here they are again'? Last night she was on the rush."

"The rush? Oh!"

"Yes, positively—from one man to another. She was on the pounce. She talked to ten in succession, making up to them in the most extraordinary way and leaving them still more crazily. She's as nervous as a cat. Put it to any man here, and see if he doesn't tell you."

"I should think it quite unpleasant to put it to any man here," I returned; "and I should have been sure you would have thought it the same. I spoke to you in the deepest confidence."

Mrs. Brissenden's look at me was for a moment of the least accommodating; then it changed to an intelligent smile. "How you *are* protecting her! But don't cry out," she added, "before you're hurt. Since your confidence has distinguished me—

though I don't quite see why—you may be sure I haven't breathed. So I all the more resent your making me a scene on the extraordinary ground that I've observed as well as yourself. Perhaps what you don't like is that my observation may be turned on *you*. I confess it is."

It was difficult to bear being put in the wrong by her, but I made an effort that I believe was not unsuccessful to recover my good humour. "It's not in the least to your observation that I object, it's to the extravagant inferences you draw from it. Of course, however, I admit I always want to protect the innocent. What does she gain, on your theory, by her rushing and pouncing? Had she pounced on Brissenden when we met him with her? Are you so very sure he hadn't pounced on *her?* They had, at all events, to me, quite the air of people settled; she was not, it was clear, at that moment meditating a change. It was we, if you remember, who had absolutely to pull them apart."

"Is it your idea to make out," Mrs. Brissenden inquired in answer to this, "that she has suddenly had the happy thought of a passion for my husband?"

A new possibility, as she spoke, came to me with a whirr of wings, and I half expressed it. "She may have a sympathy."

My interlocutress gazed at space. "You mean she may be sorry for him? On what ground?"

I had gone too far indeed; but I got off as I could. "You neglect him so! But what is she, at any rate," I went on, "nervous—as nervous as you describe her—*about?*"

"About her danger; the contingency of its being fixed upon them—an intimacy so thoroughgoing that they can scarcely afford to let it be seen even as a mere acquaintance. Think of the circumstances—*her* personal ones, I mean, and admit that it wouldn't do. It would be too bad a case. There's everything to make it so. They must live on pins and needles. Anything proved would go tremendously hard for her."

"In spite of which you're surprised that I 'protect' her?"

It was a question, however, that my companion could meet. "From people in general, no. From me in particular, yes."

In justice to Mrs. Brissenden I thought a moment. "Well, then, let us be fair all round. That you don't, as you say, breathe is a discretion I appreciate; all the more that a little inquiry, tactfully pursued, would enable you to judge whether any independent suspicion does attach. A little loose collateral evidence *might* be picked up; and your scorning to handle it is no more than I should, after all, have expected of you."

"Thank you for 'after all'!" My companion tossed her head. "I know for myself what I scorn to handle. Quite apart from that there's another matter. You must have noticed yourself that when people are so much liked——"

"There's a kind of general, amiable consensus of blindness? Yes—one can think of cases. Popularity shelters and hallows—has the effect of making a good-natured world agree not to see."

My friend seemed pleased that I so sufficiently understood. "This evidently has been a case then in which it has not only agreed not to see, but agreed not even to look. It has agreed in fact to look straight the other way. They say there's no smoke without fire, but it appears there may be fire without smoke. I'm satisfied, at all events, that one wouldn't in connection with these two find the least little puff. Isn't that just what makes the magnificence of their success—the success that reduces us to playing over them with mere moonshine?" She thought of it; seemed fairly to envy it. "I've never *seen* such luck!"

"A rare case of the beauty of impunity *as* impunity?" I laughed. "Such a case puts a price on passions otherwise to be deprecated? I'm glad indeed you admit we're 'reduced.' We *are* reduced. But what I meant to say just now was that if you'll continue to join in the genial conspiracy while I do the same—each of us making an exception only for the other—I'll pledge myself absolutely to the straight course. If before we separate I've seen reason to change my mind, I'll loyally let you know."

"What good will that do me," she asked, "if you *don't* change your mind? You won't change it if you shut your eyes to her."

"Ah, I feel I can't do that now. I *am* interested. The proof of that is," I pursued, "that I appeal to you for another impression of your own. I still don't see the logic of her general importunity."

"The logic is simply that she has a terror of appearing to encourage anyone in particular."

"Why then isn't it in her own interest, for the sake of the screen, just to *do* that? The appearance of someone in particular would be exactly the opposite of the appearance of Long. Your own admission is that that's *his* line with Lady John."

Mrs. Brissenden took her view. "Oh, she doesn't want to do anything so like the real thing. And, as for what he does, they don't feel in the same way. He's not nervous."

"Then why does he go in for a screen?"

"I mean"—she readily modified it—"that he's not so nervous as May. He hasn't the same reasons for panic. A man never has. Besides, there's not so much in Mr. Long to show——"

"What, by my notion, has taken place? Why not, if it was precisely by the change in him that my notion was inspired? Any change in *her* I know comparatively little about."

We hovered so near the case of Mr. and Mrs. Brissenden that it positively excited me, and all the more for her sustained unconsciousness. " Oh, the man's not aware of his own change. He doesn't see it as we do. It's all to his advantage."

" But *we* see it to his advantage. How should that prevent? "

" We see it to the advantage of his mind and his talk, but not to that of—— "

" Well, what? " I pressed as she pulled up.

She was thinking how to name such mysteries. " His delicacy. His consideration. His thought *for* her. He would think for her if he weren't selfish. But he *is* selfish—too much so to spare her, to be generous, to realise. It's only, after all," she sagely went on, feeding me again, as I winced to feel, with profundity of my own sort, " it's only an excessive case, a case that in him happens to show as what the doctors call ' fine,' of what goes on whenever two persons are so much mixed up. One of them always gets more out of it than the other. One of them—you know the saying—gives the lips, the other gives the cheek."

" It's the deepest of all truths. Yet the cheek profits too," I more prudently argued.

" It profits most. It takes and keeps and uses all the lips give. The cheek, accordingly," she continued to point out, " is Mr. Long's. The lips are what we began by looking for. We've found them.

They're drained—they're dry, the lips. Mr. Long finds his improvement natural and beautiful. He revels in it. He takes it for granted. He's sublime."

It kept me for a minute staring at her. "So—do you know?—are *you!*"

She received this wholly as a tribute to her acuteness, and was therefore proportionately gracious. "That's only because it's catching. You've *made* me sublime. You found me dense. You've affected me quite as Mrs. Server has affected Mr. Long. I don't pretend I show it," she added, "quite as much as he does."

"Because that would entail *my* showing it as much as, by your contention, *she* does? Well, I confess," I declared, "I do feel remarkably like that pair of lips. I feel drained—I feel dry!" Her answer to this, with another toss of her head, was extravagant enough to mean forgiveness—was that I was impertinent, and her action in support of her charge was to move away from me, taking her course again to the terrace, easily accessible from the room in which we had been talking. She passed out of the window that opened to the ground, and I watched her while, in the brighter light, she put up her pink parasol. She walked a few paces, as if to look about her for a change of company, and by this time had reached a flight of steps that descended to a lower level. On observing that here, in the act to go down, she suddenly paused, I knew she had been checked by something seen below and that this was what made her turn the next moment to give me a look. I took it as an invitation to rejoin her, and I perceived when I had done so what had led her to appeal to me. We commanded from the point in question one of the shady slopes of the park and in particular a spreading beech, the trunk of which had been inclosed with a rustic circular bench, a convenience that appeared to have offered, for the moment, a sense of leafy luxury to a lady in pale blue. She leaned back, her figure presented in profile and her head a little averted as if for talk with some one on the other side of her, someone so placed as to be lost to our view.

"There!" triumphed Mrs. Brissenden again—for the lady was unmistakably Mrs. Server. Amusement was inevitable—the fact showed her as so correctly described by the words to which I had twice had to listen. She seemed really all over the place. "I thought you said," my companion remarked, "that you had left her tucked away somewhere with M. de Dreuil."

"Well," I returned after consideration, "that *is* obviously M. de Dreuil."

"Are you so sure? I don't make out the person," my friend continued—"I only see she's not alone. I understood you moreover that you had lately left them in the house."

"They *were* in the house, but there was nothing to keep them from coming out. They've had plenty of time while we've talked; they must have passed down by some of the other steps. Perhaps also," I added, "it's another man."

But by this time she was satisfied. "It's *he!*"

"Gilbert Long? I thought you just said," I observed, "that you can make nobody out."

We watched together, but the distance was considerable, and the second figure continued to be screened. "It *must* be he," Mrs. Brissenden resumed with impatience, "since it was with him I so distinctly saw her."

"Let me once more hold you to the fact," I answered, "that she had, to my knowledge, succumbed to M. de Dreuil afterwards. The moments have fled, you see, in our fascinating discussion, and various things, on your theory of her pounce, have come and gone. Don't I moreover make out a brown shoe, in a white gaiter, protruding from the other side of her dress? It must be Lord Lutley."

Mrs. Brissenden looked and mused. "A brown shoe in a white gaiter?" At this moment Mrs. Server moved, and the next—as if it were time for another pounce—she had got up. We could, however, still distinguish but a shoulder and an outstretched leg of her gentleman, who, on her movement, appeared, as in protest, to have affirmed by an emphatic shift of his seat his preference for their remaining as they were. This carried him further round the tree. We thus lost him, but she stood there while we waited, evidently exhorting him; after a minute of which she came away as in confidence that he would follow. During this process, with a face more visible, she had looked as charming as a pretty woman almost always does in rising eloquent before the apathetic male. She hadn't yet noticed us, but something in her attitude and manner particularly spoke to me. There were implications in it to which I couldn't be blind, and I felt how my neighbour also would have caught them and been confirmed in her certitude. In fact I felt the breath of her confirmation in another elated "There!"—in a "Look at her *now!*" Incontestably, while not yet aware of us, Mrs. Server confessed with every turn of her head to a part in a relation. It stuck out of her, her part in a relation; it hung before us, her part in a relation; it was large to us beyond the breadth of the glade. And since, off her guard, she so let us have it, with whom in the world could the relation—so much of one as that—be but with Gilbert Long? The question was not settled till she had come on some distance; then the producer of our tension, emerging and coming after her, offered himself to our united, to our confounded, anxiety once more as poor Briss.

That we should have been confounded was doubtless but a proof of the impression—the singular assurance of intimacy borne toward us on the soft summer air—that we had, however delusively, received. I should myself have been as ready as my neighbour to say "Whoever he is, they're in deep!" —and on grounds, moreover, quite as recklessly, as fantastically constructive as hers. There was nothing to explain our impression but the fact of our already having seen them figure together, and of this we needed breathing-time to give them the natural benefit. It was not indeed as an absolute benefit for either that Grace Brissenden's tone marked our recognition. "Dear Guy *again?*"—but she had recovered herself enough to laugh. "I should have thought he had had more than his turn!" She had recovered herself in fact much more than I; for somehow, from this instant, convinced as she had been and turning everything to her conviction, I found myself dealing, in thought, with still larger material. It was odd what a difference was made for me by the renewed sight of dear Guy. I didn't of course analyse this sense at the time; that was still to come. Our friends meanwhile had noticed us, and something clearly passed between them—it almost produced, for an instant, a visible arrest in their advance—on the question of their having perhaps been for some time exposed.

They came on, however, and I waved them from afar a greeting, to which Mrs. Server alone replied. Distances were great at Newmarch and landscape-gardening on the grand scale; it would take them still some minutes to reach our place of vantage or to arrive within sound of speech. There was accordingly nothing marked in our turning away and strolling back to the house. We had been so intent that we confessed by this movement to a quick impulse to disown it. Yet it was remarkable that, before we went in, Mrs. Brissenden should have struck me afresh as having got all she wanted. Her recovery from our surprise was already so complete that her high lucidity now alone reigned. "You don't require, I suppose, anything more than *that?*"

"Well, I don't quite see, I'm bound to say, just where even 'that' comes in." It incommoded me singularly little, at the point to which I had jumped, that this statement was the exact reverse of the truth. Where it came in was what I happened to be in the very act of seeing—seeing to the exclusion of almost everything else. It was sufficient that I might perhaps feel myself to have done at last with Mrs. Brissenden. I desired, at all events, quite as if this benefit were assured me, to leave her the honours of the last word.

She was finely enough prepared to take them. "Why, this invention of using my husband—— !" She fairly gasped at having to explain.

"Of 'using' him?"

"Trailing him across the scent as she does all of you, one after the other. Excuse my comparing you to so many red herrings. You each have your turn; only *his* seems repeated, poor dear, till he's quite worn out with it."

I kept for a little this image in my eye. " I can see of course that his whole situation must be something of a strain for him; for I've not forgotten what you told me yesterday of his service with Lady John. To have to work in such a way for two of them at once "—it couldn't help, I admitted, being a tax on a fellow. Besides, when one came to think of it, the same man couldn't be *two* red herrings. To show as Mrs. Server's would directly impair his power to show as Lady John's. It would seem, in short, a matter for his patronesses to have out together.

Mrs. Brissenden betrayed, on this, some annoyance at my levity. " Oh, the cases are not the same, for with Lady John it amuses him: he thinks he knows."

" Knows what? "

" What she wants him for. He doesn't know "—she kept it wonderfully clear—" that she really doesn't want him for anything; for anything except, of course "—this came as a droll second thought—" himself."

" And he doesn't know, either "—I tried to remain at her level—" that Mrs. Server does."

" No," she assented, " he doesn't know what it's her idea to do with him."

"He doesn't know, in fine," I cheerfully pursued, "the truth about anything. And of course, by your agreement with me, he's not to learn it."

She recognised her agreement with me, yet looked as if she had reserved a certain measure of freedom. Then she handsomely gave up even that. "I certainly don't want him to become conscious."

"It's his unconsciousness," I declared, "that saves him."

"Yes, even from himself."

"We must accordingly feed it." In the house, with intention, we parted company; but there was something that, before this, I felt it due to my claim of consistency to bring out. "It wasn't, at all events, Gilbert Long behind the tree!"

My triumph, however, beneath the sponge she was prepared to pass again over much of our experience, was short-lived. "Of course it wasn't. We shouldn't have been treated to the scene if it *had* been. What could she possibly have put poor Briss there for but just to show it wasn't?"

## VI

I SAW other things, many things, after this, but I had already so much matter for reflection that I saw them almost in spite of myself. The difficulty with me was in the momentum already acquired by the act—as well as, doubtless, by the general habit—of observation. I remember indeed that on separating from Mrs. Brissenden I took a lively resolve to get rid of my ridiculous obsession. It was absurd to have consented to such immersion, intellectually speaking, in the affairs of other people. One had always affairs of one's own, and I was positively neglecting mine. Such, for a while, was my foremost reflection; after which, in their order or out of it, came an inevitable train of others. One of the first of these was that, frankly, my affairs were by this time pretty well used to my neglect. There were connections enough in which it had never failed. A whole cluster of such connections, effectually displacing the centre of interest, now surrounded me, and I was—though always but intellectually—drawn into their circle. I did my best for the rest of the day to turn my back on them, but with the prompt result of feeling that I meddled with them almost more in thinking them over in isolation than in hovering personally about them. Reflection was the real intensity; reflection, as to poor Mrs. Server in particular, was an indiscreet opening of doors. She became vivid in the light of the so limited vision of her that I already possessed—try positively as I would not further to extend it. It was something not to ask another question, to keep constantly away both from Mrs. Brissenden and from Ford Obert, whom I had rashly invited to a degree of participation; it was something to talk as hard as possible with other persons and on other subjects, to mingle in groups much more superficial than they supposed themselves, to give ear to broader jokes, to discuss more tangible mysteries.

The day, as it developed, was large and hot, an unstinted splendour of summer; excursions, exercise, organised amusement were things admirably spared us; life became a mere arrested ramble or stimulated lounge, and we profited to the full by the noble freedom of Newmarch, that overarching ease which in nothing was so marked as in the tolerance of talk. The air of the place itself, in such conditions, left one's powers with a sense of play; if one wanted something to play at one simply played at being there. I did this myself, with the aid, in especial, of two or three solitary strolls, unaccompanied dips, of half an hour a-piece, into outlying parts of the house and the grounds. I must add that while I resorted to such measures not to see I only fixed what I *had* seen, what I did see, the more in my mind. One of these things had been the way that, at luncheon, Gilbert Long, watching the chance given him by the loose order in which we moved to it, slipped, to the visible defeat of somebody else, into the chair of conspicuity beside clever Lady John. A second was that Mrs. Server then occupied a place as remote as possible from this couple, but not from Guy Brissenden, who had found means to seat himself next her while my notice was engaged by the others. What I was at the same time supremely struck with could doubtless only be Mrs. Server's bright ubiquity, as it had at last come to seem to me, and that of the companions she had recruited for the occasion. Attended constantly by a different gentleman, she was in the range of my vision wherever I turned—she kept repeating her picture in settings separated by such intervals that I wondered at the celerity with which she proceeded from spot to spot. She was never discernibly out of breath, though the associate of her ecstasy at the given moment might have been taken as being; and I kept getting afresh the impression which, the day before, had so promptly followed my arrival, the odd impression, as of something the matter with each party, that I had gathered, in the grounds, from the sight of her advance upon me with Obert. I had by this time of course made out—and it was absurd to shut my eyes to it—what *that* particular something, at least, was. It was that Obert had quickly perceived something to be the matter with *her*, and that she, on her side, had become aware of his discovery.

I wondered hereupon if the discovery were inevitable for each gentleman in succession, and if this were their reason for changing so often. Did everyone leave her, like Obert, with an uneasy impression of her, and were these impressions now passed about with private hilarity or profundity, though without having reached me save from the source I have named? I affected myself as constantly catching her eye, as if she wished to call my attention to the fact of who was with her and who was not. I had kept my distance since our episode with the pastels, and yet nothing could more come home to me than that I had really not, since then, been absent from her. We met without talk, but not, thanks to these pointed looks, without contact. I daresay that, for that matter, my cogitations—for I must have bristled with them—would have made me as stiff a puzzle to interpretative minds as I had suffered other phenomena to become to my own. I daresay I wandered with a tell-tale restlessness of which the practical detachment might well have mystified those who hadn't suspicions. Whenever I caught Mrs. Server's eye it was really to wonder how many suspicions *she* had. I came upon her in great dim chambers, and I came upon her before sweeps of view. I came upon her once more with the Comte de Dreuil, with Lord Lutley, with Ford Obert, with almost every other man in the house, and with several of these, as if there had not been enough for so many turns, two or three times over. Only at no moment, whatever the favouring frame, did I come upon her with Gilbert Long. It was of course an anomaly that, as an easy accident, I was not again myself set in the favouring frame. That I consistently escaped being might indeed have been the meaning most marked in our mute recognitions.

Discretion, then, I finally felt, played an odd part when it simply left one more attached, morally, to one's prey. What was most evident to me by five o'clock in the afternoon was that I was too preoccupied not to find it the best wisdom to accept my mood. It was all very well to run away; there would be no effectual running away but to have my things quickly packed and catch, if possible, a train for town. On the spot I had to *be* on it; and it began to dawn before me that there was something quite other I possibly might do with Mrs. Server than endeavour ineffectually to forget her. What was none of one's business might change its name should importunity take the form of utility. In resisted observation that was vivid thought, in inevitable thought that was vivid observation, through a succession, in short, of phases in which I shall not pretend to distinguish one of these elements from the other, I found myself cherishing the fruit of the seed dropped equally by Ford Obert and by Mrs. Briss. What was the matter with *me?*—so much as that I had ended by asking myself; and the answer had come as an unmistakable return of the anxiety produced in me by my first seeing that I had fairly let Grace Brissenden loose. My original protest against the flash of inspiration in which she had fixed responsibility on Mrs. Server had been in fact, I now saw, but the scared presentiment of something in store for myself. This scare, to express it sharply, had verily not left me from that moment; and if I had been already then anxious it was because I had felt myself foredoomed to be sure the poor lady herself would be. Why I should have minded this, should have been anxious at her anxiety and scared at her scare, was a question troubling me too little on the spot for me to suffer it to trouble me, as a painter of my state, in this place. It is sufficient that when so much of the afternoon had waned as to bring signs of the service of tea in the open air, I knew how far I was gone in pity for her. For I had at last had to take in what my two interlocutors had given me. Their impression, coinciding and, as one might say, disinterested, couldn't, after a little, fail in some degree to impose itself. It had its value. Mrs. Server *was* "nervous."

It little mattered to me now that Mrs. Briss had put it to me—that I had even whimsically put it to myself—that I was perhaps in love with her. That was as good a name as another for an interest springing up in an hour, and was moreover a decent working hypothesis. The sentiment had not indeed asserted itself at "first sight," though it might have taken its place remarkably well among the phenomena of what is known as second. The real fact was, none the less, that I was quite too sorry for her to be anything except sorry. This odd feeling was something that I may as well say I shall not even now attempt to account for—partly, it is true, because my recital of the rest of what I was to see in no small measure does so. It was a force that I at this stage simply found I had already succumbed to. If it was not the result of what I had granted to myself was the matter with her, then it was rather the very cause of my making that concession. It was a different thing from my first prompt impulse to shield her. I had already shielded her—fought for her so far as I could or as the case immediately required. My own sense of how I was affected had practically cleared up, in short, in the presence of this deeper vision of her. My divinations and inductions had finally brought home to me that in the whole huge, brilliant, crowded place I was the only person save one who was in anything that could be called a relation to her. The other person's relation was concealed, and mine, so far as she herself was concerned, was unexpressed—so that I suppose what most, at the juncture in question, stirred within me was the wonder of how I might successfully express it. I felt that so long as I didn't express it I should be haunted with the idea of something infinitely touching and tragic in her loneliness—possibly in her torment, in her terror. If she was "nervous" to the tune I had come to recognise, it could only be because she had grounds. And what might her grounds more naturally be than that, arranged and arrayed, disguised and decorated, pursuing in vain, through our careless company, her search for the right shade of apparent security, she felt herself none the less all the while the restless victim of fear and failure?

Once my imagination had seen her in this light the touches it could add to the picture might be trusted to be telling. Further observation was to convince me of their truth, but while I waited for it with my apprehension that it would come in spite of me I easily multiplied and lavished them. I made out above all what she would most be trying to hide. It was not, so to speak, the guarded primary fact—it could only be, wretched woman, that produced, that disastrous, treacherous consequence of the fact which her faculties would exhibit, and most of all the snapped cord of her faculty of talk. Guy Brissenden had, at the worst, his compromised face and figure to show and to shroud—if he were really, that is, as much aware of them as one had suspected. She had her whole compromised machinery of thought and speech, and if these signs were not, like his, external, that made her case but the harder, for she had to create, with intelligence rapidly ebbing, with wit half gone, the illusion of an unimpaired estate. She was like some unhappy lady robbed of her best jewels—obliged so to dispose and distribute the minor trinkets that had escaped as still to give the impression of a rich *écrin*. Was not that embarrassment, if one analysed a little, at the bottom of her having been all day, in the vulgar phrase and as the three of us had too cruelly noted, all over the place? *Was* indeed, for that matter, this observation confined to us, or had it at last been irrepressibly determined on the part of the company at large? This was a question, I hasten to add, that I would not now for the world have put to the test. I felt I should have known how to escape had any rumour of wonder at Mrs. Server's ways been finally conveyed to me. I might from this moment have, as much as I liked, my own sense of it, but I was definitely conscious of a sort of loyalty to her that would have rendered me blank before others: though not indeed that—oh, at last, quite the contrary!—it would have forbidden me to watch and watch. I positively dreaded the accident of my being asked by one of the men if I knew how everyone was talking about her. If everyone was talking about her, I wanted positively not to know. But nobody was, probably—they scarcely could be as yet. Without suggestive collateral evidence there would be nobody in the house so conscientiously infernal as Mrs. Brissenden, Obert and I.

Newmarch had always, in our time, carried itself as the great asylum of the finer wit, more or less expressly giving out that, as invoking hospitality or other countenance, none of the stupid, none even of the votaries of the grossly obvious, need apply; but I could luckily at present reflect that its measurements in this direction had not always been my own, and that, moreover, whatever precision they possessed, human blandness, even in such happy halls, had not been quite abolished. There was a sound law in virtue of which one could always—alike in privileged and unprivileged circles—rest more on people's density than on their penetrability. Wasn't it their density too that would be practically nearest their good nature? Whatever her successive partners of a moment might have noticed, they wouldn't have discovered in her reason for dropping them quickly a principle of fear that they might notice her failure articulately to keep up. My own actual vision, which had developed with such affluence, was that, in a given case, she could keep up but for a few minutes and was therefore obliged to bring the contact to an end before exposure. I had consistently mastered her predicament: she had at once to cultivate contacts, so that people shouldn't guess her real concentration, and to make them a literal touch and go, so that they shouldn't suspect the enfeeblement of her mind. It was obviously still worth everything to her that she was so charming. I had theorised with Mrs. Brissenden on her supposititious inanity, but the explanation of such cynicism in either of us could only be a sensibility to the truth that attractions so great might float her even a long time after intelligence pure and simple should have collapsed.

Was not my present uneasiness, none the less, a private curiosity to ascertain just how much or how little of that element she had saved from the wreck? She dodged, doubled, managed, broke off, clutching occasions, yet doubtless risking dumbnesses, vaguenesses and other betrayals, depending on attitudes, motions, expressions, a material personality, in fine, in which a plain woman would have found nothing but failure; and peace therefore might rule the scene on every hypothesis but that of her getting, to put it crudely, worse. How I remember saying to myself that if she didn't get better she surely *must* get worse!—being aware that I referred on the one side to her occult surrender and on the other to its awful penalty. It became present to me that she possibly might recover if anything should happen that would pull her up, turn her into some other channel. If, however, that consideration didn't detain me longer the fact may stand as a sign of how little I believed in any check. Gilbert Long might die, but not the intensity he had inspired. The analogy with the situation of the Brissendens here, I further considered, broke down; I at any rate rather positively welcomed the view that the sacrificed party to *that* union might really find the arrest of his decline, if not the renewal of his youth, in the loss of his wife. Would this lady indeed, as an effect of *his* death, begin to wrinkle and shrivel? It would sound brutal to say that this was what I should have preferred to hold, were it not that I in fact felt forced to recognise the slightness of such a chance. She would have loved his youth, and have made it her own, in death as in life, and he would have quitted the world, in truth, only the more effectually to leave it to her. Mrs. Server's quandary—which was now all I cared for—was exactly in her own certitude of every absence of issue. But I need give little more evidence of how it had set me thinking.

As much as anything else, perhaps, it was the fear of what one of the men might say to me that made me for an hour or two, at this crisis, continuously shy. Nobody, doubtless, would have said anything worse than that she was more of a flirt than ever, that they had all compared notes and would accordingly be interested in some hint of another, possibly a deeper, experience. It would have been almost as embarrassing to have to tell them how little experience I had had in fact as to have had to tell them how much I had had in fancy—all the more that I had as yet only my thin idea of the line of feeling in her that had led her so to spare me. Tea on the terraces represented, meanwhile, among us, so much neglect of everything else that my meditations remained for some time as unobserved as I could desire. I was not, moreover, heeding much where they carried me, and became aware of what I owed them only on at last finding myself anticipated as the occupant of an arbour into which I had strolled. Then I saw I had reached a remote part of the great gardens, and that for some of my friends also secluded thought had inducements; though it was not, I hasten to add, that either of the pair I here encountered appeared to be striking out in any very original direction. Lady John and Guy Brissenden, in the arbour, were thinking secludedly together; they were together, that is, because they were scarce a foot apart, and they were thinking, I inferred, because they were doing nothing else. Silence, by every symptom, had definitely settled on them, and whatever it was I interrupted had no resemblance to talk. Nothing—in the general air of evidence—had more struck me than that what Lady John's famous intellect seemed to draw most from Brissenden's presence was the liberty to rest. Yet it shook off this languor as soon as she saw me; it threw itself straight into the field; it went, I could see, through all the motions required of it by her ladyship's fallacious philosophy. I could mark these emotions, and what determined them, as behind clear glass.

I found, on my side, a rare intellectual joy, the oddest secret exultation, in feeling her begin instantly to play the part I had attributed to her in the irreducible drama. She broke out in a manner that could only have had for its purpose to represent to me that mere weak amiability had committed her to such a predicament. It was to humour her friend's husband that she had strayed so far, for she was somehow sorry for him, and—good creature as we all knew her—had, on principle, a kind little way of her own with silly infatuations. His *was* silly, but it was unmistakable, and she had for some time been finding it, in short, a case for a special tact. That he bored her to death I might have gathered by the way they sat there, and she could trust me to believe—couldn't she?—that she was only musing as to how she might most humanely get rid of him. She would lead him safely back to the fold if I would give her time. She seemed to ask it all, oddly, of *me*, to take me remarkably into her confidence, to refer me, for a specimen of his behaviour, to his signal abandonment of his wife the day before, his having waited over, to come down, for the train in which poor *she* was to travel. It was at all events, I felt, one of the consequences of having caught on to so much that I by this time found myself catching on to everything. I read into Lady John's wonderful manner—which quite clamoured, moreover, for an interpretation—all that was implied in the lesson I had extracted from other portions of the business. It was distinctly poor she who gave me the lead, and it was not less definite that she put it to me that I should render her a service either by remaining with them or by inventing something that would lure her persecutor away. She desired him, even at the cost of her being left alone, distracted from his pursuit.

Poor he, in his quarter, I hasten to add, contributed to my picking out this embroidery nothing more helpful than a sustained detachment. He said as little as possible, seemed heedless of what was otherwise said, and only gave me on his own account a look or two of dim suggestiveness. Yet it was these looks that most told with me, and what they, for their part, conveyed was a plea that directly contradicted Lady John's. I understood him that it was he who was bored, he who had been pursued, he for whom perversity had become a dreadful menace, he, in fine, who pleaded for my intervention. He was so willing to trust me to relieve him of his companion that I think he would simply have bolted without deferring to me if I had not taken my precautions against it. I had, as it happened, another momentary use for him than this: I wished on the one hand not to lose him and on the other not to lose Lady John, though I had quickly enough guessed this brilliant woman's real preference, of which it in fact soon became my lively wish to see the proof. The union of these two was too artificial for me not already to have connected with it the service it might render, in her ladyship's view, to that undetected cultivation, on her part, of a sentiment for Gilbert Long which, through his feigned response to it, fitted so completely to the other pieces in my collection. To see all this was at the time, I remember, to be as inhumanly amused as if one had found one could create something. I had created nothing but a clue or two to the larger comprehension I still needed, yet I positively found myself overtaken by a mild artistic glow. What had occurred was that, for my full demonstration, I needed Long, and that, by the same stroke, I became sure I should certainly get him by temporising a little.

Lady John was in love with him and had kicked up, to save her credit, the dust of a fictive relation with another man—the relation one of mere artifice and the man one in her encouragement of whom nobody would believe. Yet she was also discoverably divided between her prudence and her vanity, for if it was difficult to make poor Briss figure at all vividly as an insistent satellite, the thankless tact she had to employ gave her exactly, she argued, the right to be refreshingly fanned with an occasional flap of the flag under which she had, as she ridiculously fancied, truly conquered. If she was where I found her because her escort had dragged her there, she had made the best of it through the hope of assistance from another quarter. She had held out on the possibility that Mr. Long—whom one *could* without absurdity sit in an arbour with—might have had some happy divination of her plight. He had had such divinations before—thanks to a condition in him that made sensibility abnormal—and the least a wretched woman could do when betrayed by the excess of nature's bounty was to play admirer against admirer and be "talked about" on her own terms. She would just this once have admitted it, I was to gather, to be an occasion for pleading guilty—oh, so harmlessly!—to a consciousness of the gentleman mutely named between us. Well, the "proof" I just alluded to was that I had not sat with my friends five minutes before Gilbert Long turned up.

I saw in a moment how neatly my being there with them played *his* game; I became in this fashion a witness for him that he could almost as little leave Lady John alone as—well, as other people could. It may perfectly have been the pleasure of this reflection that again made him free and gay—produced in him, in any case, a different shade of manner from that with which, before luncheon, as the consequence perhaps of a vague *flair* for my possible penetration, I had suspected him of edging away from me. Not since my encounter with him at Paddington the afternoon before had I had so to recognise him as the transfigured talker. To see Lady John with him was to have little enough doubt of *her* recognitions, just as this spectacle also dotted each "i" in my conviction of his venial—I can only call it that—duplicity. I made up my mind on the spot that it had been no part of his plan to practise on her, and that the worst he could have been accused of was a good-natured acceptance, more apparent than real, for his own purposes, of her theory—which she from time to time let peep out—that they would have liked each other better if they hadn't been each, alas! so good. He profited by the happy accident of having pleased a person so much in evidence, and indeed it was tolerably clear to me that neither party was duped. Lady John didn't want a lover; this would have been, as people say, a larger order than, given the other complications of her existence, she could meet; but she wanted, in a high degree, the appearance of carrying on a passion that imposed alike fearless realisations and conscious renouncements, and this circumstance fully fell in with the convenience and the special situation of her friend. Her vanity rejoiced, so far as she dared to let it nibble, and the mysteries she practised, the dissimulations she elaborated, the general danger of detection in which she flattered herself that she publicly walked, were after all so much grist to the mill of that appetite.

By just so much, however, as it could never come up between them that there was another woman in Gilbert's history, by just so much would it on the other hand have been an articulate axiom that as many of the poor Brisses of the world as she might care to accommodate would be welcome to figure in her own. This personage, under that deeper induction, I suddenly became aware that I also greatly pitied—pitied almost as much as I pitied Mrs. Server; and my pity had doubtless something to do with the fact that, after I had proposed to him that we should adjourn together and we had, on his prompt, even though slightly dry response, placed the invidious arbour at a certain distance, I passed my hand into his arm. There were things I wanted of him, and the first was that he should let me show him I could be kind to him. I had made of the circumstance of tea at the house a pretext for our leaving the others, each of whom I felt as rather showily calling my attention to their good old ground for not wishing to rejoin the crowd. As to what Brissenden wished I had made up my mind; I had made up my mind as to the subject of his thoughts while they wandered, during his detention, from Lady John; and if the next of my wishes was to enter into his desire, I had decided on giving it effect by the time we reached the shortest of the vistas at the end of which the house reared a brave front.

## VII

I STAYED him there while I put it to him that he would probably in fact prefer to go back.

"You're not going then yourself?"

"No, I don't particularly want tea; and I may as well now confess to you that I'm taking a lonely, unsociable walk. I don't enjoy such occasions as these," I said, "unless I from time to time get off by myself somewhere long enough to tell myself how much I do enjoy them. That's what I was cultivating solitude for when I happened just now to come upon you. When I found you there with Lady John there was nothing for me but to make the best of it; but I'm glad of this chance to assure you that, every appearance to the contrary notwithstanding, I wasn't prowling about in search of you."

"Well," my companion frankly replied, "I'm glad you turned up. I wasn't especially amusing myself."

"Oh, I think I know how little!"

He fixed me a moment with his pathetic old face, and I knew more than ever that I was sorry for him. I was quite extraordinarily sorry, and I wondered whether I mightn't without offence or indiscretion really let him see it. It was to this end I had held him and wanted a little to keep him, and I was reassured as I felt him, though I had now released him, linger instead of leaving me. I had made him uneasy last night, and a new reason or two for my doing so had possibly even since then come up; yet these things also would depend on the way he might take them. The look with which he at present faced me seemed to hint that he would take them as I hoped, and there was no curtness, but on the contrary the dawn of a dim sense that I might possibly aid him, in the tone with which he came half-way. "You 'know'?"

"Ah," I laughed, "I know everything!"

He didn't laugh; I hadn't seen him laugh, at Newmarch, once; he was continuously, portentously grave, and I at present remembered how the effect of this had told for me at luncheon, contrasted as it was with that of Mrs. Server's desperate, exquisite levity. "You know I decidedly have too much of that dreadful old woman?"

There was a sound in the question that would have made me, to my own sense, start, though I as quickly hoped I had not done so to Brissenden's. I couldn't have persuaded myself, however, that I had escaped showing him the flush of my effort to show nothing. I had taken his disgusted allusion as to Mrs. Brissenden, and the action of that was upsetting. But nothing, fortunately, was psychologically more interesting than to grasp the next moment the truth of his reference. It was only the fact of his himself looking so much older than Lady John that had blinded me for an instant to the propriety of his not thinking of her as young. She wasn't young as *he* had a right to call people, and I felt a glow—also, I feared, too visible—as soon as I had seen whom he meant. His meaning Lady John did me somehow so much good that I believed it would have done me still more to hear him call her a harridan or a Jezebel. It was none of my business; how little was anything, when it came to that, my business!—yet indefinably, unutterably, I felt assuaged for him and comforted. I verily believe it hung in the balance a minute or two that in my impulse to draw him out, so that I might give him my sympathy, I was prepared to risk overturning the edifice of my precautions. I luckily, as it happened, did nothing of the sort; I contrived to breathe consolingly on his secret without betraying an intention. There was almost no one in the place save two or three of the very youngest women whom he wouldn't have had a right to call old. Lady John was a hag, then; Mrs. Server herself was more than on the turn; Gilbert Long was fat and forty; and I cast about for some light in which I could show that I—*à plus forte raison*—was a pantaloon. "Of course you can't quite see the fun of it, and it really isn't fair to you. You struck me as much more in your element," I ventured to add, "when, this morning, more than once, I chanced to observe you led captive by Mrs. Server."

"Oh, that's a different affair," he answered with an accent that promised a growth of confidence.

"Mrs. Server's an old woman," I continued, "but she can't seem to a fellow like you as old as Lady John. She has at any rate more charm; though perhaps not," I added, "quite so much talk."

On this he said an extraordinary thing, which all but made me start again. "Oh, she hasn't any *talk!*"

I took, as quickly as possible, refuge in a surprised demurrer. "Not *any?*"

"None to speak of."

I let all my wonder come. "But wasn't she chattering to you at luncheon?" It forced him to meet my eyes at greater length, and I could already see that my experiment—for insidiously and pardonably such I wished to make it—was on the way to succeed. I had been right then, and I knew where I stood. He couldn't have been "drawn" on his wife, and he couldn't have been drawn, in the least directly, on himself, but as he could thus easily be on Lady John, so likewise he could on other women, or on the particular one, at least, who mattered to me. I felt I really knew what I was about, for to draw him on Mrs. Server was in truth to draw him indirectly on himself. It was indeed perhaps because I had by this time in a measure expressed, in terms however general, the interest with which he inspired me, that I now found myself free to shift the ground of my indiscretion. I only wanted him to know that on the question of Mrs. Server I was prepared to go as far with him as he should care to move. How it came to me now that he was *the* absolutely safe person in the house to talk of her with! "I was too far away from you to hear," I had gone on; "and I could only judge of her flow of conversation from the animated expression of her face. It was extraordinarily animated. But that, I admit," I added, "strikes one always as a sort of *parti pris* with her. She's never *not* extraordinarily animated."

"She has no flow of conversation whatever," said Guy Brissenden.

I considered. "Really?"

He seemed to look at me quite without uneasiness now. "Why, haven't you seen for yourself——?"

"How the case stands with her on that head? Do you mean haven't I talked with her? Well, scarcely; for it's a fact that every man in the house *but* I strikes me as having been deluged with that privilege: if indeed," I laughed, "her absence of topics suffers it to be either a privilege or a deluge! She affects me, in any case, as determined to have nothing to do with me. She walks all the rest of you about; she gives you each your turn; me only she skips, she systematically ignores. I'm half consoled for it, however," I wound up, "by seeing what short innings any individual of you has. You personally strike me as having had the longest."

Brissenden appeared to wonder where I was coming out, yet not as if he feared it. There was even a particular place, if I could but guess it, where he would have liked me to come. "Oh, she's extremely charming. But of course she's strikingly odd."

"Odd?—really?"

"Why, in the sense, I mean, that I thought you suggested you've noticed."

"That of extravagant vivacity? Oh, I've had to notice it at a distance, without knowing what it represents."

He just hesitated. "You haven't any idea at all what it represents?"

"How should I have," I smiled, "when she never comes near me? I've thought *that*, as I tell you, marked. What does her avoidance of *me* represent? Has she happened, with you, to throw any light on it?"

"I think," said Brissenden after another moment, "that she's rather afraid of you."

I could only be surprised. "The most harmless man in the house?"

"*Are* you really?" he asked—and there was a touch of the comic in hearing him put it with his inveterate gravity.

"If you take me for anything else," I replied, "I doubt if you'll find anyone to back you."

My companion, on this, looked away for a little, turned about, fixed his eyes on the house, seemed, as with a drop of interest, on the point of leaving me. But instead of leaving me he brought out the next moment: "I don't want anyone to back me. I don't care. I didn't mean just now," he continued, "that Mrs. Server has said to me anything against you, or that she fears you because she dislikes you. She only told me she thought you disliked *her*."

It gave me a kind of shock. "A creature so beautiful, and so—so——"

"So what?" he asked as I found myself checked by my desire to come to her aid.

"Well, so brilliantly happy."

I had all his attention again. "Is that what she *is?*"

"Then don't you, with your opportunities, know?" I was conscious of rather an inspiration, a part of which was to be jocose. "What are you trying," I laughed, "to get out of me?"

It struck me luckily that, though he remained as proof against gaiety as ever, he was, thanks to his preoccupation, not disagreeably affected by my tone. "Of course if you've no idea, I can get nothing."

"No idea of what?"

Then it was that I at last got it straight. "Well, of what's the matter with her."

"Is there anything particular? If there *is*," I went on, "there's something that I've got out of *you!*"

"How so, if you don't know what it is?"

"Do you mean if you yourself don't?" But without detaining him on this, "Of what in especial do the signs," I asked, "consist?"

"Well, of everyone's thinking so—that there's something or other."

This again struck me, but it struck me too much. "Oh, everyone's a fool!"

He saw, in his queer wan way, how it had done so. "Then you *have* your own idea?"

I daresay my smile at him, while I waited, showed a discomfort. "Do you mean people are talking about her?"

But he waited himself. "Haven't they shown you——?"

"No, no one has spoken. Moreover I wouldn't have let them."

"Then there you *are!*" Brissenden exclaimed. "If you've kept them off, it must be because you differ with them."

"I shan't be sure of that," I returned, "till I

know what they think! However, I repeat," I added, "that I shouldn't even then care. I don't mind admitting that she much interests me."

"There you are, there you are!" he said again.

"That's all that's the matter with her so far as *I*'m concerned. You see, at any rate, how little it need make her afraid of me. She's lovely and she's gentle and she's happy."

My friend kept his eyes on me. "What is there to interest you so in that? Isn't it a description that applies here to a dozen other women? You can't say, you know, that you're interested in *them*, for you just spoke of them as so many fools."

There was a certain surprise for me in so much acuteness, which, however, doubtless admonished me as to the need of presence of mind. "I wasn't thinking of the ladies—I was thinking of the men."

"That's amiable to *me*," he said with his gentle gloom.

"Oh, my dear Brissenden, I except 'you.'"

"And why should you?"

I felt a trifle pushed. "I'll tell you some other time. And among the ladies I except Mrs. Brissenden, with whom, as you may have noticed, I've been having much talk."

"And will you tell me some other time about that too?" On which, as I but amicably shook my head for no, he had his first dimness of pleasantry. "I'll get it then from my wife."

"Never. She won't tell you."

"She has passed you her word? That won't alter the fact that she tells me everything."

He really said it in a way that made me take refuge for an instant in looking at my watch. "Are you going back to tea? If you are, I'll, in spite of my desire to roam, walk twenty steps with you." I had already again put my hand into his arm, and we strolled for a little till I threw off that I was sure Mrs. Server was waiting for him. To this he replied that if I wished to get rid of him he was as willing to take that as anything else for granted—an observation that I, on my side, answered with an inquiry, though an inquiry that had nothing to do with it. "Do you also tell everything to Mrs. Brissenden?"

It brought him up shorter than I had expected. "Do you ask me that in order that I shan't speak to her of this?"

I showed myself at a loss. "Of 'this'——?"

"Why, of what we've made out——"

"About Mrs. Server, you and I? You must act as to that, my dear fellow, quite on your own discretion. All the more that what on earth *have* we made out? I assure you I haven't a secret to confide to you about her, except that I've never seen a person more unquenchably radiant."

He almost jumped at it. "Well, that's just it!"

"But just what?"

"Why, what they're all talking about. That she *is* so awfully radiant. That she's so tremendously happy. It's the question," he explained, "of what in the world she has to make her so."

I winced a little, but tried not to show it. "My dear man, how do *I* know?"

"She *thinks* you know," he after a moment answered.

I could only stare. "Mrs. Server thinks I know what makes her happy?" I the more easily represented such a conviction as monstrous in that it truly had its surprise for me.

But Brissenden now was all with his own thought. "She *isn't* happy."

"You mean that that's what's the matter with her under her appearance——? Then what makes the appearance so extraordinary?"

"Why, exactly what I mention—that one doesn't see anything whatever in her to correspond to it."

I hesitated. "Do you mean in her circumstances?"

"Yes—or in her character. Her circumstances are nothing wonderful. She has none too much money; she has had three children and lost them; and nobody that belongs to her appears ever to have been particularly nice to her."

I turned it over. "How you *do* get on with her!"

"Do you call it getting on with her to be the more bewildered the more I see her?"

"Isn't to say you're bewildered only, on the whole, to say you're charmed? That always—doesn't it?—describes more or less any engrossed relation with a lovely lady."

"Well, I'm not sure I'm so charmed." He spoke as if he had thought this particular question over for himself; he had his way of being lucid without brightness. "I'm not at all easily charmed, you know," he the next moment added; "and I'm not a fellow who goes about much after women."

"Ah, that I never supposed! Why in the world *should* you? It's the last thing!" I laughed. "But isn't this—quite (what shall one call it?) innocently—rather a peculiar case?"

My question produced in him a little gesture of elation—a gesture emphasised by a snap of his forefinger and thumb. "I knew you knew it was special! I knew you've been thinking about it!"

"You certainly," I replied with assurance, "have, during the last five minutes, made me do so with some sharpness. I don't pretend that I don't now recognise that there *must* be something the matter. I only desire—not unnaturally—that there *should* be, to put me in the right for having thought, if, as you're so sure, such a freedom as that can be brought home to me. If Mrs. Server is beautiful and gentle and strange," I speciously went on, "what are those things but an attraction?"

I saw how he had them, whatever they were, before him, as he slowly shook his head. "They're not an attraction. They're too queer."

I caught in an instant my way to fall in with him; and not the less that I by this time felt myself committed, up to the intellectual eyes, to ascertaining just *how* queer the person under discussion might be. "Oh, of course I'm not speaking of her as a party to a silly flirtation, or an object of any sort of trivial pursuit. But there are so many different ways of being taken."

"For a fellow like you. But not for a fellow like me. For me there's only one."

"To be, you mean, in love?"

He put it a little differently. "Well, to be thoroughly pleased."

"Ah, that's doubtless the best way and the firm ground. And you mean you're *not* thoroughly pleased with Mrs. Server?"

"No—and yet I want to be kind to her. Therefore what's the matter?"

"Oh, if it's what's the matter with *you* you ask me, that extends the question. If you want to be kind to her, you get on with her, as we were saying, quite enough for my argument. And isn't the matter also, after all," I demanded, "that you simply feel she desires you to be kind?"

"She does that." And he looked at me as with the sense of drawing from me, for his relief, some greater help than I was as yet conscious of the courage to offer. "It *is* that she desires me. She likes it. And the extraordinary thing is that *I* like it."

"And why in the world shouldn't you?"

"Because she terrifies me. She has something to hide."

"But, my dear man," I asked with a gaiety singularly out of relation to the small secret thrill produced in me by these words—"my dear man, what woman who's worth anything hasn't?"

"Yes, but there are different ways. What *she* tries for is this false appearance of happiness."

I weighed it. "But isn't that the best thing?"

"It's terrible to have to keep it up."

"Ah, but if you don't *for* her? If it all comes on herself?"

"It doesn't," Guy Brissenden presently said. "I do—'for' her—help to keep it up." And then, still unexpectedly to me, came out the rest of his confession. "I want to—I try to; that's what I mean by being kind to her, and by the gratitude with which she takes it. One feels that one doesn't want her to break down."

It was on this—from the poignant touch in it—that I at last felt I had burnt my ships and didn't care how much I showed I was with him. "Oh, but she won't. You must keep her going."

He stood a little with a thumb in each pocket of his trousers, and his melancholy eyes ranging far over my head—over the tops of the highest trees. "Who am *I* to keep people going?"

"Why, you're just the man. Aren't you happy?"

He still ranged the tree-tops. "Yes."

"Well, then, you belong to the useful class. You've the wherewithal to give. It's the happy people who should help the others."

He had, in the same attitude, another pause. "It's easy for *you* to talk!"

"Because I'm not happy?"

It made him bring his eyes again down to me. "I think you're a little so now at my expense."

I shook my head reassuringly. "It doesn't cost you anything if—as I confess to it now—I do to some extent understand."

"That's more, then, than—after talking of it this way with you—I feel that *I* do!"

He had brought that out with a sudden sigh, turning away to go on; so that we took a few steps more. "You've nothing to trouble about," I then freely remarked, "but that you *are* as kind as the case requires and that you do help. I daresay that you'll find her even now on the terrace looking out for you." I patted his back, as we went a little further, but as I still preferred to stay away from the house I presently stopped again. "Don't fall below your chance. *Noblesse oblige.* We'll pull her through."

"You say 'we,'" he returned, "but you do keep out of it!"

"Why should you wish me to interfere with you?" I asked. "I wouldn't keep out of it if she wanted me as much as she wants you. That, by your own admission, is exactly what she doesn't."

"Well, then," said Brissenden, "I'll make her go for you. I think I want your assistance quite as much as she can want mine."

"Oh," I protested for this, "I've really given you already every ounce of mine I can squeeze out. And you know for yourself far more than I do."

"No, I don't!"—with which he became quite sharp; "for you know *how* you know it—which I've not a notion of. It's just what I think," he continued, facing me again, "you ought to tell me."

"I'm a little in doubt of what you're talking of, but I suppose you to allude to the oddity of my being so much interested without my having been more informed."

"You've got some clue," Brissenden said; "and a clue is what I myself want."

"Then get it," I laughed, "from Mrs. Server!"

He wondered. "Does she know?"

I had still, after all, to dodge a little. "Know what?"

"Why, that you've found out what she has to hide."

"You're perfectly free to ask her. I wonder even that you haven't done so yet."

"Well," he said with the finest stroke of unconsciousness he had yet shown me—"well, I suppose it's because I'm afraid of her."

"But not too much afraid," I risked suggesting, "to be hoping at this moment that you'll find her if you go back to where most of our party is gathered. You're not going for tea—you're going for Mrs. Server: just of whom it was, as I say, you were thinking while you sat there with Lady John. So what is it you so greatly fear?"

It was as if I could see through his dim face a sort of gratitude for my making all this out to him. "I don't know that it's anything that she may do to *me*." He could make it out in a manner for himself. "It's as if something might happen to her. It's what I told you—that she may break down. If you ask me how, or in what," he continued, "how can I tell you? In whatever it is that she's trying to do. I don't understand it." Then he wound up with a sigh that, in spite of its softness, he imperfectly stifled. "But it's something or other!"

"What would it be, then," I asked, "but what you speak of as what I've 'found out'? The effort you distinguish in her is the effort of concealment—vain, as I gather it strikes you both, so far as *I*, in my supernatural acuteness, am concerned."

Following this with the final ease to which my encouragement directly ministered, he yet gave me, before he had quite arrived, a queer sidelong glance. "Wouldn't it really be better if you were to tell me? I don't ask her myself, you see. I don't put things to her in that way."

"Oh, no—I've shown you how I do see. That's a part of your admirable consideration. But I must repeat that nothing would induce me to tell you."

His poor old face fairly pleaded. "But I want so to know."

"Ah, there it is!" I almost triumphantly laughed.

"There what is?"

"Why, everything. What I've divined, between you and Mrs. Server, as the tie. Your wanting so to know."

I felt as if he were now, intellectually speaking, plastic wax in my hand. "And her wanting me not to?"

"Wanting *me* not to," I smiled.

He puzzled it out. "And being willing, therefore——"

"That you—you only, for sympathy, for fellowship, for the wild wonder of it—*should* know? Well, for all those things, and in spite of what you call your fear, *try* her!" With which now at last I quitted him.

## VIII

I'M afraid I can't quite say what, after that, I at first did, nor just how I immediately profited by our separation. I felt absurdly excited, though this indeed was what I had felt all day; there had been in fact deepening degrees of it ever since my first mystic throb after finding myself, the day before in our railway-carriage, shut up to an hour's contemplation and collation, as it were, of Gilbert Long and Mrs. Brissenden. I have noted how my first full contact with the changed state of these associates had caused the knell of the tranquil mind audibly to ring for me. I have spoken of my sharpened perception that something altogether out of the common had happened, independently, to each, and I could now certainly flatter myself that I hadn't missed a feature of the road I had thus been beguiled to travel. It was a road that had carried me far, and verily at this hour I *felt* far. I daresay that for a while after leaving poor Briss, after what I may indeed call launching him, this was what I predominantly felt. To be where I was, to whatever else it might lead, treated me by its help to the taste of success. It appeared then that the more things I fitted together the larger sense, every way, they made—a remark in which I found an extraordinary elation. It justified my indiscreet curiosity; it crowned my underhand process with beauty. The beauty perhaps was only for *me*—the beauty of having been right; it made at all events an element in which, while the long day softly dropped, I wandered and drifted and securely floated. This element bore me bravely up, and my private triumph struck me as all one with the charm of the moment and of the place.

There was a general shade in all the lower reaches—a fine clear dusk in garden and grove, a thin suffusion of twilight out of which the greater things, the high tree-tops and pinnacles, the long crests of motionless wood and chimnied roof, rose into golden air. The last calls of birds sounded extraordinarily loud; they were like the timed, serious splashes, in wide, still water, of divers not expecting to rise again. I scarce know what odd consciousness I had of roaming at close of day in the grounds of some castle of enchantment. I had positively encountered nothing to compare with this since the days of fairy-tales and of the childish imagination of the impossible. *Then* I used to circle round enchanted castles, for then I moved in a world in which the strange " came true." It was the coming true that was the proof of the enchantment, which, moreover, was naturally never so great as when such coming was, to such a degree and by the most romantic stroke of all, the fruit of one's own wizardry. I was positively—so had the wheel revolved—proud of my work. I had thought it all out, and to have thought it was, wonderfully, to have brought it. Yet I recall how I even then knew on the spot that there was something supreme I should have failed to bring unless I had happened suddenly to become aware of the very presence of the haunting principle, as it were, of my thought. This was the light in which Mrs. Server, walking alone now, apparently, in the grey wood and pausing at sight of me, showed herself in her clear dress at the end of a vista. It was exactly as if she had been there by the operation of my intelligence, or even by that—in a still happier way—of my feeling. My excitement, as I have called it, on seeing her, was assuredly emotion. Yet what *was* this feeling, really?—of which, at the point we had thus reached, I seemed to myself to have gathered from all things an invitation to render some account.

Well, I knew within the minute that I was moved by it as by an extraordinary tenderness; so that this is the name I must leave it to make the best of. It had already been my impression that I was sorry for her, but it was marked for me now that I was sorrier than I had reckoned. All her story seemed at once to look at me out of the fact of her present lonely prowl. I met it without demur, only wanting her to know that if I struck her as waylaying her in the wood, as waiting for her there at eventide with an idea, I shouldn't in the least defend myself from the charge. I can scarce clearly tell how many fine strange things I thought of during this brief crisis of her hesitation. I wanted in the first place to make it end, and while I moved a few steps toward her I felt almost as noiseless and guarded as if I were trapping a bird or stalking a fawn. My few steps brought me to a spot where another perspective crossed our own, so that they made together a verdurous circle with an evening sky above and great lengthening, arching recesses in which the twilight thickened. Oh, it was quite sufficiently the castle of enchantment, and when I noticed four old stone seats, massive and mossy and symmetrically placed, I recognised not only the influence, in my adventure, of the grand style, but the familiar identity of this consecrated nook, which was so much of the type of all the bemused and remembered. We were in a beautiful old picture, we were in a beautiful old tale, and it wouldn't be the fault of Newmarch if some other green *carrefour,* not far off, didn't balance with this one and offer the alternative of niches, in the greenness, occupied by weather-stained statues on florid pedestals.

I sat straight down on the nearest of our benches, for this struck me as the best way to express the conception with which the sight of Mrs. Server filled me. It showed her that if I watched her I also waited for her, and that I was therefore not affected in any manner she really need deprecate. She had been too far off for me to distinguish her face, but her approach had faltered long enough to let me see that if she had not taken it as too late she would, to escape me, have found some pretext for turning off. It was just my seating myself that made the difference—it was my being so simple with her that brought her on. She came slowly and a little wearily down the vista, and her sad, shy advance, with the massed wood on either side of her, was like the reminiscence of a picture or the refrain of a ballad. What made the difference with *me*—if any difference had remained to be made—was the sense of this sharp cessation of her public extravagance. She had folded up her manner in her flounced parasol, which she seemed to drag after her as a sorry soldier his musket. It was present to me without a pang that this was the person I had sent poor Briss off to find—the person poor Briss would owe me so few thanks for his failure to have found. It was equally marked to me that, however detached and casual she might, at the first sight of me, have wished to show herself, it was to alight on poor Briss that she had come out, it was because he had not been at the house and might therefore, on his side, be wandering, that she had taken care to be unaccompanied. My demonstration was complete from the moment I thus had them in the act of seeking each other, and I was so pleased at having gathered them in that I cared little what else they had missed. I neither moved nor spoke till she had come quite near me, and as she also gave no sound the meaning of our silence seemed to stare straight out. It absolutely phrased there, in all the wonderful conditions, a relation already established; but the strange and beautiful thing was that as soon as we had recognised and accepted it this relation put us almost at our ease. "You must be weary of walking," I said at last, "and you see I've been keeping a seat for you."

I had finally got up, as a sign of welcome, but I had directly afterwards resumed my position, and it was an illustration of the terms on which we met that we neither of us seemed to mind her being meanwhile on her feet. She stood before me as if to take in—with her smile that had by this time sunk quite to dimness—more than we should, either of us, after all, be likely to be able to say. I even saw from this moment, I think, that, whatever she might understand, she would be able herself to say but little. She gave herself, in that minute, more than she doubtless knew — gave herself, I mean, to my intenser apprehension. She went through the form of expression, but what told me everything was the way the form of expression broke down. Her lovely grimace, the light of the previous hours, was as blurred as a bit of brushwork in water-colour spoiled by the upsetting of the artist's glass. She fixed me with it as she had fixed during the day forty persons, but it fluttered like a bird with a broken wing. She looked about and above, down each of our dusky avenues and up at our gilded tree-tops and our painted sky, where, at the moment, the passage of a flight of rooks made a clamour. She appeared to wish to produce some explanation of her solitude, but I was quickly enough sure that she would never find a presentable one. I only wanted to show her how little I required it. "I like a lonely walk," I went on, "at the end of a day full of people: it's always, to me, on such occasions, quite as if something has happened that the mind wants to catch and fix before the vividness fades. So I mope by myself an hour—I take stock of my impressions. But there's one thing I don't believe you know. This is the very first time, in such a place and at such an hour, that it has ever befallen me to come across a friend stricken with the same perversity and engaged in the same pursuit. Most people, don't you see?"—I kept it up as I could—"don't in the least know what has happened to them, and don't care to know. That's one way, and I don't deny it may be practically the best. But if one does care to know, that's another way. As soon as I saw you there at the end of the alley I said to myself, with quite a little thrill of elation, 'Ah, then it's *her* way too!' I wonder if you'll let me tell you," I floundered pleasantly on, "that I immediately liked you the better for it. It seemed to bring us more together. That's what I sat straight down here to show you. 'Yes,' I wished you to understand me as frankly saying, 'I *am*, as well as you, on the mope, or on the muse, or on whatever you call it, and this isn't half a bad corner for such a mood.' I can't tell you what a pleasure it is to me to see you do understand."

I kept it up, as I say, to reassure and soothe and steady her; there was nothing, however fantastic and born of the pressure of the moment, that I wouldn't have risked for that purpose. She was absolutely on my hands with her secret—I felt that from the way she stood and listened to me, silently showing herself relieved and pacified. It was marked that if I had hitherto seen her as "all over the place," she had yet nowhere seemed to me less so than at this furthermost point. But if, though only nearer to her secret and still not in possession, I felt as justified as I have already described myself, so it equally came to me that I was quite near enough, at the pass we had reached, for what I should have to take from it all. She was on my hands—it was she herself, poor creature, who was: this was the thing that just now loomed large, and the secret was a comparative detail. "I think you're very kind," she said for all answer to the speech I have reported, and the minute after this she had sunk down, in confessed collapse, to my bench, on which she sat and stared before her. The mere mechanism of her expression, the dangling paper lantern itself, was now all that was left in her face. She remained a little as if discouraged by the sight of the weariness that her surrender had let out. I hesitated, from just this fear of adding to it, to commiserate her for it more directly, and she spoke again before I had found anything to say. She brought back her attention indeed as if with an effort and from a distance. "What is it that has happened to you?"

"Oh," I laughed, "what is it that has happened to *you?*" My question had not been in the least intended for pressure, but it made her turn and look at me, and this, I quickly recognised, was all the answer the most pitiless curiosity could have desired —all the more, as well, that the intention in it had been no greater than in my words. Beautiful, abysmal, involuntary, her exquisite weakness simply opened up the depths it would have closed. It was in short a supremely unsuccessful attempt to say nothing. It said everything, and by the end of a minute my chatter—none the less out of place for being all audible—was hushed to positive awe by what it had conveyed. I saw as I had never seen before what consuming passion can make of the marked mortal on whom, with fixed beak and claws, it has settled as on a prey. She reminded me of a sponge wrung dry and with fine pores agape. Voided and scraped of everything, her shell was merely crushable. So it was brought home to me that the victim could be abased, and so it disengaged itself from these things that the abasement could be conscious. That was Mrs. Server's tragedy, that her consciousness survived—survived with a force that made it struggle and dissemble. This consciousness was all her secret—it was at any rate all mine. I promised myself roundly that I would henceforth keep clear of any other.

I none the less—from simply sitting with her there—gathered in the sense of more things than I could have named, each of which, as it came to me, made my compassion more tender. Who of us all could say that his fall might not be as deep?—or might not at least become so with equal opportunity. I for a while fairly forgot Mrs. Server, I fear, in the intimacy of this vision of the possibilities of our common nature. She became such a wasted and dishonoured symbol of them as might have put tears in one's eyes. When I presently returned to her—our session seeming to resolve itself into a mere mildness of silence—I saw how it was that whereas, in such cases in general, people might have given up much, the sort of person this poor lady was could only give up everything. She was the absolute wreck of her storm, accordingly, but to which the pale ghost of a special sensibility still clung, waving from the mast, with a bravery that went to the heart, the last tatter of its flag. There are impressions too fine for words, and I shall not attempt to say how it was that under the touch of this one I felt how nothing that concerned my companion could ever again be present to me but the fact itself of her admirable state. This was the source of her wan little glory, constituted even for her a small sublimity in the light of which mere minor identifications turned vulgar. I knew who *he* was now with a vengeance, because I had learnt precisely from that who *she* was; and nothing could have been sharper than the force with which it pressed upon me that I had really learnt more than I had bargained for. Nothing need have happened if I hadn't been so absurdly, so fatally meditative about poor Long—an accident that most people, wiser people, appeared on the whole to have steered sufficiently clear of. Compared with my actual sense, the sense with which I sat there, that other vision was gross, and grosser still the connection between the two.

Such were some of the reflections in which I indulged while her eyes—with their strange intermissions of darkness or of light: who could say which? —told me from time to time that she knew whatever

I was thinking of to be for her virtual advantage. It was prodigious what, in the way of suppressed communication, passed in these wonderful minutes between us. Our relation could be at the best but an equal confession, and I remember saying to myself that if she had been as subtle as I—which she wasn't!—she too would have put it together that I had dreadfully talked about her. She would have traced in me my demonstration to Mrs. Briss that, whoever she was, she must logically have been idiotised. It was the special poignancy of her collapse that, so far at least as I was concerned, this was a ravage the extent of which she had ceased to try to conceal. She had been trying, and more or less succeeding, all day: the little drama of her public unrest had had, when one came to consider, no other argument. It had been terror that had directed her steps; the need constantly to show herself detached and free, followed by the sterner one not to show herself, by the same token, limp and empty. This had been the distinct, ferocious logic of her renewals and ruptures—the anxious mistrust of her wit, the haunting knowledge of the small distance it would take her at once, the consequent importance of her exactly timing herself, and the quick instinct of flight before the menace of discovery. She couldn't let society alone, because that would have constituted a symptom; yet, for fear of the appearance of a worse one, she could only mingle in it with a complex diplomacy. She was accordingly exposed on every side, and to be with her a while thus quietly was to read back into her behaviour the whole explanation, which was positively simple to me now. To take up again the vivid analogy, she had been sailing all day, though scarce able to keep afloat, under the flag of her old reputation for easy response. She had given to the breeze any sad scrap of a substitute for the play of mind once supposed remarkable. The last of all the things her stillness said to me was that I could judge from so poor a show what had become of her conversability. What I did judge was that a frantic art had indeed been required to make her pretty silences pass, from one crisis to another, for pretty speeches. Half this art, doubtless, was the glittering deceit of her smile, the sublime, pathetic overdone geniality which represented so her share in any talk that, every other eloquence failing, there could only be nothing at all from the moment it abandoned its office. There *was* nothing at all. That was the truth; in accordance with which I finally—for everything it might mean to myself—put out my hand and bore ever so gently on her own. Her own rested listlessly on the stone of our seat. Of course, it had been an immense thing for her that she was, in spite of everything, so lovely.

All this was quite consistent with its eventually coming back to me that, though she took from me with appreciation what was expressed in the gesture I have noted, it was certainly in quest of a still deeper relief that she had again come forth. The more I considered her face—and most of all, so permittedly, in her passive, conscious presence—the more I was sure of this and the further I could go in the imagination of her beautiful duplicity. I ended by divining that if I was assuredly good for her, because the question of keeping up with me had so completely dropped, and if the service I so rendered her was not less distinct to her than to myself—I ended by divining that she had none the less her obscure vision of a still softer ease. Guy Brissenden had become in these few hours her positive need—a still greater need than I had lately amused myself with making out that he had found her. Each had, by their unprecedented plight, something for the other, some intimacy of unspeakable confidence, that no one else in the world could have for either. They had been feeling their way to it, but at the end of their fitful day they had grown confusedly, yet beneficently sure. The explanation here again was simple—they had the sense of a common fate. They hadn't to name it or to phrase it—possibly even couldn't had they tried; peace and support came to them, without that, in the simple revelation of each other. Oh, how I made it out that if it was indeed very well for the poor lady to feel thus in *my* company that her burden was lifted, my company would be after all but a rough substitute for Guy's! He was a still better friend, little as he could have told the reason; and if I could in this connection have put the words into her mouth, here follows something of the sense that I should have made them form.

"Yes, my dear man, I do understand you—quite perfectly now, and (by I know not what miracle) I've really done so to some extent from the first. Deep is the rest of feeling with you, in this way, that I'm watched, for the time, only as you watch me. It has all stopped, and *I* can stop. How can I make you understand what it is for me that there isn't at last a creature any more in sight, that the wood darkens about me, that the sounds drop and the relief goes on; what can it mean for you even that I've given myself up to not caring whether or no, amongst others, I'm missed and spoken of? It does help my strange case, in fine, as you see, to let you keep me here; but I should have found still more what I was in need of if I had only found, instead of you, him whom I had in mind. He is as much better than you as you are than everyone else." I finally felt, in a word, so qualified to attribute to my companion some such mute address as that, that it could only have, as the next consequence, a determining effect on me—an effect under the influence of which I spoke. "I parted with him, some way from here, some time ago. I had found him in one of the gardens with Lady John; after which we came away from her together. We strolled a little and talked, but I knew what he really wanted. He wanted to find you, and I told him he would probably do so at tea on the terrace. It was visibly with that idea—to return to the house—that he left me."

She looked at me for some time on this, taking it in, yet still afraid of it. "You found him with Lady John?" she at last asked, and with a note in her voice that made me see what—as there was a precaution I had neglected—she feared.

The perception of this, in its turn, operated with me for an instant almost as the rarest of temptations. I had puzzled out everything and put everything together; I was as morally confident and as intellectually triumphant as I have frankly here described myself; but there was no objective test to which I had yet exposed my theory. The chance to apply one — and it would be infallible — had suddenly cropped up. There would be excitement, amusement, discernment in it; it would be indeed but a more roundabout expression of interest and sympathy. It would, above all, pack the question I had for so many hours been occupied with into the compass of a needle-point. I was dazzled by my opportunity. She had had an uncertainty, in other words, as to whom I meant, and that it kept her for some seconds on the rack was a trifle compared to my chance. She would give herself away supremely if she showed she suspected me of placing my finger on the spot—if she understood the person I had not named to be nameable as Gilbert Long. What had created her peril, of course, was my naming Lady John. Well, how can I say in any sufficient way how much the extraordinary beauty of her eyes during this brevity of suspense had to do with the event? It had everything—for it was what caused me to be touched beyond even what I had already been, and I could literally bear no more of that. I therefore took no advantage, or took only the advantage I had spoken with the intention of taking. I laughed out doubtless too nervously, but it didn't compromise my tact. " Don't you know how she's perpetually pouncing on him? "

Still, however, I had not named him—which was what prolonged the tension. " Do you mean—a—do you mean——? " With which she broke off on a small weak titter and a still weaker exclamation. " There are so *many* gentlemen! "

There was something in it that might in other conditions have been as trivial as the giggle of a housemaid; but it had in fact for my ear the silver ring of poetry. I told her instantly whom I meant. " Poor Briss, you know," I said, " is always in her clutches."

Oh, how it let her off! And yet, no sooner had it done so and had I thereby tasted on the instant the sweetness of my wisdom, than I became aware of something much more extraordinary. It let her off—she showed me this for a minute, in spite of herself; but the next minute she showed me something quite different, which was, most wonderful of all, that she wished me to see her as not quite feeling why I should so much take for granted the person I *had* named. "Poor Briss?" her face and manner appeared suddenly to repeat—quite, moreover (and it was the drollest, saddest part), as if all our friends had stood about us to listen. Wherein did poor Briss so intimately concern her? What, pray, was my ground for such free reference to poor Briss? She quite repudiated poor Briss. She knew nothing at all about him, and the whole airy structure I had erected with his aid might have crumbled at the touch she thus administered if its solidity had depended only on that. I had a minute of surprise which, had it lasted another minute as surprise pure and simple, might almost as quickly have turned to something like chagrin. Fortunately it turned instead into something even more like enthusiasm than anything I had yet felt. The stroke *was* extraordinary, but extraordinary for its nobleness. I quickly saw in it, from the moment I had got my point of view, more fine things than ever. I saw for instance that, magnificently, she wished not to incriminate him. All that had passed between us had passed in silence, but it was a different matter for what might pass in sound. We looked at each other therefore with a strained smile over any question of identities. It was as if it had been one thing—to her confused, relaxed intensity—to give herself up to me, but quite another thing to give up somebody else.

And yet, superficially arrested as I was for the time, I directly afterwards recognised in this instinctive discrimination—the last, the expiring struggle of her native lucidity—a supremely convincing bit of evidence. It was still more convincing than if she had done any of the common things—stammered, changed colour, shown an apprehension of what the person named might have said to me. She had had it from me that he and I had talked about her, but there was nothing that she accepted the idea of his having been able to say. I saw—still more than this—that there was nothing to my purpose (since my purpose was to understand) that she would have had, as matters stood, coherence enough to impute to him. It was extremely curious to me to divine, just here, that she hadn't a glimmering of the real logic of Brissenden's happy effect on her nerves. It was the effect, as coming from him, that a beautiful delicacy forbade her as yet to give me her word for; and she was certainly herself in the stage of regarding it as an anomaly. Why, on the contrary, I might have wondered, shouldn't she have jumped at the chance, at the comfort, of seeing a preference trivial enough to be "worked" imputed to her? Why shouldn't she have been positively pleased that people might helpfully couple her name with that of the wrong man? Why, in short, in the language that Grace Brissenden and I had used together, was not that lady's husband the perfection of a red herring? Just because, I perceived, the relation that had established itself between them *was*, for its function, a real relation, the relation of a fellowship in resistance to doom.

Nothing could have been stranger than for *me* so to know it was while the stricken parties themselves were in ignorance; but nothing, at the same time, could have been, as I have since made out, more magnanimous than Mrs. Server's attitude. She moved, groping and panting, in the gathering dusk of her fate, but there were calculations she still could dimly make. One of these was that she must drag no one else in. I verily believe that, for that matter, she had scruples, poignant and exquisite, even about letting our friend himself see how much she liked to be with him. She wouldn't, at all events, let another see. I saw what I saw, I felt what I felt, but such things were exactly a sign that I could take care of myself. There was apparently, I was obliged to admit, but little apprehension in her of her unduly showing that *our* meeting had been anything of a blessing to her. There was no one indeed just then to be the wiser for it; I might perhaps else even have feared that she would have been influenced to treat the incident as closed. I had, for that matter, no wish to prolong it beyond her own convenience; it had already told me everything it could possibly tell. I thought I knew moreover what she would have got from it. I preferred, none the less, that we should separate by my own act; I wanted not to see her move in order to be free of me. So I stood up, to put her more at her ease, and it was while I remained before her that I tried to turn to her advantage what I had committed myself to about Brissenden.

"I had a fancy, at any rate, that he was looking for you—all the more that he didn't deny it."

She had not moved; she had let me take my hand from her own with as little sign as on her first feeling its touch. She only kept her eyes on me. "What made you have such a fancy?"

"What makes me ever have any?" I laughed. "My extraordinary interest in my fellow-creatures. I have more than most men. I've never really seen anyone with half so much. That breeds observation, and observation breeds ideas. Do you know what it has done?" I continued. "It has bred for me the idea that Brissenden's in love with you."

There was something in her eyes that struck me as betraying—and the appeal of it went to the heart—the constant dread that if entangled in talk she might show confusion. Nevertheless she brought out after a moment, as naturally and charmingly as possible: " How can that be when he's so strikingly in love with his wife? "

I gave her the benefit of the most apparent consideration. " Strikingly, you call it? "

" Why, I thought it was noticed—what he does for her."

" Well, of course she's extremely handsome—or at least extremely fresh and attractive. He *is* in love with her, no doubt, if you take it by the quarter, or by the year, like a yacht or a stable," I pushed on at random. " But isn't there such a state also as being in love by the day? "

She waited, and I guessed from the manner of it exactly why. It was the most obscure of intimations that she would have liked better that I shouldn't make her talk; but obscurity, by this time, offered me no more difficulties. The hint, none the less, a trifle disconcerted me, and, while I vaguely sought for some small provisional middle way between going and not going on, the oddest thing, as a fruit of my own delay, occurred. This was neither more nor less than the revival of her terrible little fixed smile. It came back as if with an audible click—as a gas-burner makes a pop when you light it. It told me visibly that from the moment she must talk she could talk only with its aid. The effect of its aid I indeed immediately perceived.

"How do I know?" she asked in answer to my question. "I've never *been* in love."

"Not even by the day?"

"Oh, a day's surely a long time."

"It is," I returned. "But I've none the less, more fortunately than you, been in love for a whole one." Then I continued, from an impulse of which I had just become conscious and that was clearly the result of the heart-breaking facial contortion —heart-breaking, that is, when one knew what I knew—by which she imagined herself to represent the pleasant give-and-take of society. This sense, for me, was a quick horror of forcing her, in such conditions, to talk at all. Poor Briss had mentioned to me, as an incident of his contact with her, his apprehension of her breaking down; and now, at a touch, I saw what he had meant. She *would* break down if I didn't look out. I found myself thus, from one minute to the other, as greatly dreading it for her, dreading it indeed for both of us, as I might have dreaded some physical accident or danger, her fall from an unmanageable horse or the crack beneath her of thin ice. It was impossible—that was the extraordinary impression—to come too much to her assistance. We had each of us all, in our way, hour after hour, been, as goodnaturedly as unwittingly, giving her a lift; yet what was the end of it but her still sitting there to assure me of a state of gratitude—that she couldn't even articulate—for every hint of a perch that might still be held out? What could only, therefore, in the connection, strike me as indicated was fairly to put into her mouth—if one might do so without showing too ungracefully as alarmed—the words one might have guessed her to wish to use were she able to use any. It was a small service of anticipation that I tried to render her with as little of an air as possible of being remedial. "I daresay you wonder," I remarked on these lines, "why, at all, I should have thrust Brissenden in."

"Oh, I *do* so wonder!" she replied with the refined but exaggerated glee that is a frequent form in high companies and light colloquies. I *did* help her—it was admirable to feel it. She liked my imposing on her no more complex a proposition. She liked my putting the thing to her so much better than she could have put it to me. But she immediately afterwards looked away as if—now that we *had* put it, and it didn't matter which of us best—we had nothing more to do with it. She gave me a hint of drops and inconsequences that might indeed have opened up abysses, and all the while she smiled and smiled. Yet whatever she did or failed of, as I even then observed to myself, how she remained lovely! One's pleasure in that helped one somehow not to break down on one's own side—since breaking down was in question—for commiseration. I didn't know what she might have hours of for the man—whoever he was—to whom her sacrifice had been made; but I doubted if for any other person she had ever been so beautiful as she was for me at these moments. To have kept her so, to have made her more so—how might that result of their relation not in fact have shone as a blinding light into the eyes of her lover? What would he have been bound to make out in her after all but her passion and her beauty? Wasn't it enough for such wonders as these to fill his consciousness? If they didn't fill mine—even though occupying so large a place in it—was that not only because I had not the direct benefit of them as the other party to the prodigy had it? They filled mine too, for that matter, just at this juncture, long enough for me to describe myself as rendered subject by them to a temporary loss of my thread. What *could* pass muster with her as an account of my reason for evoking the blighted identity of our friend? There came constantly into her aspect, I should say, the strangest alternatives, as I can only most conveniently call them, of presence and absence—something like intermissions of intensity, cessations and resumptions of life. They were like the slow flickers of a troubled flame, breathed upon and then left, burning up and burning down. She had really burnt down—I mean so far as her sense of things went—while I stood there.

I stood long enough to see that it didn't in the

least signify whether or no I explained, and during this interval I found myself—to my surprise—in receipt of still better assistance than any I had to give. I had happened to turn, while I awkwardly enough, no doubt, rested and shifted, to the quarter from which Mrs. Server had arrived; and there, just at the end of the same vista, I gathered material for my proper reply. Her eyes at this moment were fixed elsewhere, and that gave me still a little more time, at the end of which my reference had all its point. "I supposed you to have Brissenden in your head," I said, "because it's evidently what he himself takes for granted. But let him tell you!" He was already close to us: missing her at the house, he had started again in search of her and had successfully followed. The effect on him of coming in sight of us had been for an instant to make him hang back as I had seen Mrs. Server hang. But he had then advanced just as she had done; I had waited for him to reach us; and now she saw him. She looked at him as she always looked at all of us, yet not at either of us as if we had lately been talking of him. If it was vacancy it was eloquent; if it was vigilance it was splendid. What was most curious, at all events, was that it was now poor Briss who was disconcerted. He had counted on finding her, but not on finding her with me, and I interpreted a certain ruefulness in him as the sign of a quick, uneasy sense that he must have been in question between us. I instantly felt that the right thing was to let him know he had been, and I mentioned to him, as a joke, that he had come just in time to save himself. We had been talking of him, and I wouldn't answer for what Mrs. Server had been going to say. He took it gravely, but he took everything so gravely that I saw no symptom in that. In fact, as he appeared at first careful not to meet my eyes, I saw for a minute or two no symptom in anything—in anything, at least, but the way in which, standing beside me and before Mrs. Server's bench, he received the conscious glare of her recognition without returning it and without indeed giving her a look. He looked all about—looked, as she herself had done after our meeting, at the charming place and its marks of the hour, at the rich twilight, deeper now in the avenues, and at the tree-tops and sky, more flushed now with colour. I found myself of a sudden quite as sorry for him as I had been for Mrs. Server, and I scarce know how it was suggested to me that during the short interval since our separation something had happened that made a difference in him. Was the difference a consciousness still more charged than I had left it? I couldn't exactly say, and the question really lost itself in what soon came uppermost for me—the desire, above all, to spare them both and to spare them equally.

The difficulty, however, was to spare them in some fashion that would not be more marked than continuing to observe them. To leave them together without a decent pretext would be marked; but this, I eagerly recognised, was none the less what most concerned me. Whatever they might see in it, there was by this time little enough doubt of how it would indicate for my own mind that the wheel had completely turned. That was the point to which I had been brought by the lapse of a few hours. I had verily travelled far since the sight of the pair on the terrace had given its arrest to my first talk with Mrs. Briss. I was obliged to admit to myself that nothing could very well have been more singular than some of my sequences. I had come round to the opposite pole of the protest my companion had then drawn from me—which was the pole of agreement with herself; and it hung sharply before me that I was pledged to confess to her my revolution. I couldn't now be in the presence of the two creatures I was in the very act of finally judging to be not a whit less stricken than I had originally imagined them—I couldn't do this and think with any complacency of the redemption of my pledge; for the process by which I had at last definitely inculpated Mrs. Server was precisely such a process of providential supervision as made me morally responsible, so to speak, for her, and thereby intensified my scruples. Well, my scruples had the last word—they were what determined me to look at my watch and profess that, whatever sense of a margin Brissenden and Mrs. Server might still enjoy, it behoved me not to forget that I took, on such great occasions, an hour to dress for dinner. It was a fairly crude cover for my retreat; perhaps indeed I should rather say that my retreat was practically naked and unadorned. It formulated their relation. I left them with the formula on their hands, both queerly staring at it, both uncertain what to do with it. For some passage that would soon be a correction of this, however, one might surely feel that one could trust them. I seemed to feel my trust justified, behind my back, before I had got twenty yards away. By the time I had done this, I must add, something further had befallen me. Poor Briss had met my eyes just previous to my flight, and it was then I satisfied myself of what had happened to him at the house. He had met his wife; she had in some way dealt with him; he had been with her, however briefly, alone; and the intimacy of their union had been afresh impressed upon him. Poor Briss, in fine, looked ten years older.

# IX

I SHALL never forget the impressions of that evening, nor the way, in particular, the immediate effect of some of them was to merge the light of my extravagant perceptions in a glamour much more diffused. I remember feeling seriously warned, while dinner lasted, not to yield further to my idle habit of reading into mere human things an interest so much deeper than mere human things were in general prepared to supply. This especial hour, at Newmarch, had always a splendour that asked little of interpretation, that even carried itself, with an amiable arrogance, as indifferent to what the imagination could do for it. I think the imagination, in those halls of art and fortune, was almost inevitably accounted a poor matter; the whole place and its participants abounded so in pleasantness and picture, in all the felicities, for every sense, taken for granted there by the very basis of life, that even the sense most finely poetic, aspiring to extract the moral, could scarce have helped feeling itself treated to something of the snub that affects—when it does affect—the uninvited reporter in whose face a door is closed. I said to myself during dinner that these were scenes in which a transcendent intelligence had after all no application, and that, in short, any preposterous acuteness might easily suffer among them such a loss of dignity as overtakes the newspaper-man kicked out. We existed, all of us together, to be handsome and happy, to be really what we looked—since we looked tremendously well; to be that and neither more nor less, so not discrediting by musty secrets and aggressive doubts our high privilege of harmony and taste. We were concerned only with what was bright and open, and the expression that became us all was, at worst, that of the shaded but gratified eye, the air of being forgivingly dazzled by too much lustre.

Mrs. Server, at table, was out of my range, but I wondered if, had she not been so, I shouldn't now have been moved to recognise in her fixed expressiveness nothing more than our common reciprocal tribute. Hadn't everyone my eyes could at present take in a fixed expressiveness? Was I not very possibly myself, on this ground of physiognomic congruity, more physiognomic than anyone else? I made my excellence, on the chance, go as far as it would to cover my temporary doubts. I saw Mrs. Brissenden, in another frock, naturally, and other jewels from those of the evening before; but she gave me, across the board, no more of a look than if she had quite done with me. It struck me that she felt she *had* done—that, as to the subject of our discussion, she deemed her case by this time so established as to offer comparatively little interest. I couldn't come to her to renew the discussion; I could only come to her to make my submission; and it doubtless appeared to her—to do her justice—more delicate not to triumph over me in advance. The profession of joy, however, reigned in her handsome face none the less largely for my not having the benefit of it. If I seem to falsify my generalisation by acknowledging that her husband, on the same side, made no more public profession of joy than usual, I am still justified by the fact that there was something in a manner decorative even in Brissenden's wonted gloom. He reminded me at this hour more than ever of some fine old Velasquez or other portrait—a presentation of ugliness and melancholy that might have been royal. There was as little of the common in his dry, distinguished patience as in the case I had made out for him. Blighted and ensconed, he looked at it over the rigid convention, his peculiar perfection of necktie, shirt-front and waistcoat, as some aged remnant of sovereignty at the opera looks over the ribbon of an order and the ledge of a box.

I must add, however, that in spite of my sense of his wife's indulgence I kept quite aware of the nearer approach, as course followed course, of my hour of reckoning with her—more and more saw the moment of the evening at which, frankly amused at last at having me in a cleft stick, she would draw me a little out of the throng. Of course, also, I was much occupied in asking myself to what degree I was prepared to be perjured. *Was* I ready to pretend that my candour was still unconvinced? And was I in this case only instinctively mustering my arguments? I was certainly as sorry that Mrs. Server was out of my view as if I proposed still to fight; and I really felt, so far as that went, as if there might be something to fight for after the lady on my left had given me a piece of news. I had asked her if she happened to know, as we couldn't see, who was next Mrs. Server, and, though unable to say at the moment, she made no scruple, after a short interval, of ascertaining with the last directness. The stretch forward in which she had indulged, or the information she had caused to be passed up to her while I was again engaged on my right, established that it was Lord Lutley who had brought the lovely lady in and that it was Mr. Long who was on her other side. These things indeed were not the finest point of my companion's communication, for I saw that what she felt I would be really interested in was the fact that Mr. Long had brought in Lady John, who was naturally, therefore, his other neighbour. Beyond Lady John was Mr. Obert, and beyond Mr. Obert Mrs. Froome, not, for a wonder, this time paired, as by the immemorial tradition, so fairly comical in its candour, with Lord Lutley. Wasn't it too funny, the kind of grandmotherly view of their relation shown in their always being put together? If I perhaps questioned whether "grandmotherly" were exactly the name for the view, what yet at least was definite in the light of this evening's arrangement was that there did occur occasions on which they were put apart. My friend of course disposed of this observation by the usual exception that "proved the rule"; but it was absurd how I had thrilled with her announcement, and our exchange of ideas meanwhile helped to carry me on.

My theory had not at all been framed to embrace the phenomenon thus presented; it had been precisely framed, on the contrary, to hang together with the observed inveteracy of escape, on the part of the two persons about whom it busied itself, from public juxtaposition of more than a moment. I was fairly upset by the need to consider at this late hour whether going in for a new theory or bracing myself for new facts would hold out to me the better refuge. It is perhaps not too much to say that I should scarce have been able to sit still at all but for the support afforded me by the oddity of the separation of Lord Lutley and Mrs. Froome; which, though resting on a general appearance directly opposed to that of my friends, offered somehow the relief of a suggestive analogy. What I could directly clutch at was that if the exception did prove the rule in the one case it might equally prove it in the other. If on a rare occasion one of these couples might be divided, so, by as uncommon a chance, the other might be joined; the only difference being in the gravity of the violated law. For which pair was the betrayal greatest? It was not till dinner was nearly ended and the ladies were about to withdraw that I recovered lucidity to make out how much more machinery would have had to be put into motion consistently to prevent, than once in a way to minimise, the disconcerting accident.

All accidents, I must add, were presently to lose themselves in the unexpectedness of my finding myself, before we left the dining-room, in easy talk with Gilbert Long—talk that was at least easy for *him*, whatever it might have struck me as necessarily destined to be for me. I felt as he approached me—for he did approach me—that it was somehow "important"; I was so aware that something in the state of my conscience would have prevented me from assuming conversation between us to be at this juncture possible. The state of my conscience was that I knew too much—that no one had really any business to know what I knew. If he suspected but the fiftieth part of it there was no simple spirit in which he could challenge me. It would have been simple of course to desire to knock me down, but that was barred by its being simple to excess.

It wouldn't even have been enough for him merely to ground it on a sudden fancy. It fitted, in fine, with my cogitations that it was so significant for him to wish to speak to me that I didn't envy him his attempt at the particular shade of assurance required for carrying the thing off. He would have learned from Mrs. Server that I was not, as regarded them, at all as others were; and thus his idea, the fruit of that stimulation, could only be either to fathom, to felicitate, or—as it were—to destroy me. What was at the same time obvious was that no one of these attitudes would go quite of itself. The simple sight of him as he quitted his chair to take one nearer my own brought home to me in a flash —and much more than anything had yet done— the real existence in him of the condition it was my private madness (none the less private for Grace Brissenden's so limited glimpse of it,) to believe I had coherently stated. Is not this small touch perhaps the best example I can give of the intensity of amusement I had at last enabled my private madness to yield me? I found myself owing it, from this time on and for the rest of the evening, moments of the highest concentration.

Whatever there might have been for me of pain or doubt was washed straight out by the special sensation of seeing how "clever" poor Long not only would have to be, but confidently and actually *was;* inasmuch as this apprehension seemed to put me in possession of his cleverness, besides leaving me all my own. I made him welcome, I helped him to another cigarette, I felt above all that I should enjoy him; my response to his overture was, in other words, quickly enough to launch us. Yet I fear I can do little justice to the pleasant suppressed tumult of impression and reflection that, on my part, our ten minutes together produced. The elements that mingled in it scarce admit of discrimination. It was still more than previously a deep sense of being justified. My interlocutor was for those ten minutes immeasurably superior—superior, I mean, to himself—and he couldn't possibly have become so save through the relation I had so patiently tracked. He faced me there with another light than his own, spoke with another sound, thought with another ease and understood with another ear. I should put it that what came up between us was the mere things of the occasion, were it not for the fine point to which, in my view, the things of the occasion had been brought. While our eyes, at all events, on either side, met serenely, and our talk, dealing with the idea, dealing with the extraordinary special charm, of the social day now deepening to its end, touched our companions successively, touched the manner in which this one and that had happened to be predominantly a part of that charm; while such were our immediate conditions I wondered of course if he had not, just as consciously and essentially as I, quite another business in mind. It was not indeed that our allusion to the other business would not have been wholly undiscoverable by a third person.

So far as it took place it was of a "subtlety," as we used to say at Newmarch, in relation to which the common register of that pressure would have been, I fear, too old-fashioned a barometer. I had moreover the comfort—for it amounted to that—of perceiving after a little that we understood each other too well for our understanding really to have tolerated the interference of passion, such passion as would have been represented on his side by resentment of my intelligence and on my side by resentment of his. The high sport of such intelligence—between gentlemen, to the senses of any other than whom it must surely be closed—demanded and implied in its own intimate interest a certain amenity. Yes, accordingly, I had promptly got the answer that my wonder at his approach required: he had come to me for the high sport. He would formerly have been incapable of it, and he was beautifully capable of it now. It was precisely the kind of high sport—the play of perception, expression, sociability—in which Mrs. Server would a year or two before have borne as light a hand. I need scarcely add how little it would have found itself in that lady's present chords. He had said to me in our ten minutes everything amusing she couldn't have said. Yet if when our host gave us the sign to adjourn to the drawing-room so much as all this had grown so much clearer, I had still, figuratively speaking, a small nut or two left to crack. By the time we moved away together, however, these resistances had yielded. The answers had really only been waiting for the questions. The play of Long's mind struck me as more marked, since the morning, by the same amount, as it might have been called, as the march of poor Briss's age; and if I had, a while before, in the wood, had my explanation of this latter addition, so I had it now of the former—as to which I shall presently give it.

When music, in English society, as we know, is not an accompaniment to the voice, the voice can in general be counted on to assert its pleasant identity as an accompaniment to music; but at Newmarch we had been considerably schooled, and this evening, in the room in which most of us had assembled, an interesting pianist, who had given a concert the night before at the near county town and been brought over during the day to dine and sleep, would scarce have felt in any sensitive fibre that he was not having his way with us. It may just possibly have been an hallucination of my own, but while we sat together after dinner in a dispersed circle I could have worked it out that, as a company, we were considerably conscious of some experience, greater or smaller from one of us to the other, that had prepared us for the player's spell. Felicitously scattered and grouped, we might in almost any case have had the air of looking for a message from it—of an imagination to be flattered, nerves to be quieted, sensibilities to be soothed. The whole scene was as composed as if there were scarce one of us but had a secret thirst for the infinite to be quenched. And it was the infinite that, for the hour, the distinguished foreigner poured out to us, causing it to roll in wonderful waves of sound, almost of colour, over our receptive attitudes and faces. Each of us, I think, now wore the expression—or confessed at least to the suggestion—of some indescribable thought; which might well, it was true, have been nothing more unmentionable than the simple sense of how the posture of deference to this noble art has always a certain personal grace to contribute. We neglected nothing of it that could make our general effect ample, and whether or no we were kept quiet by the piano, we were at least admonished, to and fro, by our mutual visibility, which each of us clearly desired to make a success. I have little doubt, furthermore, that to each of us was due, as the crown of our inimitable day, the imputation of having something quite of our own to think over.

We thought, accordingly — we continued to think, and I felt that, by the law of the occasion, there had as yet been for everyone no such sovereign warrant for an interest in the private affairs of everyone else. As a result of this influence all that at dinner had begun to fade away from me came back with a rush and hovered there with a vividness. I followed many trains and put together many pieces; but perhaps what I most did was to render a fresh justice to the marvel of our civilised state. The perfection of that, enjoyed as we enjoyed it, all made a margin, a series of concentric circles of rose-colour (shimmering away into the pleasant vague of everything else that didn't matter,) for the so salient little figure of Mrs. Server, still the controlling image for me, the real principle of composition, in this affluence of fine things. What, for my part, while I listened, I most made out was the beauty and the terror of conditions so highly organised that under their rule her small lonely fight with disintegration could go on without the betrayal of a gasp or a shriek, and with no worse tell-tale contortion of lip or brow than the vibration, on its golden stem, of that constantly renewed flower of amenity which my observation had so often and so mercilessly detached only to find again in its place. This flower nodded perceptibly enough in our deeply stirred air, but there was a peace, none the less, in feeling the spirit of the wearer to be temporarily at rest. There was for the time no gentleman on whom she need pounce, no lapse against which she need guard, no presumption she need create, nor any suspicion she need destroy. In this pause in her career it came over me that I should have liked to leave her; it would have prepared for me the pleasant after-consciousness that I had seen her pass, as I might say, in music out of sight.

But we were, alas! all too much there, too much tangled and involved for that; every actor in the play that had so unexpectedly insisted on constituting itself for me sat forth as with an intimation that they were not to be so easily disposed of. It was as if there were some last act to be performed before the curtain could fall. Would the definite dramatic signal for ringing the curtain down be then only—as a grand climax and *coup de théâtre*—the due attestation that poor Briss had succumbed to inexorable time and Mrs. Server given way under a cerebral lesion? Were the rest of us to disperse decorously by the simple action of the discovery that, on our pianist's striking his last note, with its consequence of permitted changes of attitude, Gilbert Long's victim had reached the point of final simplification and Grace Brissenden's the limit of age recorded of man? I could look at neither of these persons without a sharper sense of the contrast between the tragedy of their predicament and the comedy of the situation that did everything for them but suspect it. They had truly been arrayed and anointed, they had truly been isolated, for their sacrifice. I was sufficiently aware even then that if one hadn't known it one might have seen nothing; but I was not less aware that one couldn't know anything without seeing all; and so it was that, while our pianist played, my wandering vision played and played as well. It took in again, while it went from one of them to the other, the delicate light that each had shed on the other, and it made me wonder afresh what still more delicate support they themselves might not be in the very act of deriving from their dim community. It was for the glimmer of this support that I had left them together two or three hours before; yet I was obliged to recognise that, travel between them as my fancy might, it could detect nothing in the way of a consequent result. I caught no look from either that spoke to me of service rendered them; and I caught none, in particular, from one of them to the other, that I could read as a symptom of their having compared notes. The fellow-feeling of each for the lost light of the other remained for me but a tie supposititious—the full-blown flower of my theory. It would show here as another flower, equally mature, for me to have made out a similar dim community between Gilbert Long and Mrs. Brissenden—to be able to figure them as groping side by side, proportionately, towards a fellowship of light overtaken; but if I failed of this, for ideal symmetry, that seemed to rest on the general truth that joy brings people less together than sorrow.

So much for the course of my impressions while the music lasted—a course quite consistent with my being prepared for new combinations as soon as it was over. Promptly, when that happened, the bow was unbent; and the combination I first seized, amid motion and murmur and rustle, was that, once more, of poor Briss and Lady John, the latter of whom had already profited by the general reaction to endeavour to cultivate afresh the vainest of her sundry appearances. She had laid on him the same coercive hand to which I owed my having found him with her in the afternoon, but my intervention was now to operate with less ceremony. I chanced to be near enough to them for Brissenden, on seeing me, to fix his eyes on me in silence, but in a manner that could only bring me immediately nearer. Lady John never did anything in silence, but she greeted me as I came up to them with a fine false alarm. "No, indeed," she cried, "you shan't carry him off this time!"—and poor Briss disappeared, leaving us face to face, even while she breathed defiance. He had made no joke of it, and I had from him no other recognition; it was therefore a mere touch, yet it gave me a sensible hint that he had begun, as things were going, to depend upon me, that I already in a fashion figured to him —and on amazingly little evidence after all—as his natural protector, his providence, his effective omniscience. Like Mrs. Server herself, he was materially on my hands, and it was proper I should " do " for him. I wondered if he were really beginning to look to me to avert his inexorable fate. Well, if his inexorable fate was to be an unnameable climax, it had also its special phases, and one of these I *had* just averted. I followed him a moment with my eyes and I then observed to Lady John that she decidedly took me for too simple a person. She had meanwhile also watched the direction taken by her liberated victim, and was the next instant prepared with a reply to my charge. " Because he has gone to talk with May Server? I don't quite see what you mean, for I believe him really to be in terror of her. Most of the men here *are*, you know, and I've really assured myself that he doesn't find her any less awful than the rest. He finds her the more so by just the very marked extra attention that you may have noticed she has given him."

" And does that now happen to be what he has so eagerly gone off to impress upon her? "

Lady John was so placed that she could continue to look at our friends, and I made out in her that she was not, in respect to them, without some slight elements of perplexity. These were even sufficient to make her temporarily neglect the defence of the breach I had made in her consistency. " If you mean by ' impressing upon ' her speaking to her, he hasn't gone—you can see for yourself—to impress upon her anything; they have the most extraordinary way, which I've already observed, of sitting together without sound. I don't know," she laughed, "what's the matter with such people!"

"It proves in general," I admitted, "either some coldness or some warmth, and I quite understand that that's not the way *you* sit with your friends. You steer admirably clear of every extravagance. I don't see, at any rate, why Mrs. Server is a terror——"

But she had already taken me up. "If she doesn't chatter as *I* do?" She thought it over. "But she does—to everyone but Mr. Briss. I mean to every man she can pick up."

I emulated her reflection. "Do they complain of it to you?"

"They're more civil than you," she returned; "for if, when they flee before it, they bump up against me in their flight, they don't explain that by intimating that they're come from bad to worse. Besides, I see what they suffer."

"And do you hear it?"

"What they suffer? No, I've taken care not to suffer myself. I don't listen. It's none of my business."

"Is that a way of gently expressing," I ventured to ask, "that it's also none of mine?"

"It might be," she replied, "if I had, as you appear to, the imagination of atrocity. But I don't pretend to so much as conceive what's your business."

"I wonder if it isn't just now," I said after a moment, "to convict you of an attempt at duplicity that has not even had the saving grace of success! Was it for Brissenden himself that you spoke just now as if you believed him to wish to cling to you?"

"Well, I'm kind enough for anything," she good-naturedly enough laughed. "But what," she asked more sharply, "are you trying to find out?"

Such an awful lot, the answer to this would politely have been, that I daresay the aptness of the question produced in my face a shade of embarrassment. I felt, however, the next moment that I needn't fear too much. What I, on approaching Lady John, had found myself moved to test, using her in it as a happy touchstone, was the degree of the surrounding, the latent, sense of things: an impulse confirmed by the manner in which she had momentarily circled about the phenomenon of Mrs. Server's avidity, about the mystery of the terms made with it by our friend. It was present to me that if I could catch, on the part of my interlocutress, anything of a straight scent, I might take that as the measure of a diffused danger. I mentally applied this term to the possibility of diffusion, because I suddenly found myself thinking with a kind of horror of any accident by which I might have to expose to the world, to defend against the world, to share with the world, that now so complex tangle of hypotheses that I have had for convenience to speak of as my theory. I could toss the ball myself, I could catch it and send it back, and familiarity had now made this exercise—in my own inner precincts—easy and safe. But the mere brush of Lady John's clumsier curiosity made me tremble for the impunity of my creation. If there had been, so to speak, a discernment, however feeble, of *my* discernment, it would have been irresistible to me to take this as the menace of some incalculable catastrophe or some public ugliness. It wasn't for me definitely to image the logical result of a verification by the sense of others of the matter of my vision; but the thing had only to hang before me as a chance for me to feel that I should utterly object to it, though I may appear to weaken this statement if I add that the opportunity to fix the degree of my actual companion's betrayed mystification was almost a spell. This, I conceive, was just by reason of what was at stake. How could I happily tell her what I was trying to find out?—tell her, that is, not too much for security and yet enough for relief? The best answer seemed a brave jump. I was conscious of a certain credit open with her in my appearance of intellectual sympathy.

" Well," I brought out at last, " I'm quite aching to ask you if you'll forgive me a great liberty, which

I owe to your candid challenge my opportunity to name. Will you allow me to say frankly that I think you play a dangerous game with poor Briss, in whom I confess I'm interested? I don't of course speak of the least danger to yourself; but it's an injustice to any man to make use of him quite so flagrantly. You don't in the least flatter yourself that the poor fellow is in love with you—you wouldn't care a bit if he were. Yet you're willing to make him think you like him, so far as that may be necessary to explain your so frequently ingenious appropriation of him. He doesn't like you *too* much, as yet; doesn't even like you quite enough. But your potency may, after all, work on him, and then, as your interest is so obviously quite elsewhere, what will happen will be that you'll find, to your inconvenience, that you've gone too far. A man never likes a woman enough unless he likes her *more* than enough. Unfortunately it's what the inveterate ass is sure sooner or later to do."

Lady John looked just enough interested to look detached from most of the more vulgar liabilities to offence. "Do I understand that to be the pretty name by which you describe Mr. Briss?"

"He has his share of it, for I'm thinking of the idiots that we everyone of us are. I throw out a warning against a contingency."

"Are you providing for the contingency of his ceasing to care for his wife? If you are"—and

Lady John's amusement took on a breadth—"you may be said to have a prudent mind and to be taking time by the forelock."

At this I pricked up my ears. "Do you mean because of his apparently incorruptible constancy?"

"I mean because the whole thing's so before one. She has him so in hand that they're neither of them in as much danger as would count for a mouse. It doesn't prevent his liking to dally by the way—for *she* dallies by the way, and he does everything she does. Haven't I observed her," Lady John continued, "dallying a little, so far as that goes, with *you?* You've the tact to tell me that he doesn't think me good enough, but I don't require, do I?—for such a purpose as his—to be very extraordinarily good. You may say that you wrap it up immensely and try to sugar the dose! Well, all the same, give up, for a quiet life, the attempt to be a providence. You can't be a providence and not be a bore. A real providence *knows;* whereas you," said Lady John, making her point neatly, "have to find out—and to find out even by asking 'the likes of' *me*. Your fine speech meanwhile doesn't a bit tell me what."

It affected me again that she could get so near without getting nearer. True enough it was that I wanted to find out; and though I might expect, or fear, too much of her, I wondered at her only seeing this—at her not reading deeper. The peril of the public ugliness that haunted me rose or fell, at this moment, with my varying view of her density. Or rather, to be more exact, I already saw her as necessarily stupid because I saw her as extravagantly vain. What I see now of course is that I was on my own side almost stupidly hard with her—as I may also at that hour have been subject to her other vice. Didn't I perhaps, in proportion as I felt how little she saw, think awfully well of myself, as we said at Newmarch, for seeing so much more? It comes back to me that the sense thus established of my superior vision may perfectly have gone a little to my head. If it was a frenzied fallacy I was all to blame, but if it was anything else whatever it was naturally intoxicating. I really remember in fact that nothing so much as this confirmed presumption of my impunity had appeared to me to mark the fine quality of my state. I think there must fairly have been a pitch at which I was not sure that not to partake of that state was, on the part of others, the sign of a gregarious vulgarity; as if there were a positive advantage, an undiluted bliss, in the intensity of consciousness that I had reached. *I* alone was magnificently and absurdly aware—everyone else was benightedly out of it. So I reflected that there would be almost nothing I mightn't with safety mention to my present subject of practice as an acknowledgment that I was meddlesome. I could put no clue in her hand that her notorious acuteness would make of the smallest use to her. The most she could do would be to make it of use to myself, and the clue it seemed best to select was therefore a complete confession of guilt.

"You've a lucidity of your own in which I'm forced to recognise that the highest purity of motive looks shrivelled and black. You bring out accordingly what has made me thus beat about the bush. Have you really such a fund of indulgence for Gilbert Long as we most of us, I gather—though perhaps in our blindness—seem to see it stick out again that he supposes? *May* he fondly feel that he can continue to count on it? Or, if you object to my question in that form, is it not, frankly, to making his attitude—after all so thoroughly public—more convenient to each of you that (without perhaps quite measuring what you're about,) you've gone on sacrificing poor Briss? I call it sacrificing, you see, in spite of there having been as yet no such great harm done. And if you ask me again what business of mine such inquiries may represent, why, the best thing will doubtless be to say to you that, with a smaller dose of irrepressible irony in my composition than you have in yours, I can't make so light as you of my tendency to worry on behalf of those I care for. Let me finally hasten to add that I'm not now including in that category either of the two gentlemen I've named."

I freely concede, as I continue my record, that to follow me at all, at this point, gave proof on Lady John's part of a faculty that should have prevented my thinking of her as inordinately backward. "Then who in the world *are* these objects of your solicitude?"

I showed, over and above my hesitation, my regret for the need of it. "I'm afraid I can't tell you."

At this, not unnaturally, she fairly scoffed. "Asking me everything and telling me nothing, you nevertheless look to me to satisfy you? Do you mean," she pursued, "that you speak for persons whose interest is more legitimately founded than the interest you so flatteringly attribute to myself?"

"Well, yes—let them be so described! Can't you guess," I further risked, "who constitutes at least *one* of my preoccupations?"

The condescension of her consent to think marked itself handsomely enough. "Is it your idea to pretend to me that I'm keeping Grace Brissenden awake?" There was consistency enough in her wonder. "She has not been anything but nice to me; she's not a person whose path one crosses without finding it out; and I can't imagine what has got into her if any such grievance as that is what she has been pouring out to you in your apparently so deep confabulations."

This toss of the ball was one that, I saw quickly

enough, even a taste for sport wouldn't justify my answering, and my logical interest lay moreover elsewhere. "Dear no! Mrs. Brissenden certainly feels her strength, and I should never presume to take under my charge any personal situation of hers. I had in my mind a very different identity."

Lady John, as if to be patient with me, looked about at our companions for a hint of it, wondering which of the ladies I might have been supposed to "care for" so much as to tolerate in her a preference for a rival; but the effect of this survey was, I the next instant observed, a drop of her attention from what I had been saying. Her eye had been caught by the sight of Gilbert Long within range of us, and then had been just visibly held by the fact that the person seated with him on one of the small sofas that almost of necessity made conversation intimate was the person whose name, just uttered between us, was, in default of the name she was in search of, still in the air. Gilbert Long and Mrs. Briss were in familiar colloquy—though I was aware, at the first flush, of nothing in this that should have made my interlocutress stare. That is I was aware of nothing but that I had simultaneously myself been moved to some increase of sharpness. What *could* I have known that should have caused me to wonder at the momentary existence of this particular conjunction of minds unless it were simply the fact that I hadn't seen it occur amid the many conjunctions I had already noticed—*plus* the fact that I had a few minutes before, in the interest of the full roundness of my theory, actually been missing it? These two persons had met in my presence at Paddington and had travelled together under my eyes; I had talked of Mrs. Briss with Long and of Long with Mrs. Briss; but the vivid picture that their social union forthwith presented stirred within me, though so strangely late in the day, it might have seemed, for such an emotion, more than enough freshness of impression. Yet—now that I did have it there—why should it be vivid, why stirring, why a picture at all? Was *any* temporary collocation, in a house so encouraging to sociability, out of the range of nature? Intensely prompt, I need scarcely say, were both my freshness and my perceived objections to it. The happiest objection, could I have taken time to phrase it, would doubtless have been that the particular effect of this juxtaposition—to my eyes at least—was a thing not to have been foreseen. The parties to it looked, certainly, as I felt that I hadn't prefigured them; though even this, for my reason, was not a description of their aspect. Much less was it a description for the intelligence of Lady John—to whom, however, after all, some formulation of what she dimly saw would not be so indispensable.

We briefly watched, at any rate, together, and as our eyes met again we moreover confessed that we had watched. And we could ostensibly have offered each other no explanation of that impulse save that we had been talking of those concerned as separate and that it was in consequence a little odd to find ourselves suddenly seeing them as one. For that was it—they *were* as one; as one, at all events, for *my* large reading. My large reading had meanwhile, for the convenience of the rest of my little talk with Lady John, to make itself as small as possible. I had an odd sense, till we fell apart again, as of keeping my finger rather stiffly fixed on a passage in a favourite author on which I had not previously lighted. I held the book out of sight and behind me; I spoke of things that were not at all in it—or not at all on that particular page; but my volume, none the less, was only waiting. What might be written there hummed already in my ears as a result of my mere glimpse. Had *they* also wonderfully begun to know? Had *she*, most wonderfully, and had they, in that case, prodigiously come together on it? This was a possibility into which my imagination could dip even deeper than into the depths over which it had conceived the other pair as hovering. These opposed couples balanced like bronze groups at the two ends of a chimney-piece, and the most I could say to myself in lucid deprecation of my thought was that I mustn't take them equally for granted merely *because* they balanced. Things in the real had a way of not balancing; it was all an affair, this fine symmetry, of artificial proportion. Yet even while I kept my eyes away from Mrs. Briss and Long it was vivid to me that, "composing" there beautifully, they could scarce help playing a part in my exhibition. The mind of man, furthermore—and my generalisation pressed hard, with a quick twist, on the supersubtlety as to which I had just been privately complacent—the mind of man doubtless didn't know from one minute to the other, under the appeal of phantasmagoric life, what it would profitably be at. It had struck me a few seconds before as vulgarly gross in Lady John that she was curious, or conscious, of so small a part; in spite of which I was already secretly wincing at the hint that these others had begun to find themselves less in the dark and perhaps even directly to exchange their glimmerings.

My personal privilege, on the basis of the full consciousness, had become, on the spot, in the turn of an eye, more than questionable, and I was really quite scared at the chance of having to face—of having to see *them* face—another recognition. What did this alarm imply but the complete reversal of my estimate of the value of perception? Mrs. Brissenden and Long had been hitherto magnificently without it, and I was responsible perhaps for having, in a mood practically much stupider than the stupidest of theirs, put them gratuitously and helplessly *on* it. To be without it was the most consistent, the most successful, because the most amiable, form of selfishness; and why should people admirably equipped for remaining so, people bright and insolent in their prior state, people in whom this state was to have been respected as a surface without a scratch is respected, be made to begin to vibrate, to crack and split, from within? Wasn't it enough for *me* to pay, vicariously, the tax on being absurd? Were we all to be landed, without an issue or a remedy, in a condition on which that tax would be generally levied? It was as if, abruptly, with a new emotion, I had wished to unthink every thought with which I had been occupied for twenty-four hours. Let me add, however, that even had this process been manageable I was aware of not proposing to begin it till I should have done with Lady John.

The time she took to meet my last remark is naturally not represented by this prolonged glance of mine at the amount of suggestion that just then happened to reach me from the other quarter. It at all events duly came out between us that Mrs. Server was the person I did have on my mind; and I remember that it had seemed to me at the end of a minute to matter comparatively little by which of us, after all, she was first designated. There is perhaps an oddity—which I must set down to my emotion of the moment—in my not now being able to say. I should have been hugely startled if the sight of Gilbert Long had appeared to make my companion suddenly think of her; and reminiscence of that shock is not one of those I have found myself storing up. What does abide with me is the memory of how, after a little, my apprehensions, of various kinds, dropped—most of all under the deepening conviction that Lady John was not a whit less agreeably superficial than I could even at the worst have desired. The point established for me was that, whereas she passed with herself and so many others as taking in everything, she had taken in nothing whatever that it was to my purpose she should not take. Vast, truly, was the world of observation, that we could both glean in it so actively without crossing each other's steps. There we stood close together, yet—save for the accident of a final dash, as I shall note—were at opposite ends of the field.

It's a matter as to which the truth sounds priggish, but I can't help it if—yes, positively—it affected me as hopelessly vulgar to have made any induction at all about our companions *but* those I have recorded, in such detail, on behalf of my own energy. It was better verily not to have touched them—which was the case of everyone else—than to have taken them up, with knowing gestures, only to do so little with them. That I felt the interest of May Server, that May Server felt the interest of poor Briss, and that my feeling incongruously presented itself as putting up, philosophically, with the inconvenience of the lady's—these were, in fine, circumstances to which she clearly attached ideas too commonplace for me to judge it useful to gather them in. She read all things, Lady John, heaven knows, in the light of the universal possibility of a "relation"; but most of the relations that she had up her sleeve could thrust themselves into my theory only to find themselves, the next minute, eliminated. They were of alien substance — insoluble in the whole. Gilbert Long had for her no connection, in my deeper sense, with Mrs. Server, nor Mrs. Server with Gilbert Long, nor the husband with the wife, nor the wife with the husband, nor I with either member of either pair, nor anyone with anything, nor anything with anyone. She was thus exactly where I wanted her to be, for, frankly, I became conscious, at this climax of my conclusion, that I a little wanted her to be where she had distinctly ended by betraying to me that her proper inspiration had placed her. If I have just said that my apprehensions, of various kinds, had finally and completely subsided, a more exact statement would perhaps have been that from the moment our eyes met over the show of our couple on the sofa, the question of any other calculable thing than *that* hint of a relation had simply known itself superseded. Reduced to its plainest terms, this sketch of an improved acquaintance between our comrades was designed to make Lady John think. It was designed to make me do no less, but we thought, inevitably, on different lines.

I have already so represented my successions of reflection as rapid that I may not appear to exceed in mentioning the amusement and philosophy with which I presently perceived it as unmistakable that she believed in the depth of her new sounding. It visibly went down for her much nearer to the bottom of the sea than any plumb I might be qualified to drop. Poor Briss was in love with his wife—that, when driven to the wall, she had had to recognise; but she had not had to recognise that his wife was in love with poor Briss. What was then to militate, on that lady's part, against a due consciousness, at the end of a splendid summer day, a day on which occasions had been so multiplied, of an impression of a special order? What was to prove that there was "nothing in it" when two persons sat looking so very exceptionally *much* as if there were everything in it, as if they were for the first time—thanks to finer opportunity—doing each other full justice? Mustn't it indeed at this juncture have come a little over my friend that Grace had lent herself with uncommon good nature, the previous afternoon, to the arrangement by which, on the way from town, her ladyship's reputation was to profit by no worse company, precisely, than poor Briss's? Mrs. Brissenden's own was obviously now free to profit by my companion's remembering — if the fact had reached her ears—that Mrs. Brissenden had meanwhile had Long for an escort. So much, at least, I saw Lady John as seeing, and my vision may be taken as representing the dash I have confessed myself as making from my end of our field. It offers us, to be exact, as jostling each other just sensibly—though *I* only might feel the bruise—in our business of picking up straws. Our view of the improved acquaintance was only a straw, but as I stooped to it I felt my head bump with my neighbour's. This might have made me ashamed of my eagerness, but, oddly enough, that effect was not to come. I felt in fact that, since we had even pulled against each other at the straw, I carried off, in turning away, the larger piece.

# X

IT was in the moment of turning away that I somehow learned, without looking, that Mrs. Brissenden had also immediately moved. I wanted to look and yet had my reasons for not appearing to do it too quickly; in spite of which I found my friends, even after an interval, still distinguishable as separating for the avoidance of comment. Gilbert Long, rising directly after his associate, had already walked away, but this associate, lingering where she stood and meeting me with it, availed herself of the occasion to show that she wished to speak to me. Such was the idea she threw out on my forthwith going to her. "For a few minutes—presently."

"Do you mean alone? Shall I come with you?"

She hesitated long enough for me to judge her as a trifle surprised at my being so ready—as if indeed she had rather hoped I wouldn't be; which would have been an easy pretext to her to gain time. In fact, with a face not quite like the brave face she had at each step hitherto shown me, yet unlike in a fashion I should certainly not have been able to define on the spot; with an expression, in short, that struck me as taking refuge in a general reminder that not my convenience, but her own, was in question, she replied: "Oh, no—but before it's too late. A few minutes hence. Where shall you be?" she asked with a shade, as I imagined, of awkwardness. She had looked about as for symptoms of acceptance of the evening's end on the part of the ladies, but we could both see our hostess otherwise occupied. "We don't go up quite yet. In the morning," she added as with an afterthought, "I suppose you leave early."

I debated. "I haven't thought. And you?"

She looked at me straighter now. "I haven't thought either." Then she was silent, neither turning away nor coming to the point, as it seemed to me she might have done, of telling me what she had in her head. I even fancied that her momentary silence, combined with the way she faced me—as if that might speak for her—was meant for an assurance that, whatever train she should take in the morning, she would arrange that it shouldn't be, as it had been the day before, the same as mine. I really caught in her attitude a world of invidious reference to the little journey we had already made together. She had sympathies, she had proprieties that imposed themselves, and I was not to think that any little journey was to be thought of again in those conditions. It came over me that this might have been quite a matter discussed by her, discussed and settled, with her interlocutor on the sofa. It came over me that if, before our break-up for the night, I should happen also to have a minute's talk with that interlocutor, I would equally get from it the sense of an intention unfavourable to our departing in the same group. And I wondered if this, in that case, wouldn't affect me as marking a change back to Long's old manner—a forfeiture of the conditions, whatever view might be taken of them, that had made him, at Paddington, suddenly show himself as so possible and so pleasant. If *he* "changed back," wouldn't Grace Brissenden change by the same law? And if Grace Brissenden did, wouldn't her husband? Wouldn't the miracle take the form of the rejuvenation of that husband? Would it, still by the same token, take the form of *her* becoming very old, becoming if not as old as her husband, at least as old, as one might say, as herself? Would it take the form of her becoming dreadfully plain—plain with the plainness of mere stout maturity and artificial preservation? And if it took this form for the others, which would it take for May Server? Would she, at a bound as marked as theirs, recover her presence of mind and her lost equipment?

The kind of suspense that these rising questions produced for me suffered naturally no drop after Mrs. Briss had cut everything short by rustling voluminously away. She had something to say to me, and yet she hadn't; she had nothing to say, and yet I felt her to have already launched herself in a statement. There were other persons I had made uncomfortable without at all intending it, but she at least had not suffered from me, and I had no wish that she should; according to which she had no pressure to fear. My suspense, in spite of this, remained—indeed all the more sensibly that I had suddenly lost my discomfort on the subject of redeeming my pledge to her. It had somehow left me at a stroke, my dread of her calling me, as by our agreement, to submit in respect to what we had talked of as the identification of the woman. That call had been what I looked for from her after she had seen me break with Lady John; my first idea *then* could only be that I must come, as it were, to time. It was strange that, the next minute, I should find myself sure that I was, as I may put it, free; it was at all events indisputable that as I stood there watching her recede and fairly studying, in my preoccupation, her handsome affirmative back and the special sweep of her long dress—it was indisputable that, on some intimation I could, at the instant, recognise but not seize, my consciousness was aware of having performed a full revolution. If I was free, that was what I had been only so short a time before, what I had been as I drove, in London, to the station. Was this now a foreknowledge that, on the morrow, in driving away, I should feel myself restored to that blankness? The state lost was the state of exemption from intense obsessions, and the state recovered would therefore logically match it. If the foreknowledge had thus, as by the stir of the air from my friend's whisk of her train, descended upon me, my liberation was in a manner what I was already tasting. Yet how I also felt, with it, something of the threat of a chill to my curiosity! The taste of its being all over, that really sublime success of the strained vision in which I had been living for crowded hours—was this a taste that I was sure I should particularly enjoy? Marked enough it was, doubtless, that even in the stress of perceiving myself broken with I ruefully reflected on all the more, on the ever so much, I still wanted to know!

Well, something of this quantity, in any case, would come, since Mrs. Briss did want to speak to me. The suspense that remained with me, as I have indicated, was the special fresh one she had just produced. It fed, for a little, positively, on that survey of her fine retreating person to which I have confessed that my eyes attached themselves. These seconds were naturally few, and yet my memory gathers from them something that I can only compare, in its present effect, to the scent of a strange flower passed rapidly under my nose. I seem in other words to recall that I received in that brush the very liveliest impression that my whole adventure was to yield—the impression that is my reason for speaking of myself as having at the juncture in question " studied " Mrs. Brissenden's back. Study of a profound sort would appear needed in truth to account for it. It was as handsome and affirmative that she at once met and evaded my view, but was not the affirmation (as distinguished from the handsomeness, which was a matter of stature and mass,) fairly downright and defiant? Didn't what I saw strike me as saying straight *at* me, as far as possible, " I *am* young—I am and I *will* be; see, *see* if I'm not; there, there, there!"—with " there's " as insistent and rhythmical as the undulations of her fleeing presence, as the bejewelled nod of her averted brow? If her face had not been hidden, should I not precisely have found myself right in believing that it looked, exactly, for those instants, dreadfully older than it had ever yet had to? The answer ideally cynical would have been: " Oh, any woman of your resources can look young with her back turned! But you've had to turn it to make that proclamation." She passed out of the room proclaiming, and I did stand there a little defeated, even though with her word for another chance at her. Was this word one that she would keep? I had got off—yes, to a certainty. But so too had not she?

Naturally, at any rate, I didn't stay planted; and though it seemed long it was probably for no great time after this that I roamed in my impatience. I was divided between the discourtesy of wishing the ladies would go to bed and the apprehension that if they did too soon go I might yet lose everything. Was Mrs. Briss waiting for more privacy, or was she only waiting for a complete escape? Of course, even while I asked myself that, I had to remember how much I was taking for granted on her part in the way of conscious motive. Still, if she had not a motive for escaping, why had she not had one, five minutes before, for coming to the point with me? This inquiry kept me hovering where she might at any instant find me, but that was not inconsistent with my presently passing, like herself, into another room. The first one I entered—there were great chains of them at Newmarch—showed me once more, at the end opposite the door, the object that all day had been, present or absent, most in my eyes, and that there now could be no fallacy in my recognising. Mrs. Server's unquenchable little smile had never yet been so far from quenched as when it recognised, on its own side, that I had just had time to note how Ford Obert was, for a change, taking it in. These two friends of mine appeared to have moved together, after the music, to the corner in which I should not have felt it as misrepresenting the matter to say that I surprised them. They owed nothing of the harmony that held them—unlike my other couple—to the constraint of a common seat; a small glazed table, a receptacle for minute objects of price, extended itself between them as if it had offered itself as an occasion for their drawing toward it a pair of low chairs; but their union had nevertheless such an air of accepted duration as led it slightly to puzzle me. This would have been a reason the more for not interrupting it even had I not peculiarly wished to respect it. It was grist to my mill somehow that something or other had happened as a consequence of which Obert had lost the impulse to repeat to me his odd invitation to intervene. He gave me no notice as I passed; the notice was all from his companion. It constituted, I felt, on her part, precisely as much and precisely as little of an invitation as it had constituted at the moment—so promptly following our arrival—of my first seeing them linked; which is but another way of saying that nothing in Mrs. Server appeared to acknowledge a lapse. It was nearly midnight, but she was again under arms; everything conceivable—or perhaps rather inconceivable—had passed between us before dinner, but her face was exquisite again in its repudiation of any reference.

Any reference, I saw, would have been difficult to *me*, had I unluckily been forced to approach her. What would have made the rare delicacy of the problem was that blankness itself was the most direct reference of all. I had, however, as I passed her by, a comprehension as inward as that with which I had watched Mrs. Briss's retreat. "*What* shall I see when I next see you?" was what I had mutely asked of Mrs. Briss; but "God grant I don't see *you* again at all!" was the prayer sharply determined in my heart as I left Mrs. Server behind me. I left her behind me for ever, but the prayer has not been answered. I did see her again; I see her now; I shall see her always; I shall continue to feel at moments in my own facial muscles the deadly little ache of her heroic grin. With this, however, I was not then to reckon, and my simple philosophy of the moment could be but to get out of the room. The result of that movement was that, two minutes later, at another doorway, but opening this time into a great corridor, I found myself arrested by a combination that should really have counted for me as the least of my precious anomalies, but that—as accident happened to protect me—I watched, so long as I might, with intensity. I should in this connection describe my eyes as yet again engaging the less scrutable side of the human figure, were it not that poor Briss's back, now presented to me beside his wife's—for these were the elements of the combination—had hitherto seemed to me the most eloquent of his aspects. It was when he presented his face that he looked, each time, older; but it was when he showed you, from behind, the singular stoop of his shoulders, that he looked oldest.

They had just passed the door when I emerged, and they receded, at a slow pace and with a kind of confidential nearness, down the long avenue of the lobby. Her head was always high and her husband's always low, so that I couldn't be sure—it might have been only my fancy—that the contrast of this habit was more marked in them than usual. If I had known nothing about them I should have just unimaginatively said that talk was all on one side and attention all on the other. I, of course, for that matter, *did* know nothing about them; yet I recall how it came to me, as my extemporised shrewdness hung in their rear, that I mustn't think anything too grossly simple of what might be taking place between them. My position was, in spite of myself, that of my having mastered enough possibilities to choose from. If one of these might be—for her face, in spite of the backward cock of her head, was turned to him—that she was looking her time of life straight *at* him and yet making love to him with it as hard as ever she could, so another was that he had been already so thoroughly got back into hand that she had no need of asking favours, that she was more splendid than ever, and that, the same poor Briss as before his brief adventure, he was only feeling afresh in his soul, as a response to her, the gush of the sacred fount. Presumptous choice as to these alternatives failed, on my part, in time, let me say, to flower; it rose before me in time that, whatever might be, for the exposed instant, the deep note of their encounter, only one thing concerned me in it: its being wholly their own business. So for that I liberally let it go, passing into the corridor, but proceeding in the opposite sense and aiming at an issue which I judged I should reach before they would turn in their walk. I had not, however, reached it before I caught the closing of the door furthest from me; at the sound of which I looked about to find the Brissendens gone. They had not remained for another turn, but had taken their course, evidently, back to the principal drawing-room, where, no less presumably, the procession of the ladies bedward was even then forming. Mrs. Briss would fall straight into it, and I *had* accordingly lost her. I hated to appear to pursue her, late in the day as it may appear to affirm that I put my dignity before my curiosity.

Free again, at all events, to wait or to wander, I lingered a minute where I had stopped—close to a wide window, as it happened, that, at this end of the passage, stood open to the warm darkness and overhung, from no great height, one of the terraces. The night was mild and rich, and though the lights within were, in deference to the temperature, not too numerous, I found the breath of the outer air a sudden corrective to the grossness of our lustre and the thickness of our medium, our general heavy humanity. I felt its taste sweet, and while I leaned for refreshment on the sill I thought of many things. One of those that passed before me was the way that Newmarch and its hospitalities were sacrificed, after all, and much more than smaller circles, to material frustrations. We were all so fine and formal, and the ladies in particular at once so little and so much clothed, so beflounced yet so denuded, that the summer stars called to us in vain. We had ignored them in our crystal cage, among our tinkling lamps; no more free really to alight than if we had been dashing in a locked railway-train across a lovely land. I remember asking myself if I mightn't still take a turn under them, and I remember that on appealing to my watch for its sanction I found midnight to have struck. That then was the end, and my only real alternatives were bed or the smoking-room. The difficulty with bed was that I was in no condition to sleep, and the difficulty about rejoining the men was that—definitely, yes—there was one of them I desired not again to see. I felt it with sharpness as I leaned on the sill; I felt it with sadness as I looked at the stars; I felt once more what I had felt on turning a final back five minutes before, so designedly, on Mrs. Server. I saw poor Briss as he had just moved away from me, and I knew, as I had known in the other case, that my troubled sense would fain feel I had practically done with him. It would be well, for aught I could do *for* him, that I should have seen the last of him.

What remained with me from that vision of his pacing there with his wife was the conviction that his fate, whatever it was, held him fast. It wouldn't let him go, and all I could ask of it now was that it should let *me*. I *would* go—I was going; if I had not had to accept the interval of the night I should indeed already have gone. The admonitions of that moment—only confirmed, I hasten to add, by what was still to come—were that I should catch in the morning, with energy, an earlier train to town than anyone else was likely to take, and get off alone by it, bidding farewell for a long day to Newmarch. I should be in small haste to come back, for I should leave behind me my tangled theory, no loose thread of which need I ever again pick up, in no stray mesh of which need my foot again trip. It was on my way to the place, in fine, that my obsession had met me, and it was by retracing those steps that I should be able to get rid of it. Only I must break off sharp, must escape all reminders by forswearing all returns.

That was very well, but it would perhaps have been better still if I had gone straight to bed. In that case I *should* have broken off sharp—too sharp to become aware of something that kept me a minute longer at the window and that had the instant effect of making me wonder if, in the interest of observation, I mightn't snap down the electric light that, playing just behind me, must show where I stood. I resisted this impulse and, with the thought that my position was in no way compromising, chanced being myself observed. I presently saw moreover that I was really not in evidence: I could take in freely what I had at first not been sure of, the identity of the figure stationed just within my range, but just out of that of the light projected from my window. One of the men of our company had come out by himself for a stroll, and the man was Gilbert Long. He had paused, I made out, in his walk; his back was to the house, and, resting on the balustrade of the terrace with a cigarette in his lips, he had given way to a sense of the fragrant gloom. He moved so little that I was sure—making no turn that would have made me draw back; he only smoked slowly in his place and seemed as lost in thought as I was lost in my attention to him. I scarce knew what this told me; all I felt was that, however slight the incident and small the evidence, it essentially fitted in. It had for my imagination a value, for my theory a price, and it in fact constituted an impression under the influence of which this theory, just impatiently shaken off, perched again on my shoulders. It was of the deepest interest to me to see Long in such detachment, in such apparent concentration. These things marked and presented him more than any had yet done, and placed him more than any yet in relation to other matters. They showed him, I thought, as serious, his situation as grave. I couldn't have said what they proved, but I was as affected by them as if they proved everything. The proof simply acted from the instant the vision of him alone there in the warm darkness was caught. It was just with all that was in the business that he *was*, that he had fitfully needed to be, alone. Nervous and restless after separating, under my eyes, from Mrs. Briss, he had wandered off to the smoking-room, as yet empty; *he* didn't know what to do either, and was incapable of bed and of sleep. He had observed the communication of the smoking-room with the terrace and had come out into the air; this was what suited him, and, with pauses and meditations, much, possibly, by this time to turn over, he prolonged his soft vigil. But he at last moved, and I found myself startled. I gave up watching and retraced my course. I felt, none the less, fairly humiliated. It had taken but another turn of an eye to re-establish all my connections.

I had not, however, gone twenty steps before I met Ford Obert, who had entered the corridor from the other end and was, as he immediately let me know, on his way to the smoking-room.

"Is everyone then dispersing?"

"Some of the men, I think," he said, "are following me; others, I believe—wonderful creatures!—have gone to array themselves. Others still, doubtless, have gone to bed."

"And the ladies?"

"Oh, they've floated away—soared aloft; to high jinks—isn't that the idea?—in their own quarters. Don't they too, at these hours, practise sociabilities of sorts? They make, at any rate, here, an extraordinary picture on that great staircase."

I thought a moment. "I wish I had seen it. But I do see it. Yes—splendid. Is the place wholly cleared of them?"

"Save, it struck me, so far as they may have left some 'black plume as a token'——"

"Not, I trust," I returned, "of any 'lie' their 'soul hath spoken!' But not one of them lingers?"

He seemed to wonder. "'Lingers?' For what?"

"Oh, I don't know—in this house!"

He looked at our long vista, still lighted—appeared to feel with me our liberal ease, which implied that unseen powers waited on our good pleasure and sat up for us. There is nothing like it in fact, the liberal ease at Newmarch. Yet Obert reminded me—if I needed the reminder—that I mustn't after all presume on it. "Was one of them to linger for *you?*"

"Well, since you ask me, it was what I hoped. But since you answer for it that my hope has not been met, I bow to a superior propriety."

"You mean you'll come and smoke with me? Do then come."

"What, if I do," I asked with an idea, "will you give me?"

"I'm afraid I can promise you nothing more that *I* deal in than a bad cigarette."

"And what then," I went on, "will you take from me?"

He had met my eyes, and now looked at me a little with a smile that I thought just conscious. "Well, I'm afraid I *can't* take any more——"

"Of the sort of stuff," I laughed, "you've already had? Sorry stuff, perhaps—a poor thing but mine own! Such as it is, I only ask to keep it for myself, and that isn't what I meant. I meant what flower will you gather, what havoc will you play——?"

"Well?" he said as I hesitated.

"Among superstitions that I, after all, cherish. *Mon siège est fait*—a great glittering crystal palace. How many panes will you reward me for amiably sitting up with you by smashing?"

It might have been my mere fancy—but it *was* my fancy—that he looked at me a trifle harder. "How on earth can I tell what you're talking about?"

I waited a moment, then went on: "Did you happen to count them?"

"Count whom?"

"Why, the ladies as they filed up. Was the number there?"

He gave a jerk of impatience. "Go and see for yourself!"

Once more I just waited. "But suppose I should find Mrs. Server——?"

"Prowling there on the chance of you? Well—I thought she was what you wanted."

"Then," I returned, "you *could* tell what I was talking about!" For a moment after this we faced each other without more speech, but I presently continued: "You didn't really notice if any lady stayed behind?"

"I think you ask too much of me," he at last brought out. "Take care of your ladies, my dear man, yourself! Go," he repeated, "and see."

"Certainly—it's better; but I'll rejoin you in three minutes." And while he went his way to the smoking-room I proceeded without more delay to assure myself, performing in the opposite sense the journey I had made ten minutes before. It was extraordinary what the sight of Long alone in the outer darkness had done for me: my expression of it would have been that it had put me "on" again at the moment of my decidedly feeling myself off. I believed that if I hadn't seen him I could now have gone to bed without seeing Mrs. Briss; but my renewed impression had suddenly made the difference. If that was the way he struck me, how might not, if I could get at her, she? And she might, after all, in the privacy at last offered us by empty rooms, be waiting for me. I went through them all, however, only to find them empty indeed. In conformity with the large allowances of every sort that were the law of Newmarch, they were still open and lighted, so that if I had believed in Mrs. Briss's reappearance I might conveniently, on the spot, have given her five minutes more. I am not sure, for that matter, that I didn't. I remember at least wondering if I mightn't ring somewhere for a servant and cause a question to be sent up to her. I didn't ring, but I must have lingered a little on the chance of the arrival of servants to extinguish lights and see the house safe. They had not arrived, however, by the time I again felt that I must give up.

## XI

I GAVE up by going, decidedly, to the smoking-room, where several men had gathered and where Obert, a little apart from them, was in charmed communion with the bookshelves. They are wonderful, everywhere, at Newmarch, the book-shelves, but he put a volume back as he saw me come in, and a moment later, when we were seated, I said to him again, as a recall of our previous passage, "Then you *could* tell what I was talking about!" And I added, to complete my reference, "Since you thought Mrs. Server was the person whom, when I stopped you, I was sorry to learn from you I had missed."

His momentary silence appeared to admit the connection I established. "Then you find you *have* missed her? She wasn't there for you?"

"There's no one 'there for me'; so that I fear that if you weren't, as it happens, here for me, my amusement would be quite at an end. I had, in fact," I continued, "already given it up as lost when I came upon you, a while since, in conversation with the lady we've named. At that, I confess, my prospects gave something of a flare. I said to myself that since *your* interest hadn't then wholly dropped, why, even at the worst, should mine? Yours *was* mine, wasn't it? for a little, this morning. Or was it mine that was yours? We exchanged, at any rate, some lively impressions. Only, before we had done, your effort dropped or your discretion intervened: you gave up, as none of your business, the question that had suddenly tempted us."

"And you gave it up too," said my friend.

"Yes, and it was on the idea that it was mine as little as yours that we separated."

"Well then?" He kept his eyes, with his head thrown back, on the warm bindings, admirable for old gilt and old colour, that covered the opposite wall.

"Well then, if I've correctly gathered that you're, in spite of our common renunciation, still interested, I confess to you that I am. I took my detachment too soon for granted. I haven't been detached. I'm not, hang me! detached now. And it's all because you were originally so suggestive."

"Originally?"

"Why, from the moment we met here yesterday—the moment of my first seeing you with Mrs. Server. The look you gave me then was really the beginning of everything. Everything"—and I spoke now with real conviction—"was traceably to spring from it."

"What do you mean," he asked, "by everything?"

"Well, this failure of detachment. What you said to me as we were going up yesterday afternoon to dress—what you said to me then is responsible for it. And since it comes to that," I pursued, "I make out for myself now that you're not detached either—unless, that is, simply detached from *me*. I had indeed a suspicion of that as I passed through the room there."

He smoked through another pause. "You've extraordinary notions of responsibility."

I watched him a moment, but he only stared at the books without looking round. Something in his voice had made me more certain, and my certainty made me laugh. "I see you *are* serious!"

But he went on quietly enough. "You've extraordinary notions of responsibility. I deny altogether mine."

"You *are* serious—you *are!*" I repeated with a gaiety that I meant as inoffensive and that I believe remained so. "But no matter. You're no worse than I."

"I'm clearly, by your own story, not half so bad. But, as you say, no matter. I don't care."

I ventured to keep it up. "Oh, don't you?"

His good nature was proof. "I don't care."

"Then why didn't you so much as look at me a while ago?"

"Didn't I look at you?"

"You know perfectly you didn't. Mrs. Server did—with her unutterable intensity; making me feel afresh, by the way, that I've never seen a woman compromise herself so little by proceedings so compromising. But though you saw her intensity, it never diverted you for an instant from your own."

He lighted before he answered this a fresh cigarette. "A man engaged in talk with a charming woman scarcely selects that occasion for winking at somebody else."

"You mean he contents himself with winking at *her?* My dear fellow, that wasn't enough for you yesterday, and it wouldn't have been enough for you this morning, among the impressions that led to our last talk. It was just the fact that you did wink, that you *had* winked, at me that wound me up."

"And what about the fact that you had winked at *me?* *Your* winks—come"—Obert laughed—"are portentous!"

"Oh, if we recriminate," I cheerfully said after a moment, "we agree."

"I'm not so sure," he returned, "that we agree."

"Ah, then, if we differ it's still more interesting. Because, you know, we didn't differ either yesterday or this morning."

Without hurry or flurry, but with a decent confusion, his thoughts went back. "I thought you said just now we did—recognising, as you ought, that you were keen about a chase of which I washed my hands."

"No—I wasn't keen. You've just mentioned that you remember my giving up. I washed my hands too."

It seemed to leave him with the moral of this. "Then, if our hands are clean, what are we talking about?"

I turned, on it, a little more to him, and looked at him so long that he had at last to look at me; with which, after holding his eyes another moment, I made my point. "Our hands are not clean."

"Ah, speak for your own!"—and as he moved back I might really have thought him uneasy. There was a hint of the same note in the way he went on: "I assure you I decline all responsibility. I see the responsibility as quite beautifully yours."

"Well," I said, "I only want to be fair. You were the first to bring it out that she was changed."

"Well, she isn't changed!" said my friend with an almost startling effect, for me, of suddenness. "Or rather," he immediately and incongruously added, "she *is*. She's changed back."

"'Back'?" It made me stare.

"Back," he repeated with a certain sharpness and as if to have done at last, for himself, with the muddle of it.

But there was that in me that could let him see he had far from done; and something, above all, told me now that he absolutely mustn't have before I had. I quickly moreover saw that I must, with an art, make him want not to. "Back to what she was when you painted her?"

He had to think an instant for this. "No—not quite to that."

"To what then?"

He tried in a manner to oblige me. "To something else."

It seemed so, for my thought, the gleam of something that fitted, that I was almost afraid of quenching the gleam by pressure. I must then get everything I could from him without asking too much. "You don't quite know to *what* else?"

"No—I don't quite know." But there was a sound in it, this time, that I took as the hint of a wish to know—almost a recognition that I might help him.

I helped him accordingly as I could and, I may add, as far as the positive flutter he had stirred in me suffered. It fitted—it fitted! "If her change is to something other, I suppose then a change back is not quite the exact name for it."

"Perhaps not." I fairly thrilled at his taking the suggestion as if it were an assistance. "She isn't at any rate what I thought her yesterday."

It was amazing into what depths this dropped for

me and with what possibilities it mingled. "I remember what you said of her yesterday."

I drew him on so that I brought back for him the very words he had used. "She was so beastly unhappy." And he used them now visibly not as a remembrance of what he had said, but for the contrast of the fact with what he at present perceived; so that the value this gave for me to what he at present perceived was immense.

"And do you mean that that's gone?"

He hung fire, however, a little as to saying so much what he meant, and while he waited he again looked at me. "What do *you* mean? Don't you think so yourself?"

I laid my hand on his arm and held him a moment with a grip that betrayed, I daresay, the effort in me to keep my thoughts together and lose not a thread. It betrayed at once, doubtless, the danger of that failure and the sharp foretaste of success. I remember that with it, absolutely, I struck myself as knowing again the joy of the intellectual mastery of things unamenable, that joy of determining, almost of creating results, which I have already mentioned as an exhilaration attached to some of my plunges of insight. "It would take long to tell you what I mean."

The tone of it made him fairly watch me as I had been watching him. "Well, haven't we got the whole night?"

"Oh, it would take more than the whole night—even if we had it!"

"By which you suggest that we haven't it?"

"No—we haven't it. I want to get away."

"To go to bed? I thought you were so keen."

"I *am* keen. Keen is no word for it. I don't want to go to bed. I want to get away."

"To leave the house — in the middle of the night?"

"Yes—absurd as it may seem. You excite me too much. You don't know what you do to me."

He continued to look at me; then he gave a laugh which was not the contradiction, but quite the attestation, of the effect produced on him by my grip. If I had wanted to hold him I held him. It only came to me even that I held him too much. I felt this in fact with the next thing he said. "If you're too excited, then, to be coherent now, will you tell me to-morrow?"

I took time myself now to relight. Ridiculous as it may sound, I had my nerves to steady; which is a proof, surely, that for real excitement there are no such adventures as intellectual ones. "Oh, to-morrow I shall be off in space!"

"Certainly we shall neither of us be here. But can't we arrange, say, to meet in town, or even to go up together in such conditions as will enable us to talk?"

I patted his arm again. "Thank you for your patience. It's really good of you. Who knows if I shall be alive to-morrow? We *are* meeting. We *do* talk."

But with all I had to think of I must have fallen, on this, into the deepest of silences, for the next thing I remember is his returning: "We don't!" I repeated my gesture of reassurance, I conveyed that I should be with him again in a minute, and presently, while he gave me time, he came back to something of his own. "My wink, at all events, would have been nothing for any question between us, as I've just said, without yours. That's what I call your responsibility. It was, as we put the matter, the torch of your analogy——"

"Oh, the torch of my analogy!"

I had so groaned it—as if for very ecstasy—that it pulled him up, and I could see his curiosity as indeed reaffected. But he went on with a coherency that somewhat admonished me: "It was your making me, as I told you this morning, think over what you had said about Brissenden and his wife: it was *that*——"

"That made you think over"—I took him straight up—"what you yourself had said about our troubled lady? Yes, precisely. That *was* the torch of my analogy. What I showed you in the one case seemed to tell you what to look for in the other. You thought it over. I accuse you of nothing worse than of *having* thought it over. But you see what thinking it over does for it."

The way I said this appeared to amuse him. "I see what it does for *you!*"

"No, you don't! Not at all yet. That's just the embarrassment."

"Just whose?" If I had thanked him for his patience he showed that he deserved it. "Just yours?"

"Well, say mine. But when you do——!" And I paused as for the rich promise of it.

"When I do see where you are, you mean?"

"The only difficulty is whether you *can* see. But we must try. You've set me whirling round, but we must go step by step. Oh, but it's all in your germ!"—I kept that up. "If she isn't now beastly unhappy——"

"She's beastly happy?" he broke in, getting firmer hold, if not of the real impression he had just been gathering under my eyes, then at least of something he had begun to make out that my argument required. "Well, that *is* the way I see her difference. Her difference, I mean," he added, in his evident wish to work with me, "her difference from her other difference! There!" He laughed as if, also, he had found himself fairly fantastic. "Isn't *that* clear for you?"

"Crystalline—for *me*. But that's because I know why."

I can see again now the long look that, on this, he gave me. I made out already much of what was in it. "So then do I!"

"But how in the world——? I know, for myself, *how* I know."

"So then do I," he after a moment repeated.

"And can you tell me?"

"Certainly. But what I've already named to you—the torch of your analogy."

I turned this over. "You've made evidently an admirable use of it. But the wonderful thing is that you seem to have done so without having all the elements."

He on his side considered. "What do you call all the elements?"

"Oh, it would take me long to tell you!" I couldn't help laughing at the comparative simplicity with which he asked it. "That's the sort of thing we just now spoke of taking a day for. At any rate, such as they are, these elements," I went on, "I believe myself practically in possession of them. But what I don't quite see is how *you* can be."

Well, he was able to tell me. "Why in the world shouldn't your analogy have put me?" He spoke with gaiety, but with lucidity. "I'm not an idiot either."

"I see." But there was so much!

"Did you think I *was?*" he amiably asked.

"No. I see," I repeated. Yet I didn't, really, fully; which he presently perceived.

"You made me think of your view of the Brissenden pair till I could think of nothing else."

"Yes—yes," I said. "Go on."

"Well, as you had planted the theory in me, it began to bear fruit. I began to watch them. I continued to watch them. I did nothing but watch them."

The sudden lowering of his voice in this confession—as if it had represented a sort of darkening of his consciousness—again amused me. "You too? How then we've been occupied! For I, you see, have watched—or had, until I found you just now with Mrs. Server—everyone, everything *but* you."

"Oh, I've watched *you*," said Ford Obert as if he had then perhaps after all the advantage of me. "I admit that I made you out for myself to be back on the scent; for I thought I made you out baffled."

To learn whether I really had been was, I saw, what he would most have liked; but I also saw that he had, as to this, a scruple about asking me. What I most saw, however, was that to tell him I should have to understand. "What scent do you allude to?"

He smiled as if I might have fancied I could fence. "Why, the pursuit of the identification that's none of our business—the identification of her lover."

"Ah, it's as to that," I instantly replied, "you've

judged me baffled? I'm afraid," I almost as quickly added, "that I must admit I *have* been. Luckily, at all events, it *is* none of our business."

"Yes," said my friend, amused on his side, "nothing's our business that we can't find out. I saw you hadn't found him. And what," Obert continued, "does he matter now?"

It took but a moment to place me for seeing that my companion's conviction on this point was a conviction decidedly to respect; and even that amount of hesitation was but the result of my wondering how he had reached it. "What, indeed?" I promptly replied. "But how did you see I had failed?"

"By seeing that I myself had. For I've been looking too. He isn't here," said Ford Obert.

Delighted as I was that he should believe it, I was yet struck by the complacency of his confidence, which connected itself again with my observation of their so recent colloquy. "Oh, for you to be so sure, has Mrs. Server squared you?"

"*Is* he here?" he for all answer to this insistently asked.

I faltered but an instant. "No; he isn't here. It's no thanks to one's scruples, but perhaps it's lucky for one's manners. I speak at least for mine. If you've watched," I pursued, "you've doubtless sufficiently seen what has already become of mine. He isn't here, at all events," I repeated, "and we must do without his identity. What, in fact, are we showing each other," I asked, "but that we *have* done without it?"

"*I* have!" my friend declared with supreme frankness and with something of the note, as I was obliged to recognise, of my own constructive joy. "I've done perfectly without it."

I saw in fact that he had, and it struck me really as wonderful. But I controlled the expression of my wonder. "So that if you spoke therefore just now of watching them——"

"I meant of course"—he took it straight up—"watching the Brissendens. And naturally, above all," he as quickly subjoined, "the wife."

I was now full of concurrence. "Ah, naturally, above all, the wife."

So far as was required it encouraged him. "A woman's lover doesn't matter—doesn't matter at least to anyone but himself, doesn't matter to you or to me or to her—when once she has given him up."

It made me, this testimony of his observation, show, in spite of my having by this time so counted on it, something of the vivacity of my emotion. "She *has* given him up?"

But the surprise with which he looked round put me back on my guard. "Of what else then are we talking?"

"Of nothing else, of course," I stammered.

"But the way you see——!" I found my refuge in the gasp of my admiration.

"I do see. But"—he *would* come back to that —"only through your having seen first. You gave me the pieces. I've but put them together. You gave me the Brissendens—bound hand and foot; and I've but made them, in that sorry state, pull me through. I've blown on my torch, in other words, till, flaring and smoking, it has guided me, through a magnificent chiaroscuro of colour and shadow, out into the light of day."

I was really dazzled by his image, for it represented his personal work. "You've done more than I, it strikes me—and with less to do it with. If I gave you the Brissendens I gave you all I had."

"But all you had was immense, my dear man. The Brissendens are immense."

"Of course the Brissendens are immense! If they hadn't been immense they wouldn't have been —*nothing* would have been — anything." Then after a pause, "Your image is splendid," I went on—"your being out of the cave. But what is it exactly," I insidiously threw out, "that you *call* the 'light of day'?"

I remained a moment, however, not sure whether I had been too subtle or too simple. He had another of his cautions. "What do *you*——?"

But I was determined to make him give it me

all himself, for it was from my not prompting him that its value would come. "You tell me," I accordingly rather crudely pleaded, "first."

It gave us a moment during which he so looked as if I asked too much, that I had a fear of losing all. He even spoke with some impatience. "If you really haven't found it for yourself, you know. I scarce see what you *can* have found."

Then I had my inspiration. I risked an approach to roughness, and all the more easily that my words were strict truth. "Oh, don't be afraid—greater things than yours!"

It succeeded, for it played upon his curiosity, and he visibly imagined that, with impatience controlled, he should learn what these things were. He relaxed, he responded, and the next moment I was in all but full enjoyment of the piece wanted to make all my other pieces right—right because of that special beauty in my scheme through which the whole depended so on each part and each part so guaranteed the whole. "What I call the light of day is the sense I've arrived at of her vision."

"Her vision?"—I just balanced in the air.

"Of what they have in common. *His*—poor chap's—extraordinary situation too."

"Bravo! And you see in that——?"

"What, all these hours, has touched, fascinated, drawn her. It has been an instinct with her."

"Bravissimo!"

It saw him, my approval, safely into port. "The instinct of sympathy, pity—the response to fellowship in misery; the sight of another fate as strange, as monstrous as her own."

I couldn't help jumping straight up—I stood before him. "So that whoever may have *been* the man, the man *now*, the actual man——"

"Oh," said Obert, looking, luminous and straight, up at me from his seat, "the man now, the actual man——!" But he stopped short, with his eyes suddenly quitting me and his words becoming a formless ejaculation. The door of the room, to which my back was turned, had opened, and I quickly looked round. It was Brissenden himself who, to my supreme surprise, stood there, with rapid inquiry in his attitude and face. I saw, as soon as he caught mine, that I was what he wanted, and, immediately excusing myself for an instant to Obert, I anticipated, by moving across the room, the need, on poor Briss's part, of my further demonstration. My whole sense of the situation blazed up at the touch of his presence, and even before I reached him it had rolled over me in a prodigious wave that I had lost nothing whatever. I can't begin to say how the fact of his appearance crowned the communication my interlocutor had just made me, nor in what a bright confusion of many things I found myself facing poor Briss. One of these things was precisely that he had never been so much poor Briss as at this moment. That ministered to the confusion as well as to the brightness, for if his being there at all renewed my sources and replenished my current—spoke all, in short, for my gain—so, on the other hand, in the light of what I had just had from Obert, his particular aspect was something of a shock. I can't present this especial impression better than by the mention of my instant certitude that what he had come for was to bring me a message and that somehow—yes, indubitably—this circumstance seemed to have placed him again at the very bottom of his hole. It was down in that depth that he let me see him—it was out of it that he delivered himself. Poor Briss! poor Briss!—I had asked myself before he spoke with what kindness enough I could meet him. Poor Briss! poor Briss!—I am not even now sure that I didn't first meet him by *that* irrepressible murmur. It was in it all for me that, thus, at midnight, he had traversed on his errand the length of the great dark house. I trod with him, over the velvet and the marble, through the twists and turns, among the glooms and glimmers and echoes, every inch of the way, and I don't know what humiliation, for him, was constituted there, between us, by his long pilgrimage. It was the final expression of his sacrifice.

"My wife has something to say to you."

"Mrs. Briss? Good!"—and I could only hope

the candour of my surprise was all I tried to make it. "Is she with you there?"

"No, but she has asked me to say to you that if you'll presently be in the drawing-room she'll come."

Who could doubt, as I laid my hand on his shoulder, fairly patting it, in spite of myself, for applause—who could doubt where I would presently be? "It's most uncommonly good of both of you."

There was something in his inscrutable service that, making him almost august, gave my dissimulated eagerness the sound of a heartless compliment. *I* stood for the hollow chatter of the vulgar world, and he—oh, he was as serious as he was conscious; which was enough. "She says you'll know what she wishes—and she was sure I'd find you here. So I may tell her you'll come?"

His courtesy half broke my heart. "Why, my dear man, with all the pleasure——! So many thousand thanks. I'll be with her."

"Thanks to *you*. She'll be down. Good-night." He looked round the room—at the two or three clusters of men, smoking, engaged, contented, on their easy seats and among their popped corks; he looked over an instant at Ford Obert, whose eyes, I thought, he momentarily held. It was absolutely as if, for me, he were seeking such things—out of what was closing over him—for the last time. Then he turned again to the door, which, just not to fail humanly to accompany him a step, I had opened. On the other side of it I took leave of him. The passage, though there was a light in the distance, was darker than the smoking-room, and I had drawn the door to.

"Good-night, Brissenden. I shall be gone to-morrow before you show."

I shall never forget the way that, struck by my word, he let his white face fix me in the dusk. "'Show'? *What* do I show?"

I had taken his hand for farewell, and, inevitably laughing, but as the falsest of notes, I gave it a shake. "You show nothing! You're magnificent."

He let me keep his hand while things unspoken and untouched, unspeakable and untouchable, everything that had been between us in the wood a few hours before, were between us again. But so we could only leave them, and, with a short, sharp "Good-bye!" he completely released himself. With my hand on the latch of the closed door I watched a minute his retreat along the passage, and I remember the reflection that, before rejoining Obert, I made on it. I seemed perpetually, at Newmarch, to be taking his measure from behind.

Ford Obert has since told me that when I came back to him there were tears in my eyes, and I didn't know at the moment how much the words with which he met me took for granted my consciousness of them. "He looks a hundred years old!"

"Oh, but you should see his shoulders, always, as he goes off! *Two* centuries—ten! Isn't it amazing?"

It was so amazing that, for a little, it made us reciprocally stare. "I should have thought," he said, "that he would have been on the contrary——"

"Visibly rejuvenated? So should I. I must make it out," I added. "I *shall.*"

But Obert, with less to go upon, couldn't wait. It was wonderful, for that matter—and for all I had to go upon—how I myself could. I did so, at this moment, in my refreshed intensity, by the help of confusedly lighting another cigarette, which I should have no time to smoke. "I should have thought," my friend continued, "that he too might have changed back."

I took in, for myself, so much more of it than I could say! "Certainly. You wouldn't have thought he would have changed forward." Then with an impulse that bridged over an abyss of connections I jumped to another place. "Was what you most saw while you were there with *her*—was this that her misery, the misery you first phrased to me, has dropped?"

"Dropped, yes." He was clear about it. "I called her beastly unhappy to you though I even then knew that beastly unhappiness wasn't quite all of it. It was part of it, it was enough of it; for she was—well, no doubt you could tell *me*. Just now, at all events"—and recalling, reflecting, deciding, he used, with the strongest effect, as he so often did in painting, the simplest term—"just now she's all right."

"All right?"

He couldn't know how much more than was possible my question gave him to answer. But he answered it on what he had; he repeated: "All right."

I wondered, in spite of the comfort I took, as I had more than once in life had occasion to take it before, at the sight of the painter-sense deeply applied. My wonder came from the fact that Lady John had also found Mrs. Server all right, and Lady John had a vision as closed as Obert's was open. It didn't suit my book for both these observers to have been affected in the same way. "You mean you saw nothing whatever in her that was the least bit strange?"

"Oh, I won't say as much as that. But nothing that was more strange than that she *should* be—well, after all, all right."

"All there, eh?" I after an instant risked.

I couldn't put it to him more definitely than that, though there was a temptation to try to do so. For Obert to have found her all there an hour or two after I had found her all absent, made me again, in my nervousness, feel even now a trifle menaced. Things *had*, from step to step, to hang together, and just here they seemed—with all allowances—to hang a little apart. My whole superstructure, I could only remember, reared itself on my view of Mrs. Server's condition; but it was part of my predicament—really equal in its way to her own—that I couldn't without dishonouring myself give my interlocutor a practical lead. The question of her happiness was essentially subordinate; what I stood or fell by was that of her faculty. But I couldn't, on the other hand—and remain " straight "—insist to my friend on the whereabouts of this stolen property. If he hadn't missed it in her for himself I mightn't put him on the track of it; since, with the demonstration he had before my eyes received of the rate at which Long was, as one had to call it, intellectually living, nothing would be more natural than that he should make the cases fit. Now my personal problem, unaltered in the least particular by anything, was for me to have worked to the end without breathing in another ear that Long had been her lover. That was the only thing in the whole business that was simple. It made me cling an instant the more, both for bliss and bale, to the bearing of this fact of Obert's insistence. Even as a sequel to his vision of her change, almost everything was wrong for her being all right except the one fact of my recent view, from the window, of the man unnamed. I saw him again sharply in these seconds, and to notice how he still kept clear of our company was almost to add certitude to the presumption of his rare reasons. Mrs. Server's being now, by a wonderful turn, all right would at least decidedly offer to these reasons a basis. It would be something Long's absence would fit. It would supply ground, in short, for the possibility that, by a process not less wonderful, he himself was all wrong. If he *was* all wrong my last impression of him would be amply accounted for. If he was all wrong—if he, in any case, felt himself going so—what more consequent than that he should have wished to hide it, and that the most immediate way for this should have seemed to him, markedly gregarious as he usually was, to keep away from the smokers? It came to me unspeakably that he *was* still hiding it and *was* keeping away. How, accordingly, must he not—and must not Mrs. Briss—have been in the spirit of this from the moment that, while I talked with Lady John, the sight of these two seated together had given me its message! But Obert's answer to my guarded challenge had meanwhile come. "Oh, when a woman's so clever——!"

That was all, with its touch of experience and its hint of philosophy; but it was stupefying. She was already then positively again "so clever?" This was really more than I could as yet provide an explanation for, but I was pressed; Brissenden would have reached his wife's room again, and I temporised. "It was her cleverness that held you so that when I passed you couldn't look at me?"

He looked at me at present well enough. "I knew you were passing, but I wanted precisely to mark for you the difference. If you really want to know," the poor man confessed, "I was a little ashamed of myself. I had given her away to you, you know, rather, before."

"And you were bound you wouldn't do it again?"

He smiled in his now complete candour. "Ah, there was no reason." Then he used, happily, to right himself, my own expression. "She was all there."

"I see—I see." Yet I really didn't see enough not to have for an instant to turn away.

"Where are you going?" he asked.

"To do what Brissenden came to me for."

"But I don't *know*, you see, what Brissenden came to you for."

"Well, with a message. She was to have seen me this evening, but, as she gave me no chance, I was afraid I had lost it and that, so rather awkwardly late, she didn't venture. But what he arrived for just now, at her request, was to say she does venture."

My companion stared. "At this extraordinary hour?"

"Ah, the hour," I laughed, "is no more extraordinary than any other part of the business: no more so, for instance, than this present talk of yours and mine. What part of the business isn't extraordinary? If it *is*, at all events, remarkably late, that's *her* fault."

Yet he not unnaturally, in spite of my explanation, continued to wonder. "And—a—where is it then you meet?"

"Oh, in the drawing-room or the hall. So good-night."

He got up to it, moving with me to the door; but his mystification, little as I could, on the whole, soothe it, still kept me. "The household sits up for you?"

I wondered myself, but found an assurance. "She must have squared the household! And it won't probably take us very long."

His mystification frankly confessed itself, at this, plain curiosity. The ground of such a conference, for all the point I had given his ingenuity, simply baffled him. "Do you mean you propose to discuss with her——?"

"My dear fellow," I smiled with my hand on the door, "it's *she*—don't you see?—who proposes."

"But what in the world——?"

"Oh, *that* I shall have to wait to tell you."

"With all the other things?" His face, while he sounded mine, seemed to say that I must then take his expectation as serious. But it seemed to say also that he was—definitely, yes—more at a loss than consorted with being quite sure of me. "Well, it will make a lot, really——!" But he broke off. "You do," he sighed with an effort at resignation, "know more than I!"

"And haven't I admitted that?"

"I'll be hanged if you *don't* know who he is!" the poor fellow, for all answer, now produced.

He said it as if I had, after all, not been playing fair, and it made me for an instant hesitate. "No, I really don't know. But it's exactly what I shall perhaps now learn."

"You mean that what she has proposed is to *tell* you?"

His darkness had so deepened that I saw only now what I should have seen sooner—the misconception that, in my excessive estimate of the distance he had come with me, I had not at first caught. But it was a misconception that only enriched his testimony; it involved such a conviction of the new link between our two sacrificed friends that it immediately constituted for me the strongest light he would, in our whole talk, have thrown. Yes, he had not yet thrown so much as in this erroneous supposition of the source of my summons. It took me of course, at the same time, but a few seconds to remind myself again of the innumerable steps he had necessarily missed. His question meanwhile, rightly applied by my own thought, brought back to that thought, by way of answer, an immense suggestion, which moreover, for him too, was temporarily answer enough. "She'll tell me who he *won't* have been!"

He looked vague. "Ah, but *that*——"

"That," I declared, "will be luminous."

He made it out. "As a sign, you think, that he must be the very one she denies?"

"The very one!" I laughed; and I left him under this simple and secure impression that my appointment was with Mrs. Server.

## XII

I WENT from one room to the other, but to find only, at first, as on my previous circuit, a desert on which the sun had still not set. Mrs. Brissenden was nowhere, but the whole place waited as we had left it, with seats displaced and flowers dispetalled, a fan forgotten on a table, a book laid down upon a chair. It came over me as I looked about that if she *had* "squared" the household, so large an order, as they said, was a sign sufficient of what I was to have from her. I had quite rather it were her doing—not mine; but it showed with eloquence that she had after all judged some effort or other to be worth her while. Her renewed delay moreover added to my impatience of mind in respect to the nature of this effort by striking me as already part of it. What, I asked myself, could be so much worth her while as to have to be paid for by so much apparent reluctance? But at last I saw her through a vista of open doors, and as I forthwith went to her—she took no step to meet me—I was doubtless impressed afresh with the "pull" that in social intercourse a woman always has. She was able to assume on the spot by mere attitude and air the appearance of having been ready and therefore inconvenienced. Oh, I saw soon enough that she was ready and that one of the forms of her readiness would be precisely to offer herself as having acted entirely to oblige me—to give me, as a sequel to what had already passed between us, the opportunity for which she had assured me I should thank her before I had done with her. Yet, as I felt sure, at the same time, that she had taken a line, I was curious as to how, in her interest, our situation could be worked. What it had originally left us with was her knowing I was wrong. I had promised her, on my honour, to be candid, but even if I were disposed to cease to contest her identification of Mrs. Server I was scarce to be looked to for such an exhibition of gratitude as might be held to repay her for staying so long out of bed. There were in short elements in the business that I couldn't quite clearly see handled as favours to me. Her dress gave, with felicity, no sign whatever of preparation for the night, and if, since our last words, she had stood with any anxiety whatever before her glass, it had not been to remove a jewel or to alter the place of a flower. She was as much under arms as she had been on descending to dinner—as fresh in her array as if that banquet were still to come. She met me in fact as admirably—that was the truth that covered every other—as if she had been able to guess the most particular curiosity with which, from my end of the series of rooms, I advanced upon her.

A part of the mixture of my thoughts during these seconds had been the possibility—absurd, preposterous though it looks when phrased here—of some change in her person that would correspond, for me to the other changes I had had such keen moments of flattering myself I had made out. I had just had them over in the smoking-room, some of these differences, and then had had time to ask myself if I were not now to be treated to the vision of the greatest, the most wonderful, of all. I had already, on facing her, after my last moments with Lady John, seen difference peep out at me, and I had seen the impression of it confirmed by what had afterwards happened. It had been in her way of turning from me after that brief passage; it had been in her going up to bed without seeing me again; it had been once more in her thinking, for reasons of her own, better of that; and it had been most of all in her sending her husband down to me. Well, wouldn't it finally be, still more than most of all——? But I scarce had known, at this point, what grossness or what fineness of material correspondence to forecast. I only had waited there with these general symptoms so present that almost any further development of them occurred to me as conceivable. So much as this was true, but I was after a moment to become aware of something by which I was as strongly affected as if I had been quite unprepared. Yes, literally, that final note, in the smoking-room, the note struck in Obert's ejaculation on poor Briss's hundred years, had failed to achieve for me a worthy implication. I was forced, after looking at Grace Brissenden a minute, to recognise that my imagination had not risen to its opportunity. The full impression took a minute—a minute during which she said nothing; then it left me deeply and above all, as I felt, discernibly conscious of the prodigious thing, *the* thing, I had not thought of. This it was that gave her such a beautiful chance not to speak: she was so quite sufficiently occupied with seeing what I hadn't thought of, and with seeing me, to make up for lost time, breathlessly think of it while she watched me.

All I had at first taken in was, as I say, her untouched splendour; I don't know why that should have impressed me—as if it had been probable she would have appeared in her dressing-gown; it was the only thing to have expected. And it in fact plumed and enhanced her assurance, sustained her propriety, lent our belated interview the natural and casual note. But there was another service it still more rendered her: it so covered, at the first blush, the real message of her aspect, that she enjoyed the luxury—and I felt her enjoy it—of seeing my perception in arrest. Amazing, when I think of it, the number of things that occurred in these stayed seconds of our silence; but they are perhaps best represented by the two most marked intensities of my own sensation: the first the certitude that she had at no moment since her marriage so triumphantly asserted her defeat of time, and the second the conviction that I, losing with her while, as it were, we closed, a certain advantage I should never recover, had at no moment since the day before made so poor a figure on my own ground. Ah, it may have been only for six seconds that she caught me gaping at her renewed beauty; but six seconds, it was inevitable to feel, were quite enough for every purpose with which she had come down to me. She might have been a large, fair, rich, prosperous person of twenty-five; she was at any rate near enough to it to put me for ever in my place. It was a success, on her part, that, though I couldn't as yet fully measure it, there could be no doubt of whatever, any more than of my somehow paying for it. Her being there at all, at such an hour, in such conditions, became, each moment, on the whole business, more and more a part of her advantage; the case for her was really in almost any aspect she could now make it wear to my imagination. My wealth of that faculty, never so stimulated, was thus, in a manner, her strength; by which I mean the impossibility of my indifference to the mere immense suggestiveness of our circumstances. How can I tell now to what tune the sense of all these played into my mind?—the huge oddity of the nameless idea on which we foregathered, the absence and hush of everything except that idea, so magnified in consequence and yet still, after all, altogether fantastic. There remained for her, there spoke for her too, her vividly "unconventional" step, the bravery of her rustling, on an understanding so difficult to give an account of, through places and times only made safe by the sleep of the unsuspecting. My imagination, in short, since I have spoken of it, couldn't do other than work for her from the moment she had, so simply yet so wonderfully, not failed me. Therefore it was all with me again, the vision of her reasons. They were in fact sufficiently in the sound of what she presently said. "Perhaps you don't know—but I mentioned in the proper quarter that I should sit up a little. They're of a kindness here, luckily——! So it's all right." It was all right, obviously—she made it so; but she made it so as well that, in spite of the splendour she showed me, she should be a little nervous. "We shall only take moreover," she added, "a minute."

I should perhaps have wondered more what she proposed to do in a minute had I not felt it as already more or less done. Yes, she might have been twenty-five, and it was a short time for *that* to have taken. However, what I clutched at, what

I clung to, was that it was a nervous twenty-five. I might pay for her assurance, but wasn't there something of mine for which *she* might pay? I was nervous also, but, as I took in again, with a glance through our great chain of chambers, the wonderful conditions that protected us, I did my best to feel sure that it was only because I was so amused. That—in so high a form—was what it came to in the end. "I supposed," I replied, "that you'd have arranged; for, in spite of the way things were going, I hadn't given you up. I haven't understood, I confess," I went on, "why you've preferred a conference so intensely nocturnal—of which I quite feel, however, that, if it has happened to suit you, it isn't for me to complain. But I felt sure of you—that was the great thing—from the moment, half an hour ago, you so kindly spoke to me. I gave you, you see," I laughed, "what's called 'rope.'"

"I don't suppose you mean," she exclaimed, "for me to hang myself!—for that, I assure you, is not at all what I'm prepared for." Then she seemed again to give me the magnificence of her youth. It wasn't, throughout, I was to feel, that she at all had abysses of irony, for she in fact happily needed none. Her triumph was in itself ironic enough, and all her point in her sense of her freshness. "Were you really so impatient?" But as I inevitably hung fire a little she continued before I could answer;

which somewhat helped me indeed by showing the one flaw in her confidence. More extraordinary perhaps than anything else, moreover, was just my perception of this; which gives the value of all that each of us so visibly felt the other to have put together, to have been making out and gathering in, since we parted, on the terrace, after seeing Mrs. Server and Briss come up from under their tree. We *had*, of a truth, arrived at our results—though mine were naturally the ones for me to believe in; and it was prodigious that we openely met not at all where we had last left each other, but exactly on what our subsequent suppressed processes had achieved. We hadn't named them—hadn't alluded to them, and we couldn't, no doubt, have done either; but they were none the less intensely there between us, with the whole bright, empty scene given up to them. Only she had her shrewd sense that mine, for reasons, might have been still more occult than her own. Hadn't I possibly burrowed the deeper—to come out in some uncalculated place behind her back? That was the flaw in her confidence. She had in spite of it her firm ground, and I could feel, to do her justice, how different a complacency it was from such smug ignorance as Lady John's. If I didn't fear to seem to drivel about my own knowledge I should say that she had, in addition to all the rest of her " pull," the benefit of striking me as worthy of me. She was *in* the mystic circle—not one of us more; she knew the size of it; and it was our now being in it alone together, with everyone else out and with the size greater than it had yet been at all—it was this that gave the hour, in fine, so sharp a stamp.

But she had meanwhile taken up my allusion to her having preferred so to wait. "I wanted to see you quietly; which was what I tried—not altogether successfully, it rather struck me at the moment—to make you understand when I let you know about it. You stared so that I didn't quite know what was the matter. Nothing could be quiet, I saw, till the going to bed was over, and I felt it coming off then from one minute to the other. I didn't wish publicly to be called away for it from this putting of our heads together, and, though you may think me absurd, I had a dislike to having our question of May up so long as she was hanging about. I knew of course that she would hang about till the very last moment, and that was what I perhaps a little clumsily—if it was my own fault!—made the effort to convey to you. She may be hanging about still," Mrs. Briss continued, with her larger look round—her looks round were now immense; "but at any rate I shall have done what I could. I had a feeling—perfectly preposterous, I admit!—against her seeing us together; but if she comes down again, as I've so boldly done, and finds us, she'll have no one but herself to thank. It's a funny house, for that matter," my friend rambled on, "and I'm not sure that anyone *has* gone to bed. One does what one likes; I'm an old woman, at any rate, and *I* do!" She explained now, she explained too much, she abounded, talking herself stoutly into any assurance that failed her. I had meanwhile with every word she uttered a sharper sense of the pressure, behind them all, of a new consciousness. It was full of everything she didn't say, and what she said was no representation whatever of what was most in her mind. We had indeed taken a jump since noon—we had indeed come out further on. Just this fine dishonesty of her eyes, moreover—the light of a part to play, the excitement (heaven knows what it struck me as being!) of a happy duplicity—may well have been what contributed most to her present grand air.

It was in any case what evoked for me most the contrasted image, so fresh with me, of the other, the tragic lady—the image that had so embodied the unutterable opposite of everything actually before me. What was actually before me was the positive pride of life and expansion, the amplitude of conscious action and design; not the arid channel forsaken by the stream, but the full-fed river sweeping to the sea, the volume of water, the stately current, the flooded banks into which the source had swelled. There was nothing Mrs. Server had been able to risk, but there was a rich indifference to risk in the mere carriage of Grace Brissenden's head. Her reference, for that matter, to our discussed subject had the effect of relegating to the realm of dim shades the lady representing it, and there was small soundness in her glance at the possibility on the part of this person of an anxious prowl back. There was indeed—there could be—small sincerity in any immediate demonstration from a woman so markedly gaining time and getting her advantages in hand. The connections between the two, certainly, were indirect and intricate, but it was positive to me that, for the spiritual ear, my companion's words had the sound of a hard bump, a contact from the force of which the weaker vessel might have been felt to crack. At last, merciful powers, it was in pieces! The shock of the brass had told upon the porcelain, and I fancied myself for an instant facing Mrs. Briss over the damage—a damage from which I was never, as I knew, to see the poor banished ghost recover. As strange as anything was this effect almost of surprise for me in the freedom of her mention of "May." For what had she come to me, if for anything, but to insist on her view of May, and what accordingly was more to the point than to mention her? Yet it was almost already as if to mention her had been to get rid of her. She was mentioned, however, inevitably and none the less promptly, anew—even as if simply to receive a final shake before being quite dropped. My friend kept it up. "If you were so bent on not losing what I might have to give you that you fortunately stuck to the ship, for poor Briss to pick you up, wasn't this also"—she roundly put it to me—"a good deal because you've been nursing all day the grievance with which I this morning so comfortably furnished you?"

I just waited, but fairly for admiration. "Oh, I certainly had my reasons—as I've no less certainly had my luck—for not indeed deserting our dear little battered, but still just sufficiently buoyant vessel, from which everyone else appears, I recognise, to *s'être sauvé*. She'll float a few minutes more! But (before she sinks!) do you mean by my grievance——"

"Oh, you know what I mean by your grievance!" *She* had no intention, Mrs. Briss, of sinking. "I was to give you time to make up your mind that Mrs. Server was our lady. You so resented, for some reason, my suggesting it that I scarcely believed you'd consider it at all; only I hadn't forgotten, when I spoke to you a while since, that you had nevertheless handsomely promised me that you would do your best."

"Yes, and, still more handsomely, that if I changed my mind, I would eat, in your presence, for my error, the largest possible slice of humble pie. If you didn't see this morning," I continued, "quite why I should have cared so much, so I don't quite see why, in your different way, *you* should; at the same time that I do full justice to the good faith with which you've given me my chance. Please believe that if I *could* candidly embrace that chance I should feel all the joy in the world in repaying you. It's only, alas! because I cling to my candour that I venture to disappoint you. If I cared this morning it was really simple enough. You didn't convince me, but I should have cared just as much if you had. I only didn't see what *you* saw. I needed more than you could then give me. I knew, you see, what I needed—I mean before I struck! It was the element of collateral support that we both lacked. I couldn't do without it as you could. This was what I, clumsily enough, tried to show you I felt. You, on your side," I pursued, "grasped admirably the evident truth that that element *could* be present only in such doses as practically to escape detection." I kept it up as she had done, and I remember striking myself as scarce less excitedly voluble. I was conscious of being at a point at which I should have to go straight, to go fast, to go it, as the phrase is, blind, in order to go at all. I was also conscious—and it came from the look with which she listened to me and that told me more than she wished—I felt sharply, though but instinctively, in fine, that I should still, whatever I practically had lost, make my personal experience most rich and most complete by putting it definitely to her that, sorry as I might be not to oblige her, I had, even at this hour, no submission to make. I doubted in fact whether my making one *would* have obliged her; but I felt that, for all so much had come and gone, I was not there to take, for her possible profit, any new tone with her. She would sufficiently profit, at the worst, by the old. My old motive—old with the prodigious antiquity the few hours had given it—had quite left me; I seemed to myself to know little now of my desire to " protect " Mrs. Server. She was certainly, with Mrs. Briss at least, past all protection; and the conviction had grown with me, in these few minutes, that there was now no rag of the queer truth that Mrs. Briss hadn't secretly — by which I meant morally — handled. But I none the less, on a perfectly simple reasoning, stood to my guns, and with no sense whatever, I must add, of now breaking my vow of the morning. I had made another vow since then—made it to the poor lady herself as we sat together in the wood; passed my word to *her* that there was no approximation I pretended even to myself to have made. How then was I to pretend to Mrs. Briss, and what facts *had* I collected on which I could respectably ground an acknowledgment to her that I had come round to her belief? If I had " caught " our incriminated pair together—really together—even for three minutes, I would, I sincerely considered, have come round. But I was to have performed this revolution on nothing less, as I now went on to explain to her. "Of course if you've got new evidence I shall be delighted to hear it; and of course I can't help wondering whether the possession of it and the desire to overwhelm me with it aren't, together, the one thing you've been nursing till now."

Oh, how intensely she didn't like such a tone! If she hadn't looked so handsome I would say she made a wry face over it, though I didn't even yet see where her dislike would make her come out. Before she came out, in fact, she waited as if it were a question of dashing her head at a wall. Then, at last, she charged. "It's nonsense. I've nothing to tell you. I feel there's nothing in it and I've given it up."

I almost gaped—by which I mean that I looked as if I did—for surprise. "You agree that it's not she——?" Then, as she again waited, "It's *you* who've come round?" I insisted.

"To your doubt of its being May? Yes—I've come round."

"Ah, pardon me," I returned; "what I expressed this morning was, if I remember rightly, not at all a 'doubt,' but a positive, intimate conviction that was inconsistent with *any* doubt. I was emphatic—purely and simply—that I didn't see it."

She looked, however, as if she caught me in a weakness here. "Then why did you say to me that if you should reconsider——"

"You should handsomely have it from me, and my grounds? Why, as I've just reminded you, as a form of courtesy to you—magnanimously to help you, as it were, to feel as comfortable as I conceived you naturally would desire to feel in your own conviction. Only for that. And now," I smiled, "I'm to understand from you that, in spite of that immense allowance, you *haven't*, all this while, felt comfortable?"

She gave, on this, in a wonderful, beautiful way, a slow, simplifying headshake. "Mrs. Server isn't in it!"

The only way then to take it from her was that her concession was a prelude to something still better; and when I had given her time to see this dawn upon me I had my eagerness and I jumped into the breathless. "You've made out then who *is?*"

"Oh, I don't make out, you know," she laughed, "so much as you! *She* isn't," she simply repeated.

I looked at it, on my inspiration, quite ruefully—almost as if I now wished, after all, she were. "Ah, but, do you know? it really strikes me you make out marvels. You made out this morning quite what I couldn't. I hadn't put together anything so extraordinary as that—in the total absence of everything—it *should* have been our friend."

Mrs. Briss appeared, on her side, to take in the intention of this. "What do you mean by the total absence? When I made my mistake," she declared as if in the interest of her dignity, "I didn't think everything absent."

"I see," I admitted. "I see," I thoughtfully repeated. "And do you, then, think everything now?"

"I had my honest impression of the moment," she pursued as if she had not heard me. "There were appearances that, as it at the time struck me, fitted."

"Precisely"—and I recalled for her the one she had made most of. "There was in especial the appearance that she was at a particular moment using Brissenden to show whom she was not using. You felt *then*," I ventured to observe, "the force of that."

I ventured less than, already, I should have liked to venture; yet I none the less seemed to see her try on me the effect of the intimation that I was going far. "Is it your wish," she inquired with much nobleness, "to confront me, to my confusion, with my inconsistency?" Her nobleness offered itself somehow as such a rebuke to my mere logic that, in my momentary irritation, I might have been on the point of assenting to her question. This imminence of my assent, justified by my horror of her huge egotism, but justified by nothing else and precipitating everything, seemed as marked for these few seconds as if we each had our eyes on it. But I sat so tight that the danger passed, leaving my silence to do what it could for my manners. She proceeded meanwhile to add a very handsome account of her own. "You should do me the justice to recognise how little I need have spoken another word to you, and how little, also, this amiable explanation to you is in the interest of one's natural pride. It seems to me I've come to you here altogether in the interest of *yours*. You talk about humble pie, but I think that, upon my word—with all I've said to you—it's I who have had to eat it. The magnanimity you speak of," she continued with all her grandeur—"I really don't see, either, whose it is but mine. I don't see what account of anything I'm in any way obliged to give."

I granted it quickly and without reserve. "You're not obliged to give any—you're quite right: you do it only because you're such a large, splendid creature. I quite feel that, beside you"—I did, at least, treat myself to the amusement of saying—"I move in a tiny circle. Still, I won't have it"—I could also, again, keep it up—"that our occasion has nothing for you but the taste of abasement. You gulp your mouthful down, but hasn't it been served on gold plate? You've had a magnificent day—a brimming cup of triumph, and you're more beautiful and fresh, after it all, and at an hour when fatigue would be almost positively graceful, than you were even this morning, when you met me as a daughter of the dawn. That's the sort of sense," I laughed, "that must sustain a woman!" And I wound up on a complete recovery of my good-humour. "No, no. I thank you—thank you immensely. But I don't pity you. You can afford to lose." I wanted her perplexity—the proper sharp dose of it—to result both from her knowing and her not knowing sufficiently what I meant; and when I in fact saw how perplexed she could be and how little, again, she could enjoy it, I felt anew my private wonder at her having cared and dared to meet me. Where *was* enjoyment, for her, where the insolence of success, if the breath of irony could chill them? Why, since she was bold, should she be susceptible, and how, since she was susceptible, could she be bold? I scarce know what, at this moment, determined the divination; but everything, the distinct and the dim alike, had cleared up the next instant at the touch of the real truth. The certitude of the source of my present opportunity had rolled over me before we exchanged another word. The source was simply Gilbert Long, and she was there because he had directed it. This connection hooked itself, like a sudden picture and with a click that fairly resounded through our empty rooms, into the array of the other connections, to the immense enrichment, as it was easy to feel, of the occasion, and to the immense confirmation of the very idea that, in the course of the evening, I had come near dismissing from my mind as too fantastic even for the rest of the company it should enjoy there. What I now was sure of flashed back, at any rate, every syllable of sense I could have desired into the suggestion I had, after the music, caught from the juxtaposition of these two. Thus solidified, this conviction, it spread and spread to a distance greater than I could just then traverse under Mrs. Briss's eyes, but which, exactly for that reason perhaps, quickened my pride in the kingdom of thought I had won. I was really not to have felt more, in the whole business, than I felt at this moment that by my own right hand I had gained the kingdom. Long and she were together, and I was alone thus in face of them, but there was none the less not a single flower of the garden that my woven wreath should lack.

I must have looked queer to my friend as I grinned to myself over this vow; but my relish of the way I was keeping things together made me perhaps for the instant unduly rash. I cautioned myself, however, fortunately, before it could leave her—scared a little, all the same, even with Long behind her—an advantage to take, and, in infinitely less time than I have needed to tell it, I had achieved my flight into luminous ether and, alighting gracefully on my feet, reported myself at my post. I had in other words taken in both the full prodigy of the *entente* between Mrs. Server's lover and poor Briss's wife, and the finer strength it gave the last-named as the representative of their interest. I may add too that I had even taken time fairly not to decide which of these two branches of my vision—that of the terms of their intercourse, or that of their need of it—was likely to prove, in delectable retrospect, the more exquisite. All this, I admit, was a good deal to have come and gone while my privilege trembled, in its very essence, in the scale. Mrs. Briss had but a back to turn, and everything was over. She had, in strictness, already uttered what saved her honour, and her revenge on impertinence might easily be her withdrawing with one of her sweeps. I couldn't certainly in that case hurry after her without spilling my cards. As my accumulations of lucidity, however, were now such as to defy all leakage, I promptly recognised the facilities involved in a superficial sacrifice; and with one more glance at the beautiful fact that she knew the strength of Long's hand, I again went steadily and straight. She was acting not only for herself, and since she had another also to serve and, as I was sure, report to, I should sufficiently hold her. I knew moreover that I held her as soon as I had begun afresh. "I don't mean that anything alters the fact that you lose gracefully. It *is* awfully charming, your thus giving yourself up, and yet, justified as I am by it, I can't help regretting a little the excitement I found it this morning to pull a different way from you. Shall I tell you," it suddenly came to me to put to her, "what, for some reason, a man feels aware of?" And then as, guarded, still uneasy, she would commit herself to no permission: "That pulling against you also had its thrill. You defended your cause. Oh," I quickly added, "I know—who should know better?—that it was bad. Only—what shall I say?—*you* weren't bad, and one had to fight. And then there was what one was fighting for! Well, you're not bad now, either; so that you may ask me, of course, what more I want." I tried to think a moment. "It isn't that, thrown back on the comparative dullness of security, I find—as people have been known to—my own cause less good: no, it isn't that." After which I had my illumination. "I'll tell you what it is: it's the come-down of ceasing to work with you!"

She looked as if she were quite excusable for not following me. "To 'work'?"

I immediately explained. "Even fighting was working, for we struck, you'll remember, sparks, and sparks were what we wanted. There we are then," I cheerfully went on. "Sparks are what we still want, and you've not come to me, I trust, with a mere spent match. I depend upon it that you've another to strike." I showed her without fear all I took for granted. "Who, then, *has?*"

She was superb in her coldness, but her stare was partly blank. "Who then has what?"

"Why, done it." And as even at this she didn't

light I gave her something of a jog. "You haven't, with the force of your revulsion, I hope, literally lost our thread." But as, in spite of my thus waiting for her to pick it up she did nothing, I offered myself as fairly stooping to the carpet for it and putting it back in her hand. "Done what we spent the morning wondering at. Who then, if it isn't, certainly, Mrs. Server, *is* the woman who has made Gilbert Long—well, what you know?"

I had needed the moment to take in the special shade of innocence she was by this time prepared to show me. It was an innocence, in particular, in respect to the relation of anyone, in all the vast impropriety of things, to anyone. "I'm afraid I know nothing."

I really wondered an instant how she could expect help from such extravagance. "But I thought you just recognised that you do enjoy the sense of your pardonable mistake. You knew something when you knew enough to see you had made it."

She faced me as with the frank perception that, of whatever else one might be aware, I abounded in traps, and that this would probably be one of my worst. "Oh, I think one generally knows when one has made a mistake."

"That's all then I invite you—*a* mistake, as you properly call it—to allow me to impute to you. I'm not accusing you of having made fifty. You made none whatever, I hold, when you agreed with me with such eagerness about the striking change in him."

She affected me as asking herself a little, on this, whether vagueness, the failure of memory, the rejection of nonsense, mightn't still serve her. But she saw the next moment a better way. It all came back to her, but from so very far off. "The change, do you mean, in poor Mr. Long?"

"Of what other change—except, as you may say, your own—have you met me here to speak of? Your own, I needn't remind you, is part and parcel of Long's."

"Oh, my own," she presently returned, "is a much simpler matter even than that. My own is the recognition that I just expressed to you and that I can't consent, if you please, to your twisting into the recognition of anything else. It's the recognition that I know nothing of any other change. I stick, if you'll allow me, to my ignorance."

"I'll allow you with joy," I laughed, "if you'll let me stick to it *with* you. Your own change is quite sufficient—it gives us all we need. It will give us, if we retrace the steps of it, everything, everything!"

Mrs. Briss considered. "I don't quite see, do I? why, at this hour of the night, we should begin to retrace steps."

"Simply because it's the hour of the night you've

happened, in your generosity and your discretion, to choose. I'm struck, I confess," I declared with a still sharper conviction, "with the wonderful charm of it for our purpose."

"And, pray, what do you call with such solemnity," she inquired, "our purpose?"

I had fairly recovered at last—so far from being solemn—an appropriate gaiety. "I can only, with positiveness, answer for mine! That has remained all day the same—to get at the truth: not, that is, to relax my grasp of that tip of the tail of it which you so helped me this morning to fasten to. If you've ceased to *care* to help me," I pursued, "that's a difference indeed. But why," I candidly, pleadingly asked, "*should* you cease to care?" It was more and more of a comfort to feel her imprisoned in her inability really to explain her being there. To show herself as she was explained it only so far as she could express that; which was just the freedom she could least take. "What on earth is between us, anyhow," I insisted, "but our confounded interest? That's only quickened, for me, don't you see? by the charming way you've come round; and I don't see how it can logically be anything less than quickened for yourself. We're like the messengers and heralds in the tale of Cinderella, and I protest, I assure you, against any sacrifice of our dénoûment. We've still the glass shoe to fit."

I took pleasure at the moment in my metaphor;

but this was not the case, I soon enough perceived, with my companion. "How can I tell, please," she demanded, "what you consider you're talking about?"

I smiled; it was so quite the question Ford Obert, in the smoking-room, had begun by putting me. I hadn't to take time to remind myself how I had dealt with *him*. "And you knew," I sighed, "so beautifully, you glowed over it so, this morning!" She continued to give me, in every way, her disconnection from this morning, so that I had only to proceed: "You've not availed yourself of this occasion to pretend to me that poor Mr. Long, as you call him, is, after all, the same limited person——"

"That he always was, and that you, yesterday, so suddenly discovered him to have ceased to be?" —for with this she had waked up. But she was still thinking how she could turn it. "You see too much."

"Oh, I know I do—ever so much too much. And much as I see, I express only half of it—so you may judge!" I laughed. "But what will you have? I see what I see, and this morning, for a good bit, you did me the honour to do the same. I returned, also, the compliment, didn't I? by seeing something of what *you* saw. We put it, the whole thing, together, and we shook the bottle hard. I'm to take from you, after this," I wound up, "that what it contains is a perfectly colourless fluid?"

I paused for a reply, but it was not to come so happily as from Obert. "You talk too much!" said Mrs. Briss.

I met it with amazement. "Why, whom have I told?"

I looked at her so hard with it that her colour began to rise, which made me promptly feel that she wouldn't press that point. "I mean you're carried away—you're abused by a fine fancy: so that, with your art of putting things, one doesn't know where one is—nor, if you'll allow me to say so, do I quite think *you* always do. Of course I don't deny you're awfully clever. But you build up," she brought out with a regret so indulgent and a reluctance so marked that she for some seconds fairly held the blow—"you build up houses of cards."

I had been impatient to learn what, and, frankly, I was disappointed. This broke from me, after an instant, doubtless, with a bitterness not to be mistaken. "Long *isn't* what he seems?"

"Seems to whom?" she asked sturdily.

"Well, call it—for simplicity—to *me*. For you see"—and I spoke as to show *what* it was to see—"it all stands or falls by that."

The explanation presently appeared a little to have softened her. If it all stood or fell only by *that*, it stood or fell by something that, for her comfort, might be not so unsuccessfully disposed of. She exhaled, with the swell of her fine person, a comparative blandness—seemed to play with the idea of a smile. She had, in short, her own explanation. "The trouble with you is that you over-estimate the penetration of others. How can it approach your own?"

"Well, yours had for a while, I should say, distinct moments of keeping up with it. Nothing is more possible," I went on, "than that I do talk too much; but I've done so—about the question in dispute between us—only to *you*. I haven't, as I conceived we were absolutely not to do, mentioned it to anyone else, nor given anyone a glimpse of our difference. If you've not understood yourself as pledged to the same reserve, and have consequently," I went on, "appealed to the light of other wisdom, it shows at least that, in spite of my intellectual pace, you must more or less have followed me. What am I *not*, in fine, to think of your intelligence," I asked, "if, deciding for a resort to headquarters, you've put the question to Long himself?"

"The question?" She was straight out to sea again.

"Of the identity of the lady."

She slowly, at this, headed about. "To Long himself?"

# XIII

I HAD felt I could risk such directness only by making it extravagant—by suggesting it as barely imaginable that she could so have played our game; and during the instant for which I had now pulled her up I could judge I had been right. It was an instant that settled everything, for I saw her, with intensity, with gallantry too, surprised but not really embarrassed, recognise that of course she must simply lie. I had been justified by making it so possible for her to lie. "It would have been a short cut," I said, "and even more strikingly perhaps—to do it justice—a bold deed. But it would have been, in strictness, a departure—wouldn't it?—from our so distinguished little compact. Yet while I look at you," I went on, "I wonder. Bold deeds are, after all, quite in your line; and I'm not sure I don't rather want not to have missed so much possible comedy. 'I have it for you from Mr. Long himself that, every appearance to the contrary notwithstanding, his stupidity is unimpaired'—isn't that, for the beauty of it, after all, what you've veraciously to give me?" We stood face to face a moment, and I laughed out. "The beauty of it would be great!"

I had given her time; I had seen her safely to shore. It was quite what I had meant to do, but she now took still better advantage than I had expected of her opportunity. She not only scrambled up the bank, she recovered breath and turned round. "Do you imagine he would have told me?"

It was magnificent, but I felt she was still to better it should I give her a new chance. "Who the lady really is? Well, hardly; and that's why, as you so acutely see, the question of your having risked such a step has occurred to me only as a jest. Fancy indeed"—I piled it up—"your saying to him: 'We're all noticing that you're so much less of an idiot than you used to be, and we've different views of the miracle'!"

I had been going on, but I was checked without a word from her. Her look alone did it, for, though it was a look that partly spoiled her lie, it—by that very fact—sufficed to my confidence. "I've not spoken to a creature."

It was beautifully said, but I felt again the abysses that the mere saying of it covered, and the sense of these wonderful things was not a little, no doubt, in my immediate cheer. "Ah, then, we're all right!" I could have rubbed my hands over it. "I mean, however," I quickly added, "only as far as that. I don't at all feel comfortable about your new theory itself, which puts me so wretchedly in the wrong."

"Rather!" said Mrs. Briss almost gaily. "Wretchedly indeed in the wrong!"

"Yet oniy—equally of course," I returned after a brief brooding, "if I come within a conceivability of accepting it. Are you conscious that, in default of Long's own word—equivocal as that word would be—you press it upon me without the least other guarantee?"

"And pray," she asked, "what guarantee had *you?*"

"For the theory with which we started? Why, our recognised fact. The change in the man. You may say," I pursued, "that I was the first to speak for him; but being the first didn't, in your view, constitute a weakness when it came to your speaking yourself for Mrs. Server. By which I mean," I added, "speaking against her."

She remembered, but not for my benefit. "Well, you then asked me *my* warrant. And as regards Mr. Long and your speaking against *him*——"

"Do you describe what I say as 'against' him?" I immediately broke in.

It took her but an instant. "Surely—to have made him out horrid."

I could only want to fix it. "'Horrid'——?"

"Why, having such secrets." She was roundly ready now. "Sacrificing poor May."

"But *you,* dear lady, sacrificed poor May! It didn't strike you as horrid *then.*"

"Well, that was only," she maintained, "because you talked me over."

I let her see the full process of my taking—or not taking—this in. "And who is it then that—if, as you say, you've spoken to no one—has, as I may call it, talked you under?"

She completed, on the spot, her statement of a moment before. "Not a creature has spoken to me."

I felt somehow the wish to make her say it in as many ways as possible—I seemed so to enjoy her saying it. This helped me to make my tone approve and encourage. "You've communicated so little with anyone!" I didn't even make it a question.

It was scarce yet, however, quite good enough. "So little? I've not communicated the least mite."

"Precisely. But don't think me impertinent for having for a moment wondered. What I should say to you if you had, you know, would be that you just accused me."

"Accused you?"

"Of talking too much."

It came back to her dim. "Are we accusing each other?"

Her tone seemed suddenly to put us nearer together than we had ever been at all. "Dear no," I laughed—"not each other; only with each other's help, a few of our good friends."

"A few?" She handsomely demurred. "But one or two at the best."

"Or at the worst!"—I continued to laugh. "And not even those, it after all appears, very much!"

She didn't like my laughter, but she was now grandly indulgent. "Well, I accuse no one."

I was silent a little; then I concurred. "It's doubtless your best line; and I really quite feel, at all events, that when you mentioned a while since that I talk too much you only meant too much to *you.*"

"Yes—I wasn't imputing to you the same direct appeal. I didn't suppose," she explained, "that—to match your own supposition of *me*—you had resorted to May herself."

"You didn't suppose I had asked her?" The point was positively that she didn't; yet it made us look at each other almost as hard as if she did. "No, of course you couldn't have supposed anything so cruel—all the more that, as you knew, I had not admitted the possibility."

She accepted my assent; but, oddly enough, with a sudden qualification that showed her as still sharply disposed to make use of any loose scrap of her embarrassed acuteness. "Of course, at the same time, you yourself saw that your not admitting the possibility would have taken the edge from your cruelty. It's not the innocent," she suggestively remarked, "that we fear to frighten."

"Oh," I returned, "I fear, mostly, I think, to frighten *any* one. I'm not particularly brave. I haven't, at all events, in spite of my certitude, interrogated Mrs. Server, and I give you my word of honour that I've not had any denial from her to prop up my doubt. It still stands on its own feet, and it was its own battle that, when I came here at your summons, it was prepared to fight. Let me accordingly remind you," I pursued, "in connection with that, of the one sense in which you were, as you a moment ago said, talked over by me. I persuaded you apparently that Long's metamorphosis was not the work of Lady John. I persuaded you of nothing else."

She looked down a little, as if again at a trap. "You persuaded me that it was the work of somebody." Then she held up her head. "It came to the same thing."

If I had credit then for my trap it at least might serve. "The same thing as what?"

"Why, as claiming that it *was* she."

"Poor May—'claiming'? When I insisted it wasn't!"

Mrs. Brissenden flushed. "You didn't insist it wasn't anybody!"

"Why should I when I didn't believe so? I've left you in no doubt," I indulgently smiled, "of my beliefs. It was somebody—and it still is."

She looked about at the top of the room. "The mistake's now yours."

I watched her an instant. "Can you tell me then what one does to recover from such mistakes?"

"One thinks a little."

"Ah, the more I've thought the deeper I've sunk! And that seemed to me the case with you this morning," I added, "the more *you* thought."

"Well, then," she frankly declared, "I must have stopped thinking!"

It was a phenomenon, I sufficiently showed, that thought only could meet. "Could you tell me then at what point?"

She had to think even to do that. "At what point?"

"What in particular determined, I mean, your arrest? You surely didn't—launched as you were—stop short all of yourself."

She fronted me, after all, still so bravely that I believed her for an instant not to be, on this article, without an answer she could produce. The unexpected therefore broke for me when she fairly produced none. "I confess I don't make out," she simply said, "while you seem so little pleased that I agree with you."

I threw back, in despair, both head and hands. "But, you poor, dear thing, you don't in the *least* agree with me! You flatly contradict me. You deny my miracle."

"I don't believe in miracles," she panted.

"So I exactly, at this late hour, learn. But I

don't insist on the name. Nothing *is*, I admit, a miracle from the moment one's on the track of the cause, which was the scent we were following. Call the thing simply my fact."

She gave her high head a toss. "If it's yours it's nobody else's!"

"Ah, there's just the question—if we could know all! But my point is precisely, for the present, that you do deny it."

"Of course I deny it," said Mrs. Briss.

I took a moment, but my silence held her. "Your 'of course' would be what I would again contest, what I would denounce and brand as the word too much—the word that spoils, were it not that it seems best, that it in any case seems necessary, to let all question of your consistency go."

On that I had paused, and, as I felt myself still holding her, I was not surprised when my pause had an effect. "You do let it go?"

She had tried, I could see, to put the inquiry as all ironic. But it was not all ironic; it was, in fact, little enough so to suggest for me some intensification —not quite, I trust, wanton—of her suspense. I should be at a loss to say indeed how much it suggested or half of what it told. These things again almost violently moved me, and if I, after an instant, in my silence, turned away, it was not only to keep her waiting, but to make my elation more private. I turned away to that tune that I literally, for a few minutes, quitted her, availing myself thus, superficially, of the air of weighing a consequence. I wandered off twenty steps and, while I passed my hand over my troubled head, looked vaguely at objects on tables and sniffed absently at flowers in bowls. I don't know how long I so lost myself, nor quite why —as I must for some time have kept it up—my companion didn't now really embrace her possible alternative of rupture and retreat. Or rather, as to her action in this last matter, I am, and was on the spot, clear: I knew at that moment how much *she* knew she must not leave me without having got from me. It came back in waves, in wider glimpses, and produced in so doing the excitement I had to control. It could *not* but be exciting to talk, as we talked, on the basis of those suppressed processes and unavowed references which made the meaning of our meeting so different from its form. We knew ourselves—what moved me, that is, was that she knew me—to mean, at every point, immensely more than I said or than she answered; just as she saw me, at the same points, measure the space by which her answers fell short. This made my conversation with her a totally other and a far more interesting thing than any colloquy I had ever enjoyed; it had even a sharpness that had not belonged, a few hours before, to my extraordinary interview with Mrs. Server. She couldn't afford to quarrel with me for catechising her; she couldn't afford not to have kept, in her way, faith with me; she couldn't afford, after inconceivable passages with Long, not to treat me as an observer to be squared. She had come down to square me; she was hanging on to square me; she was suffering and stammering and lying; she was both carrying it grandly off and letting it desperately go: all, all to square me. And I caught moreover perfectly her vision of her way, and I followed her way even while I judged it, feeling that the only personal privilege I could, after all, save from the whole business was that of understanding. I couldn't save Mrs. Server, and I couldn't save poor Briss; I *could*, however, guard, to the last grain of gold, my precious sense of their loss, their disintegration and their doom; and it was for this I was now bargaining.

It was of giving herself away just enough not to spoil for me my bargain over my treasure that Mrs. Briss's bribe would consist. She would let me see as far as I would if she could feel sure I would *do* nothing; and it was exactly in this question of how much I might have scared my couple into the sense I *could* "do" that the savour of my suspense most dwelt. I could have made them uneasy, of course, only by making them fear my intervention; and yet the idea of their being uneasy was less wonderful than the idea of my having, with all my precautions, communicated to them a consciousness. This was so the last thing I had wanted to do that I felt, during my swift excursion, how much time I should need in the future for recovery of the process—all of the finest wind-blown intimations, woven of silence and secrecy and air—by which their suspicion would have throbbed into life. I could only, provisionally and sketchily, figure it out, this suspicion, as having, little by little—not with a sudden start—felt itself in the presence of my own, just as my own now returned the compliment. What came back to me, as I have said, in waves and wider glimpses, was the marvel of their exchange of signals, the phenomenon, scarce to be represented, of their breaking ground with each other. They both had their treasure to guard, and they had looked to each other with the instinct of help. They had felt, on either side, the victim possibly slip, and they had connected the possibility with an interest discernibly inspired in me by this personage, and with a relation discoverably established by that interest. It wouldn't have been a danger, perhaps, if the two victims hadn't slipped together; and more amazing, doubtless, than anything else was the recognition by my sacrificing couple of the opportunity drawn by my sacrificed from being conjoined in my charity. How could they know, Gilbert Long and Mrs. Briss, that actively to communicate a consciousness to my other friends had no part in my plan? The most I had dreamed of, I could honourably feel, was to assure myself of their independent possession of one. These things were with me while, as I have noted, I made Grace Brissenden wait, and it was also with me that, though I condoned her deviation, she must take it from me as a charity. I had presently achieved another of my full revolutions, and I faced her again with a view of her overture and my answer to her last question. The terms were not altogether what my pity could have wished, but I sufficiently kept everything together to have to see that there were limits to my choice. "Yes, I let it go, your change of front, though it vexes me a little—and I'll in a moment tell you why—to have to. But let us put it that it's on a condition."

"Change of front?" she murmured while she looked at me. "Your expressions are not of the happiest."

But I saw it was only again to cover a doubt. My condition, for her, was questionable, and I felt it would be still more so on her hearing what it was. Meanwhile, however, in spite of her qualification of it, I had fallen back, once and for all, on pure benignity. "It scarce matters if I'm clumsy when you're practically so bland. I wonder if you'll understand," I continued, "if I make you an explanation."

"Most probably," she answered, as handsome as ever, "not."

"Let me at all events try you. It's moreover the one I just promised; which was no more indeed than the development of a feeling I've already permitted myself to show you. I lose"—I brought it out—"by your agreeing with me!"

"'Lose'?"

"Yes; because while we disagreed you were, in spite of that, on the right side."

"And what do you call the right side?"

"Well"—I brought it out again—"on the same side as my imagination."

But it gave her at least a chance. "Oh, your imagination!"

"Yes—I know what you think of it; you've sufficiently hinted how little that is. But it's precisely because you regard it as rubbish that I now appeal to you."

She continued to guard herself by her surprises. "Appeal? I thought you were on the ground, rather," she beautifully smiled, "of dictation."

"Well, I'm that too. I dictate my terms. But my terms are in themselves the appeal." I was ingenious but patient. "See?"

"How in the world can I see?"

"*Voyons*, then. Light or darkness, my imagination rides me. But of course if it's all wrong I want to get rid of it. You can't, naturally, help me to destroy the faculty itself, but you can aid in the defeat of its application to a particular case. It was because you so smiled, before, on that application, that I valued even my minor difference with you;

and what I refer to as my loss is the fact that your frown leaves me struggling alone. The best thing for me, accordingly, as I feel, is to get rid altogether of the obsession. The way to do that, clearly, since *you've* done it, is just to quench the fire. By the fire I mean the flame of the fancy that blazed so for us this morning. What the deuce have you, for yourself, poured on it? Tell me," I pleaded, "and teach me."

Equally with her voice her face echoed me again. "Teach you?"

"To abandon my false gods. Lead me back to peace by the steps *you've* trod. By so much as they must have remained traceable to you, shall I find them of interest and profit. They must in fact be most remarkable: won't they even—for what *I* may find in them—be more remarkable than those we should now be taking together if we hadn't separated, if we hadn't pulled up?" That was a proposition I could present to her with candour, but before her absence of precipitation had permitted her much to consider it I had already followed it on. "You'll just tell me, however, that since I do pull up and turn back with you we shall just have *not* separated. Well, then, so much the better—I see you're right. But I want," I earnestly declared, "not to lose an inch of the journey."

She watched me now as a Roman lady at the circus may have watched an exemplary Christian. "The journey has been a very simple one," she said at last. "With my mind made up on a single point, it was taken at a stride."

I was all interest. "On a single point?" Then, as, almost excessively deliberate, she still kept me: "You mean the still commonplace character of Long's—a—consciousness?"

She had taken at last again the time she required. "Do you know what I think?"

"It's exactly what I'm pressing you to make intelligible."

"Well," said Mrs. Briss, "I think you're crazy."

It naturally struck me. "Crazy?"

"Crazy."

I turned it over. "But do you call that intelligible?"

She did it justice. "No: I don't suppose it *can* be so for you if you *are* insane."

I risked the long laugh which might have seemed that of madness. "'If I am' is lovely!" And whether or not it was the special sound, in my ear, of my hilarity, I remember just wondering if perhaps I mightn't be. "Dear woman, it's the point at issue!"

But it was as if she too had been affected. "It's not at issue for me now."

I gave her then the benefit of my stirred speculation. "It always happens, of course, that one is one's self the last to know. You're perfectly convinced?"

She not ungracefully, for an instant, faltered; but since I really would have it——! "Oh, so far as what we've talked of is concerned, perfectly!"

"And it's actually what you've come down then to tell me?"

"Just exactly what. And if it's a surprise to you," she added, "that I *should* have come down—why, I can only say I was prepared for anything."

"Anything?" I smiled.

"In the way of a surprise."

I thought; but her preparation was natural, though in a moment I could match it. "Do you know that's what I was too?"

"Prepared——?"

"For anything in the way of a surprise. But only *from* you," I explained. "And of course—yes," I mused, "I've got it. If I *am* crazy," I went on—"it's indeed simple."

She appeared, however, to feel, from the influence of my present tone, the impulse, in courtesy, to attenuate. "Oh, I don't pretend it's simple!"

"No? I thought that was just what you did pretend."

"I didn't suppose," said Mrs. Briss, "that you'd like it. I didn't suppose that you'd accept it or even listen to it. But I owed it to you——" She hesitated.

"You owed it to me to let me know what you thought of me even should it prove very disagreeable?"

That perhaps was more than she could adopt. "I owed it to myself," she replied with a touch of austerity.

"To let me know I'm demented?"

"To let you know I'm *not*." We each looked, I think, when she had said it, as if she had done what she said. "That's all."

"All?" I wailed. "Ah, don't speak as if it were so little. It's much. It's everything."

"It's anything you will!" said Mrs. Briss impatiently. "Good-night."

"Good-night?" I was aghast. "You leave me on it?"

She appeared to profess for an instant all the freshness of her own that she was pledged to guard. "I must leave you on something. I couldn't come to spend a whole hour."

"But do you think it's so quickly done—to persuade a man he's crazy?"

"I haven't expected to persuade you."

"Only to throw out the hint?"

"Well," she admitted, "it would be good if it could work in you. But I've told you," she added as if to wind up and have done, "what determined me."

"I beg your pardon"—oh, I protested! "That's

just what you've not told me. The reason of your change——"

"I'm not speaking," she broke in, "of my change."

"Ah, but *I* am!" I declared with a sharpness that threw her back for a minute on her reserves. "It's your change," I again insisted, "that's the interesting thing. If I'm crazy, I must once more remind you, you were simply crazy *with* me; and how can I therefore be indifferent to your recovery of your wit or let you go without having won from you the secret of your remedy?" I shook my head with kindness, but with decision. "You mustn't leave me till you've placed it in my hand."

The reserves I had spoken of were not, however, to fail her. "I thought you just said that you let my inconsistency go."

"Your moral responsibility for it—perfectly. But how can I show a greater indulgence than by positively desiring to enter into its history? It's in that sense that, as I say," I developed, "I do speak of your change. There must have been a given moment when the need of it—or when, in other words, the truth of my personal state—dawned upon you. That moment is the key to your whole position—the moment for us to fix."

"Fix it," said poor Mrs. Briss, "when you like!"

"I had much rather," I protested, "fix it when

*you* like. I want—you surely must understand if I want anything of it at all—to get it absolutely right." Then as this plea seemed still not to move her, I once more compressed my palms. "You *won't* help me?"

She bridled at last with a higher toss. "It wasn't with such views I came. I don't believe," she went on a shade more patiently, "I don't believe—if you want to know the reason—that you're really sincere."

Here indeed was an affair. "Not sincere—*I?*"

"Not properly honest. I mean in giving up."

"Giving up what?"

"Why, everything."

"Everything? Is it a question"—I stared—"of *that?*"

"You would if you *were* honest."

"Everything?" I repeated.

Again she stood to it. "Everything."

"But is that quite the readiness I've professed?"

"If it isn't then, what is?"

I thought a little. "Why, isn't it simply a matter rather of the renunciation of a confidence?"

"In your sense and your truth?" This, she indicated, was all she asked. "Well, what is that but everything?"

"Perhaps," I reflected, "perhaps." In fact, it no doubt was. "We'll take it then for everything, and it's as so taking it that I renounce. I keep nothing at all. Now do you believe I'm honest?"

She hesitated. "Well—yes, if you say so."

"Ah," I sighed, "I see you don't! What can I do," I asked, "to prove it?"

"You can easily prove it. You can let me go."

"Does it strike you," I considered, "that I should take your going as a sign of your belief?"

"Of what else, then?"

"Why, surely," I promptly replied, "my assent to your leaving our discussion where it stands would constitute a very different symptom. Wouldn't it much rather represent," I inquired, "a failure of belief on my own part in *your* honesty? If you can judge me, in short, as only pretending——"

"Why shouldn't you," she put in for me, "also judge *me?* What have I to gain by pretending?"

"I'll tell you," I returned, laughing, "if you'll tell me what *I* have."

She appeared to ask herself if she could, and then to decide in the negative. "If I don't understand you in any way, of course I don't in that. Put it, at any rate," she now rather wearily quavered, "that one of us has as little to gain as the other. I believe you," she repeated. "There!"

"Thanks," I smiled, "for the way you say it. If you don't, as you say, understand me," I insisted, "it's because you think me crazy. And if you think me crazy I don't see how you *can* leave me."

She presently met this. "If I believe you're sincere in saying you give up I believe you've recovered. And if I believe you've recovered I don't think you crazy. It's simple enough."

"Then why isn't it simple to understand me?"

She turned about, and there were moments in her embarrassment, now, from which she fairly drew beauty. Her awkwardness was somehow noble; her sense of her predicament was in itself young. "Is it *ever?*" she charmingly threw out.

I felt she must see at this juncture how wonderful I found her, and even that that impression—one's whole consciousness of her personal victory—was a force that, in the last resort, was all on her side. "It was quite worth your while, this sitting up to this hour, to show a fellow how you bloom when other women are fagged. If that was really, with the truth that we're so pulling about laid bare, what you did most want to show, why, then, you've splendidly triumphed, and I congratulate and thank you. No," I quickly went on, "I daresay, to do you justice, the interpretation of my tropes and figures *isn't* 'ever' perfectly simple. You doubtless *have* driven me into a corner with my dangerous explosive, and my only fair course must be therefore to sit on it till you get out of the room. I'm sitting on it now; and I think you'll find you can get out as soon as you've told me *this*. Was the moment your change of view dawned upon you the moment of our exchanging a while ago, in the drawing-room, our few words?"

The light that, under my last assurances, had so considerably revived faded in her a little as she saw me again tackle the theme of her inconstancy; but the prospect of getting rid of me on these terms made my inquiry, none the less, worth trying to face. "That moment?" She showed the effort to think back.

I gave her every assistance. "It was when, after the music, I had been talking to Lady John. You were on a sofa, not far from us, with Gilbert Long; and when, on Lady John's dropping me, I made a slight movement toward you, you most graciously met it by rising and giving me a chance while Mr. Long walked away."

It was as if I had hung the picture before her, so that she had fairly to look at it. But the point that she first, in her effort, took up was not, superficially, the most salient. "Mr. Long walked away?"

"Oh, I don't mean to say that that had anything to do with it."

She continued to think. "To do with what?"

"With the way the situation comes back to me now as possibly marking your crisis."

She wondered. "Was it a 'situation'?"

"That's just what I'm asking you. *Was* it? Was it *the* situation?"

But she had quite fallen away again. " I remember the moment you mean—it was when I said I would come to you here. But why should it have struck you as a crisis? "

" It didn't in the least at the time, for I didn't then know you were no longer ' with ' me. But in the light of what I've since learned from you I seem to recover an impression which, on the spot, was only vague. The impression," I explained, " of your taking a decision that presented some difficulty, but that was determined by something that had then—and even perhaps a little suddenly—come up for you. That's the point "—I continued to unfold my case—" on which my question bears. *Was* this ' something ' your conclusion, then and there, that there's nothing in anything? "

She kept her distance. " ' In anything '? "

" And that I could only be, accordingly, out of my mind? Come," I patiently pursued; " such a perception as that had, at some instant or other, to *begin;* and I'm only trying to aid you to recollect when the devil it did! "

" Does it particularly matter? " Mrs. Briss inquired.

I felt my chin. " That depends a little—doesn't it?—on what you mean by ' matter '! It matters for your meeting my curiosity, and that matters, in its turn, as we just arranged, for my releasing you. You may ask of course if my curiosity itself matters;

but to that, fortunately, my reply can only be of the clearest. The satisfaction of my curiosity is the pacification of my mind. We've granted, we've accepted, I again press upon you, in respect to that precarious quantity, its topsy-turvy state. Only give me a lead; I don't ask you for more. Let me for an instant see play before me any feeble reflection whatever of the flash of new truth that unsettled you."

I thought for a moment that, in her despair, she would find something that would do. But she only found: "It didn't come in a flash."

I remained all patience. "It came little by little? It began then perhaps earlier in the day than the moment to which I allude? And yet," I continued, "we were pretty well on in the day, I must keep in mind, when I had your last news of your credulity."

"My credulity?"

"Call it then, if you don't like the word, your sympathy."

I had given her time, however, to produce at last something that, it visibly occurred to her, might pass. "As soon as I was not with you—I mean with you personally—you *never* had my sympathy."

"Is my person then so irresistible?"

Well, she was brave. "It *was*. But it's not, thank God, now!"

"Then there we are again at our mystery! I don't think, you know," I made out for her, "it was my person, really, that gave its charm to my theory; I think it was much more my theory that gave its charm to my person. My person, I flatter myself, has remained through these few hours—hours of tension, but of a tension, you see, purely intellectual—as good as ever; so that if we're not, even in our anomalous situation, in danger from any such source, it's simply that my theory is dead and that the blight of the rest is involved."

My words were indeed many, but she plumped straight through them. "As soon as I was away from you I hated you."

"Hated *me?*"

"Well, hated what you call 'the rest'—hated your theory."

"I see. Yet," I reflected, "you're not at present—though you wish to goodness, no doubt, you *were*—away from me."

"Oh, I don't care now," she said with courage; "since—for you see I believe you—we're away from your delusions."

"You wouldn't, in spite of your belief,"—I smiled at her—"like to be a little further off yet?" But before she could answer, and because also, doubtless, the question had too much the sound of a taunt, I came up, as if for her real convenience, quite in another place. "Perhaps my idea—my timing, that is, of your crisis—is the result, in my mind, of my own association with that particular instant.

It comes back to me that what I was most full of while your face signed to me and your voice then so graciously confirmed it, and while too, as I've said, Long walked away—what I was most full of, as a consequence of another go, just ended, at Lady John, was, once more, this same Lady John's want of adjustability to the character you and I, in our associated speculation of the morning, had so candidly tried to fit her with. I was still even then, you see, speculating—all on my own hook, alas!—and it had just rolled over me with renewed force that she was nothing whatever, not the least little bit, to our purpose. The moment, in other words, if you understand, happened to be one of *my* moments; so that, by the same token, I simply wondered if it mightn't likewise have happened to be one of yours."

"It *was* one of mine," Mrs. Briss replied as promptly as I could reasonably have expected; "in the sense that—as you've only to consider—it was to lead more or less directly to these present words of ours."

If I had only to consider, nothing was more easy; but each time I considered, I was ready to show, the less there seemed left by the act. "Ah, but you had then *already* backed out. *Won't* you understand—for you're a little discouraging—that I want to catch you at the earlier stage?"

"To 'catch' me?" I had indeed expressions!

"Absolutely catch! Focus you under the first shock of the observation that was to make everything fall to pieces for you."

"But I've told you," she stoutly resisted, "that there was no 'first' shock."

"Well, then, the second or the third."

"There was no shock," Mrs. Briss magnificently said, "at all."

It made me somehow break into laughter. "You found it so natural then—and you so rather liked it—to make up your mind of a sudden that you had been steeped in the last intellectual intimacy with a maniac?"

She thought once more, and then, as I myself had just previously done, came up in another place. "I had at the moment you speak of wholly given up any idea of Lady John."

But it was so feeble it made me smile. "Of course you had, you poor innocent! You couldn't otherwise, hours before, have strapped the saddle so tight on another woman."

"I had given up everything," she stubbornly continued.

"It's exactly what, in reference to that juncture, I perfectly embrace."

"Well, even in reference to that juncture," she resumed, "you may catch me as much as you like." With which, suddenly, during some seconds, I saw her hold herself for a leap. "You talk of 'focussing,' but what else, even in those minutes, were you in fact engaged in?"

"Ah, then, you do recognise them," I cried—"those minutes?"

She took her jump, though with something of a flop. "Yes—as, consenting thus to be catechised, I cudgel my brain for your amusement—I do recognise them. I remember what I thought. You focussed—I felt you focus. I saw you wonder whereabouts, in what you call our associated speculation, I would by that time be. I asked myself whether you'd understand if I should try to convey to you simply by my expression such a look as would tell you all. By 'all' I meant the fact that, sorry as I was for you—or perhaps for myself—it had struck me as only fair to let you know as straight as possible that I was nowhere. That was why I stared so, and I of course couldn't explain to you," she lucidly pursued, "to whom my stare had reference."

I hung on her lips. "But you can *now?*"

"Perfectly. To Mr. Long."

I remained suspended. "Ah, but this is lovely! It's what I want."

I saw I should have more of it, and more in fact came. "You were saying just now what you were full of, and I can do the same. I was full of *him.*"

I, on my side, was now full of eagerness. "Yes? He had left you full as he walked away?"

She winced a little at this renewed evocation of his retreat, but she took it as she had not done before, and I felt that with another push she would be fairly afloat. "He had reason to walk!"

I wondered. "What had you said to him?"

She pieced it out. "Nothing—or very little. But I had listened."

"And to *what?*"

"To what he says. To his platitudes."

"His platitudes?" I stared. "Long's?"

"Why, don't you know he's a prize fool?"

I mused, sceptical but reasonable. "He *was.*"

"He *is!*"

Mrs. Briss was superb, but, as I quickly felt I might remind her, there was her possibly weak judgment. "Your confidence is splendid; only mustn't I remember that your sense of the finer kinds of cleverness isn't perhaps absolutely secure? Don't you know?—you also, till just now, thought *me* a prize fool."

If I had hoped, however, here to trip her up, I had reckoned without the impulse, and even perhaps the example, that she properly owed to me. "Oh, no—not anything of that sort, you, at all. Only an intelligent man gone wrong."

I followed, but before I caught up, "Whereas Long's only a stupid man gone right?" I threw out.

It checked her too briefly, and there was indeed something of my own it brought straight back. "I thought that just what you told me, this morning or yesterday, was that you had never known a case of the conversion of an idiot."

I laughed at her readiness. Well, I had wanted to make her fight! "It's true it would have been the only one."

"Ah, you'll have to do without it!" Oh, she was brisk now. "And if you know what I think of him, you know no more than *he* does."

"You mean you told him?"

She hung fire but an instant. "I told him, practically—and it was in fact all I did have to say to him. It was enough, however, and he disgustedly left me on it. Then it was that, as you gave me the chance, I tried to telegraph you—to say to you on the spot and under the sharp impression: 'What on earth do you mean by your nonsense? It doesn't hold water!' It's a pity I didn't succeed!" she continued—for she had become almost voluble. "It would have settled the question, and I should have gone to bed."

I weighed it with the grimace that, I feared, had become almost as fixed as Mrs. Server's. "It would have settled the question perhaps; but I should have lost this impression of you."

"Oh, this impression of me!"

"Ah, but don't undervalue it: it's what I want! What was it then Long had said?"

She had it more and more, but she had it as

nothing at all. "Not a word to repeat—you wouldn't believe! He does say nothing at all. One can't remember. It's what I mean. I tried him on purpose, while I thought of you. But he's perfectly stupid. I don't see how we can have fancied——!" I had interrupted her by the movement with which again, uncontrollably tossed on one of my surges of certitude, I turned away. *How* deep they must have been in together for her to have so at last gathered herself up, and in how doubly interesting a light, above all, it seemed to present Long for the future! That was, while I warned myself, what I most read in—literally an implication of the enhancement of this latter side of the prodigy. If his cleverness, under the alarm that, first stirring their consciousness but dimly, had so swiftly developed as to make next of each a mirror for the other, and then to precipitate for them, in some silence deeper than darkness, the exchange of recognitions, admissions and, as they certainly would have phrased it, tips—if his excited acuteness was henceforth to protect itself by dissimulation, what wouldn't perhaps, for one's diversion, be the new spectacle and wonder? I could in a manner already measure this larger play by the amplitude freshly determined in Mrs. Briss, and I was for a moment actually held by the thought of the possible finish our friend would find it in him to give to a represented, a fictive ineptitude. The sharpest jostle to my thought, in this rush, might well have been, I confess, the reflection that as it was I who had arrested, who had spoiled their unconsciousness, so it was natural they should fight against me for a possible life in the state I had given them instead. I had spoiled their unconsciousness, I had destroyed it, and it was consciousness alone that could make them effectively cruel. Therefore, if they were cruel, it was I who had determined it, inasmuch as, consciously, they could only want, they could only intend, to live. Wouldn't that question have been, I managed even now to ask myself, the very basis on which they had inscrutably come together? "It's life, you know," each had said to the other, "and I, accordingly, can only cling to mine. But you, poor dear—shall *you* give up?" "Give up?" the other had replied: "for what do you take me? I shall fight by your side, please, and we can compare and exchange weapons and manœuvres, and you may in every way count upon me."

That was what, with greater vividness, was for the rest of the occasion before me, or behind me; and that I had done it all and had only myself to thank for it was what, from this minute, by the same token, was more and more for me the inner essence of Mrs. Briss's attitude. I know not what heavy admonition of my responsibility had thus suddenly descended on me; but nothing, under it, was indeed more sensible than that practically it paralysed me. And I could only say to myself that this was the price—the price of the secret success, the lonely liberty and the intellectual joy. There were things that for so private and splendid a revel—that of the exclusive king with his Wagner opera—I could only let go, and the special torment of my case was that the condition of light, of the satisfaction of curiosity and of the attestation of triumph, was in this direct way the sacrifice of feeling. There was no point at which my assurance could, by the scientific method, judge itself complete enough not to regard feeling as an interference and, in consequence, as a possible check. If it had to go I knew well who went with it, but I wasn't there to save *them*. I was there to save my priceless pearl of an inquiry and to harden, to that end, my heart. I should need indeed all my hardness, as well as my brightness, moreover, to meet Mrs. Briss on the high level to which I had at last induced her to mount, and, even while I prolonged the movement by which I had momentarily stayed her, the intermission of her speech became itself for me a hint of the peculiar pertinence of caution. It lasted long enough, this drop, to suggest that her attention was the sharper for my having turned away from it, and I should have feared a renewed challenge if she hadn't, by good luck, presently gone on: "There's really nothing in him at all!"

## XIV

I HAD faced her again just in time to take it, and I immediately made up my mind how best to do so. "Then I go utterly to pieces!"

"You shouldn't have perched yourself," she laughed—she could by this time almost coarsely laugh—"in such a preposterous place!"

"Ah, that's my affair," I returned, "and if I accept the consequences I don't quite see what you've to say to it. That I do accept them—so far as I make them out as not too intolerable and you as not intending them to be—that I do accept them is what I've been trying to signify to you. Only my fall," I added, "is an inevitable shock. You remarked to me a few minutes since that you didn't recover yourself in a flash. I differ from you, you see, in that *I* do; I take my collapse all at once. Here then I am. I'm smashed. I don't see, as I look about me, a piece I can pick up. I don't attempt to account for my going wrong; I don't attempt to account for yours with me; I don't attempt to account for anything. If Long *is* just what he always was it settles the matter, and the special clincher for us can be but your honest final impression, made precisely more aware of itself by repentance for the levity with which you had originally yielded to my contagion."

She didn't insist on her repentance; she was too taken up with the facts themselves. "Oh, but add to my impression everyone else's impression! Has anyone noticed anything?"

"Ah, I don't know what anyone has noticed. I haven't," I brooded, "ventured—as you know—to ask anyone."

"Well, if you had you'd have seen—seen, I mean, all they don't see. If they had been conscious they'd have talked."

I thought. "To me?"

"Well, I'm not sure to you; people have such a notion of what you embroider on things that they're rather afraid to commit themselves or to lead you on: they're sometimes in, you know," she luminously reminded me, "for more than they bargain for, than they quite know what to do with, or than they care to have on their hands."

I tried to do justice to this account of myself. "You mean I see so much?"

It was a delicate matter, but she risked it. "Don't you sometimes see horrors?"

I wondered. "Well, names are a convenience. People catch me in the act?"

"They certainly think you critical."

"And is criticism the vision of horrors?"

She couldn't quite be sure where I was taking her. "It isn't, perhaps, so much that you see them——"

I started. "As that I perpetrate them?"

She was sure now, however, and wouldn't have it, for she was serious. "Dear no—you don't perpetrate anything. Perhaps it would be better if you did!" she tossed off with an odd laugh. "But —always by people's idea—you like them."

I followed. "Horrors?"

"Well, you don't——"

"Yes——?"

But she wouldn't be hurried now. "You take them too much for what they are. You don't seem to want——"

"To come down on them strong? Oh, but I often do!"

"So much the better then."

"Though I do like—whether for that or not," I hastened to confess, "to look them first well in the face."

Our eyes met, with this, for a minute, but she made nothing of that. "When they *have* no face, then, you can't do it! It isn't at all events now a question," she went on, "of people's keeping anything back, and you're perhaps in any case not the person to whom it would first have come."

I tried to think then who the person would be. "It would have come to Long himself?"

But she was impatient of this. "Oh, one doesn't know what comes—or what doesn't—to Long himself! I'm not sure he's too modest to misrepresent—if he had the intelligence to play a part."

"Which he hasn't!" I concluded.

"Which he hasn't. It's to *me* they might have spoken—or to each other."

"But I thought you exactly held they *had* chattered in accounting for his state by the influence of Lady John."

She got the matter instantly straight. "Not a bit. That chatter was mine only—and produced to meet yours. There had so, by your theory, to be a woman——"

"That, to oblige me, you invented *her?* Precisely. But I thought——"

"You needn't have thought!" Mrs. Briss broke in. "I didn't invent her."

"Then what are you talking about?"

"I didn't invent her," she repeated, looking at me hard. "She's true." I echoed it in vagueness, though instinctively again in protest; yet I held my breath, for this was really the point at which I felt my companion's forces most to have mustered. Her manner now moreover gave me a great idea of them, and her whole air was of taking immediate advantage of my impression. "Well, see here: since you've wanted it, I'm afraid that, however little you may like it, you'll have to take it. You've pressed me for explanations and driven me much harder than you must have seen I found convenient. If I've seemed to beat about the bush it's because I hadn't only myself to think of. One can be simple for one's self—one can't be, always, for others."

"Ah, to whom do you say it?" I encouragingly sighed; not even yet quite seeing for what issue she was heading.

She continued to make for the spot, whatever it was, with a certain majesty. "I should have preferred to tell you nothing more than what I *have* told you. I should have preferred to close our conversation on the simple announcement of my recovered sense of proportion. But you *have*, I see, got me in too deep."

"O-oh!" I courteously attenuated.

"You've made of me," she lucidly insisted, "too big a talker, too big a thinker, of nonsense."

"Thank you," I laughed, "for intimating that I trifle so agreeably."

"Oh, *you've* appeared not to mind! But let me then at last not fail of the luxury of admitting that *I* mind. Yes, I mind particularly. I may be bad, but I've a grain of gumption."

"'Bad'?" It seemed more closely to concern me.

"Bad I may be. In fact," she pursued at this high pitch and pressure, "there's no doubt whatever I *am*."

" I'm delighted to hear it," I cried, " for it was exactly something strong I wanted of you ! "

" It *is* then strong "—and I could see indeed she was ready to satisfy me. " You've worried me for my motive and harassed me for my ' moment,' and I've had to protect others and, at the cost of a decent appearance, to pretend to be myself half an idiot. I've had even, for the same purpose—if you must have it—to depart from the truth; to give you, that is, a false account of the manner of my escape from your tangle. But now the truth shall be told, and others can take care of themselves ! " She had so wound herself up with this, reached so the point of fairly heaving with courage and candour, that I for an instant almost miscalculated her direction and believed she was really throwing up her cards. It was as if she had decided, on some still finer lines, just to rub my nose into what I had been spelling out; which would have been an anticipation of my own journey's crown of the most disconcerting sort. I wanted my personal confidence, but I wanted nobody's confession, and without the journey's crown where *was* the personal confidence? Without the personal confidence, moreover, where was the personal honour? That would be really the single thing to which I could attach authority, for a confession might, after all, be itself a lie. Anybody, at all events, could fit the shoe to one. My friend's intention, however, remained but briefly equivocal;

my danger passed, and I recognised in its place a still richer assurance. It was not the unnamed, in short, who were to be named. "Lady John *is* the woman."

Yet even this was prodigious. "But I thought your present position was just that she's *not!*"

"Lady John *is* the woman," Mrs. Briss again announced.

"But I thought your present position was just that nobody is!"

"Lady John *is* the woman," she a third time declared.

It naturally left me gaping. "Then there *is* one?" I cried between bewilderment and joy.

"A woman? There's *her!*" Mrs. Briss replied with more force than grammar. "I know," she briskly, almost breezily added, "that I said she wouldn't do (as I had originally said she would do better than any one), when you a while ago mentioned her. But that was to save her."

"And you don't care now," I smiled, "if she's lost!"

She hesitated. "She *is* lost. But she can take care of herself."

I could but helplessly think of her. "I'm afraid indeed that, with what you've done with her, *I* can't take care of her. But why is she now to the purpose," I articulately wondered, "any more than she was?"

"Why? On the very system you yourself laid down. When we took him for brilliant, she couldn't be. But now that we see him as he is——"

"We can only see her also as *she* is?" Well, I tried, as far as my amusement would permit, so to see her; but still there were difficulties. "Possibly!" I at most conceded. "Do you owe your discovery, however, wholly to my system? My system, where so much made for protection," I explained, "wasn't intended to have the effect of exposure."

"It appears to have been at all events intended," my companion returned, "to have the effect of driving me to the wall; and the consequence of *that* effect is nobody's fault but your own."

She was all logic now, and I could easily see, between my light and my darkness, how she would remain so. Yet I was scarce satisfied. "And it's only on 'that effect'——?"

"That I've made up my mind?" She was positively free at last to enjoy my discomfort. "Wouldn't it be surely, if your ideas were worth anything, enough? But it isn't," she added, "only on that. It's on something else."

I had after an instant extracted from this the single meaning it could appear to yield. "I'm to understand that you *know?*"

"That they're intimate enough for anything?" She faltered, but she brought it out. "I know."

It was the oddest thing in the world for a little,

the way this affected me without my at all believing it. It was preposterous, hang though it would with her somersault, and she had quite succeeded in giving it the note of sincerity. It was the mere sound of it that, as I felt even at the time, made it a little of a blow—a blow of the smart of which I was conscious just long enough inwardly to murmur: "What if she *should* be right?" She had for these seconds the advantage of stirring within me the memory of her having indeed, the day previous, at Paddington, "known" as I hadn't. It had been really on what she *then* knew that we originally started, and an element of our start had been that I admired her freedom. The form of it, at least—so beautifully had she recovered herself—was all there now. Well, I at any rate reflected, it wasn't the form that need trouble me, and I quickly enough put her a question that related only to the matter. "Of course if she is—it *is* smash!"

"And haven't you yet got used to its being?"

I kept my eyes on her; I traced the buried figure in the ruins. "She's good enough for a fool; and so"—I made it out—"is he! If he *is* the same ass—yes—they *might* be."

"*And* he is," said Mrs. Briss, "the same ass!"

I continued to look at her. "He would have no need then of her having transformed and inspired him."

"Or of her having *de*formed and idiotised herself," my friend subjoined.

Oh, how it sharpened my look! "No, no—she wouldn't need that."

"The great point is that *he* wouldn't!" Mrs. Briss laughed.

I kept it up. "She would do perfectly."

Mrs. Briss was not behind. "My dear man, she has *got* to do!"

This was brisker still, but I held my way. "Almost anyone would do."

It seemed for a little, between humour and sadness, to strike her. "Almost anyone *would.* Still," she less pensively declared, "we want the right one."

"Surely; the right one"—I could only echo it. "But how," I then proceeded, "has it happily been confirmed to you?"

It pulled her up a trifle. "'Confirmed'——?"

"That he's her lover."

My eyes had been meeting hers without, as it were, hers quite meeting mine. But at this there had to be intercourse. "By my husband."

It pulled *me* up a trifle. "Brissenden knows?"

She hesitated; then, as if at my tone, gave a laugh. "Don't you suppose I've told him?"

I really couldn't but admire her. "Ah—so you *have* talked!"

It didn't confound her. "One's husband isn't

talk. You're cruel moreover," she continued, "to my joke. It was Briss, poor dear, who talked—though, I mean, only to me. *He* knows."

I cast about. "Since when?"

But she had it ready. "Since this evening."

Once more I couldn't but smile. "Just in time then! And the *way* he knows——?"

"Oh, the way!"—she had at this a slight drop. But she came up again. "I take his word."

"You haven't then asked him?"

"The beauty of it was—half an hour ago, upstairs—that I *hadn't* to ask. He came out with it himself, and *that*—to give you the whole thing—was, if you like, my moment. He dropped it on me," she continued to explain, "without in the least, sweet innocent, knowing what he was doing; more, at least, that is, than give her away."

"Which," I concurred, "was comparatively nothing!"

But she had no ear for irony, and she made out still more of her story. "He's simple—but he sees."

"And when he sees"—I completed the picture—"he luckily tells."

She quite agreed with me that it was lucky, but without prejudice to his acuteness and to what had been in him moreover a natural revulsion. "He has seen, in short; there comes some chance when one does. His, as luckily as you please, came this evening. If you ask me what it showed him you ask more than *I've* either cared or had time to ask. Do you consider, for that matter"—she put it to me—"that one does ask?" As her high smoothness—such was the wonder of this reascendancy—almost deprived me of my means, she was wise and gentle with me. "Let us leave it alone."

I fairly, while my look at her turned rueful, scratched my head. "Don't you think it a little late for that?"

"Late for everything!" she impatiently said. "But there you are."

I fixed the floor. There indeed I was. But I tried to stay there—just there only—as short a time as possible. Something, moreover, after all, caught me up. "But if Brissenden already knew——?"

"If he knew——?" She still gave me, without prejudice to her ingenuity—and indeed it was a part of this—all the work she could.

"Why, that Long and Lady John were thick?"

"Ah, then," she cried, "you admit they *are!*"

"Am I not admitting everything you tell me? But the more I admit," I explained, "the more I must understand. It's *to* admit, you see, that I inquire. If Briss came down with Lady John yesterday to oblige Mr. Long——"

"He didn't come," she interrupted, "to oblige Mr. Long!"

"Well, then, to oblige Lady John herself——"

"He didn't come to oblige Lady John herself!"

"Well, then, to oblige his clever wife——"

"He didn't come to oblige his clever wife! He came," said Mrs. Briss, "just to amuse himself. He *has* his amusements, and it's odd," she remarkably laughed, "that you should grudge them to him!"

"It would be odd indeed if I did! But put his proceeding," I continued, "on any ground you like; you described to me the purpose of it as a screening of the pair."

"I described to you the purpose of it as nothing of the sort. I didn't describe to you the purpose of it," said Mrs. Briss, "at all. I described to you," she triumphantly set forth, "the *effect* of it—which is a very different thing."

I could only meet her with admiration. "You're of an astuteness——!"

"Of course I'm of an astuteness! I *see* effects. And I saw that one. How much Briss himself had seen it is, as I've told you, another matter; and what he had, at any rate, quite taken the affair for was the sort of flirtation in which, if one is a friend to either party, and one's own feelings are not at stake, one may now and then give people a lift. Haven't I asked you before," she demanded, "if you suppose he would have given one had he had an idea where these people *are?*"

"I scarce know what you have asked me before!" I sighed; "and 'where they are' is just what you haven't told me."

"It's where my husband was so annoyed unmistakably to discover them." And as if she had quite fixed the point she passed to another. "He's peculiar, dear old Briss, but in a way by which, if one uses him—by which, I mean, if one depends on him—at all, one gains, I think, more than one loses. Up to a certain point, in any case that's the least a case for subtlety, he sees nothing at all; but beyond it—when once he does wake up—he'll go through a house. Nothing then escapes him, and what he drags to light is sometimes appalling."

"Rather," I thoughtfully responded — "since witness this occasion!"

"But isn't the interest of this occasion, as I've already suggested," she propounded, "simply that it makes an end, bursts a bubble, rids us of an incubus and permits us to go to bed in peace? I thank God," she moralised, "for dear old Briss to-night."

"So do I," I after a moment returned; "but I shall do so with still greater fervour if you'll have for the space of another question a still greater patience." With which, as a final movement from her seemed to say how much this was to ask, I had on my own side a certain exasperation of soreness for all I had to acknowledge—even were it mere acknowledgment—that she had brought rattling down. "Remember," I pleaded, "that you're costing me a perfect palace of thought!"

I could see too that, held unexpectedly by something in my tone, she really took it in. Couldn't I even almost see that, for an odd instant, she regretted the blighted pleasure of the pursuit of truth with me? I needed, at all events, no better proof either of the sweet or of the bitter in her comprehension than the accent with which she replied: "Oh, those who live in glass houses——"

"Shouldn't—no, I know they shouldn't—throw stones; and that's precisely why I don't." I had taken her immediately up, and I held her by it and by something better still. "You, from your fortress of granite, can chuck them about as you will! All the more reason, however," I quickly added, "that, before my frail, but, as I maintain, quite sublime structure, you honour me, for a few seconds, with an intelligent look at it. I seem myself to see it again, perfect in every part," I pursued, "even while I thus speak to you, and to feel afresh that, weren't the wretched accident of its weak foundation, it wouldn't have the shadow of a flaw. I've spoken of it in my conceivable regret," I conceded, "as already a mere heap of disfigured fragments; but that was the extravagance of my vexation, my despair. It's in point of fact so beautifully fitted that it comes apart piece by piece—which, so far as that goes, you've seen it do in the last quarter of an hour at your own touch, quite handing me the pieces, one by one, yourself and watching me stack them along the ground. They're not even in this state—see!" I wound up—"a pile of ruins!" I wound up, as I say, but only for long enough to have, with the vibration, the exaltation, of my eloquence, my small triumph as against her great one. "I should almost like, piece by piece, to hand them back to you." And this time I completed my figure. "I believe that, for the very charm of it, you'd find yourself placing them by your own sense in their order and rearing once more the splendid pile. Will you take just *one* of them from me again," I insisted, "and let me see if only to have it in your hands doesn't positively start you off? That's what I meant just now by asking you for another answer." She had remained silent, as if really in the presence of the rising magnificence of my metaphor, and it was not too late for the one chance left me. "There was nothing, you know, I had so fitted as your account of poor Mrs. Server when, on our seeing them, from the terrace, together below, you struck off your explanation that old Briss was *her* screen for Long."

"Fitted?"—and there was sincerity in her surprise. "I thought my stupid idea the one for which you had exactly no use!"

"I had no use," I instantly concurred, "for your stupid idea, but I had great use for your stupidly, alas! having it. *That* fitted beautifully," I smiled, "till the piece came out. And even now," I added, "I don't feel it quite accounted for."

"Their being there together?"

"No. Your not liking it that they were."

She stared. "Not liking it?"

I could see how little indeed she minded now, but I also kept the thread of my own intellectual history. "Yes. Your not liking it is what I speak of as the piece. I hold it, you see, up before you. What, artistically, would you do with it?"

But one might take a horse to water——! I held it up before her, but I couldn't make her look at it. "How do you know what I mayn't, or may, have liked?"

It did bring me to. "Because you were conscious of not telling me? Well, even if you didn't——!"

"That made no difference," she inquired with a generous derision, "because you could always imagine? Of course you could always imagine—which is precisely what is the matter with you! But I'm surprised at your coming to me with it once more as evidence of anything."

I stood rebuked, and even more so than I showed her, for she need, obviously, only decline to take one of my counters to deprive it of all value as coin. When she pushed it across I had but to pocket it again. "It *is* the weakness of my case," I feebly and I daresay awkwardly mused at her, "that any particular thing you don't grant me becomes straightway the strength of yours. Of course, however"—and I gave myself a shake—"I'm absolutely rejoicing (am I not?) in the strength of yours. The weakness of my own is what, under your instruction, I'm now going into; but don't you see how much weaker it will show if I draw from you the full expression of your indifference? How *could* you in fact care when what you were at the very moment urging on me so hard was the extravagance of Mrs. Server's conduct? That extravagance then proved her, to your eyes, the woman who had a connection with Long to keep the world off the scent of—though you maintained that in spite of the dust she kicked up by it she was, at a pinch, now and then to be caught with him. That instead of being caught with him she was caught only with Brissenden annoyed you naturally for the moment; but what was that annoyance compared to your appreciation of her showing—by undertaking your husband, of all people!—just the more markedly *as* extravagant?"

She had been sufficiently interested this time to follow me. "What was it indeed?"

I greeted her acquiescence, but I insisted. "And yet if she *is* extravagant—what do you do with it?"

"I thought you wouldn't hear of it!" she exclaimed.

I sought to combine firmness with my mildness. "What do you do with it?"

But she could match me at this. "I thought you wouldn't hear of it!"

"It's not a question of *my* dispositions. It's a question of her having been, or not been, for you 'all over the place,' and of everyone's also being, for you, on the chatter about it. You go by that in respect to Long—by your holding, that is, that nothing has been noticed; therefore mustn't you go by it in respect to *her*—since I understand from you that everything has?"

"Everything always is," Mrs. Briss agreeably replied, "in a place and a party like this; but so little—anything in particular—that, with people moving 'every which' way, it comes to the same as if nothing was. Things are not, also, gouged out to *your* tune, and it depends, still further, on what you mean by 'extravagant.'"

"I mean whatever you yourself meant."

"Well, I myself mean no longer, you know, what I did mean."

"She isn't then——?"

But suddenly she was almost sharp with me. "Isn't what?"

"What the woman we so earnestly looked for would have to be."

"All gone?" She had hesitated, but she went on with decision. "No, she isn't all gone, since there was enough of her left to make up to poor Briss."

"Precisely—and it's just what we saw, and just what, with her other dashes of the same sort, led us to have to face the question of her being—well, what I say. Or rather," I added, "what *you* say. That is," I amended, to keep perfectly straight, "what you say you *don't* say."

I took indeed too many precautions for my friend not to have to look at them. "Extravagant?" The irritation of the word had grown for her, yet I risked repeating it, and with the effect of its giving her another pause. "I tell you she *isn't* that!"

"Exactly; and it's only to ask you what in the world then she *is*."

"She's horrid!" said Mrs. Briss.

"'Horrid'?" I gloomily echoed.

"Horrid. It wasn't," she then developed with decision, "a 'dash,' as you say, 'of the same sort'—though goodness knows of what sort you mean: it wasn't, to be plain, a 'dash' at all." My companion *was* plain. "She settled. She stuck." And finally, as I could but echo her again: "She made love to him."

"But—a—really?"

"Really. That's how I knew."

I was at sea. "'Knew'? But you saw."

"I knew—that is I learnt—more than I saw. I knew she couldn't be gone."

It in fact brought light. "Knew it by *him?*"

"He told me," said Mrs. Briss.

It brought light, but it brought also, I fear, for me, another queer grimace. "Does he then regularly tell?"

"Regularly. But what he tells," she did herself the justice to declare, "is not always so much to the point as the two things I've repeated to you."

Their weight then suggested that I should have them over again. "His revelation, in the first place, of Long and Lady John?"

"And his revelation in the second"—she spoke of it as a broad joke—"of May Server and himself."

There was something in her joke that was a chill to my mind; but I nevertheless played up. "And what does he say that's further interesting about *that?*"

"Why, that she's awfully sharp."

I gasped—she turned it out so. "*She*—Mrs. Server?"

It made her, however, equally stare. "Why, isn't it the very thing you maintained?"

I felt her dreadful logic, but I couldn't—with my exquisite image all contrasted, as in a flash from flint, with this monstrosity—so much as entertain her question. I could only stupidly again sound it. "Awfully sharp?"

"You after all then now don't?" It was she

herself whom the words at present described! "Then what on earth *do* you think?" The strange mixture in my face naturally made her ask it, but everything, within a minute, had somehow so given way under the touch of her supreme assurance, the presentation of her own now finished system, that I dare say I couldn't at the moment have in the least trusted myself to tell her. She left me, however, in fact, small time—she only took enough, with her negations arrayed and her insolence recaptured, to judge me afresh, which she did as she gathered herself up into the strength of twenty-five. I didn't after all—it appeared part of my smash—know the weight of her husband's years, but I knew the weight of my own. They might have been a thousand, and nothing but the sense of them would in a moment, I saw, be left me. "My poor dear, you *are* crazy, and I bid you good-night!"

Nothing but the sense of them—on my taking it from her without a sound and watching her, through the lighted rooms, retreat and disappear—*was* at first left me; but after a minute something else came, and I grew conscious that her verdict lingered. She had so had the last word that, to get out of its planted presence, I shook myself, as I had done before, from my thought. When once I had started to my room indeed—and to preparation for a livelier start as soon as the house should stir again—I almost breathlessly hurried. Such a last word

—the word that put me altogether nowhere—was too unacceptable not to prescribe afresh that prompt test of escape to other air for which I had earlier in the evening seen so much reason. I *should* certainly never again, on the spot, quite hang together, even though it wasn't really that I hadn't three times her method. What I too fatally lacked was her tone.

THE END

# OTHER GROVE PRESS DRAMA AND THEATER PAPERBACKS